Exploring the
WORLD OF MEDICINE

A fascinating and comprehensive guide for children and parents

By Era Hitin

Translated From The Hebrew By Denise Levin

KIP – Kotarim International Publishing, Ltd.

Exploring the WORLD OF MEDICINE

A fascinating and comprehensive guide for children and parents

By Era Hitin

Graphic Design by: Laura Gryncwajg

KIP – Kotarim International Publishing, Ltd.

Publisher: Moshe Alon

ISBN 978-965-7589-21-2

2015

To Yudka
Tali and Tovi, Ella, Amir and Alon
Omer and Shiri, Uri, Eitan and Ram
From my heart and soul.

Heartfelt Thanks

A special thank you to my daughter-in-law Shiri for her devoted help in all the stages of preparing this book, starting with her initiative and encouragement to turn the idea into a reality, through her support as I wrote it and her never-failing ongoing assistance, until the manuscript finally was converted into a printed book.

Thank you to my son, Omer, who supported me and helped me during critical moments.

I wish to also extend my thanks

to doctors, Dr. Yael Levi, Prof. Itamar Shalit, Prof. Yitzhak Versano, Prof. Benjamin Volovitz, Dr. Boaz Geva , Prof. Ovdi Dagan, and Prof. Yaakov Amir;

to health care professionals, Dr. Nadine Khatib, Clinical Pharmacist and Senior Medical Officer at the Tel Aviv Sourasky Medical Center, Israel and Mr. David Tveta, Director of the Kaplan Medical Center Roentgen School, Rehovot, Israel, who willingly, with a feeling of mission, devoted time to reviewing the chapters in their fields of expertise, made important corrections and remarks, and contributed their knowledge to integrating its medical-educational approach.

My thanks also go to Mr. Liran Mendel, who was unknown to me until he pitched in wholeheartedly, to Ms. Denise Levin, who translated the book from Hebrew into English, to Ms. Phillis Komspam, who typed the Hebrew original, for her cooperation and her efforts all along the way, to computer expert Ms. Malka Segal, for her patience and good spirits in placing all the photos and illustrations in their correct places in the book, to my friends and acquaintances, in particular to Ms. Sonia Kasher, Ms. Bilha Nitzan, Ms. Edna Hokon, Ms. Genny Yerushalmi, Ms. Laura Ramati, Dalia and Eli Sirota and to Dr. Edith Kiper who contributed a word here, a piece of advice there, and otherwise helped.

My book was published thanks to all these wonderful people.

And a great big thank you to my husband, Yudka, who was, as always, constantly by my side.

Dear Readers,

This book, written originally in Hebrew, is here translated into English. You'll find a new language in it, that of the wonderful world of medicine. The book you are about to read doesn't tell a story. Instead, it gives answers to questions you always wondered about, but hadn't the courage to ask.

Every medical test uses its own instruments. "How does it work?" "How is it built?"

"What's my doctor searching for in my throat?" "What's he looking for in my ear?" "How did that germ or virus get into my body?"

These are questions that everyone wonders about. These are questions that concern each and every one of us.

The book, **Exploring the WORLD OF MEDICINE**, opens a window into this wide world.

It collects together detailed information on the most important and fascinating areas in the world of medicine, uncovers their mysteries and brings you closer to them.

Strange medical and scientific concepts, and questions about how medical equipment works, all become familiar and clear.

As you read on, you uncover the interesting and fascinating world of medicine.

Happy reading!

Table of Contents

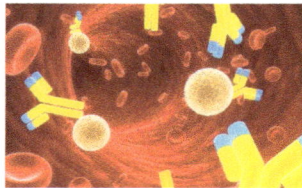

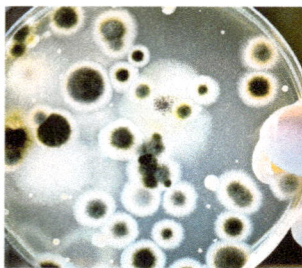

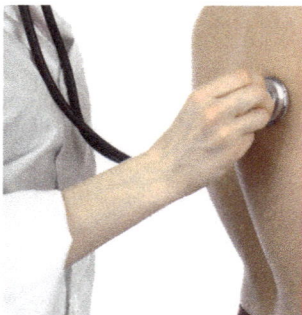

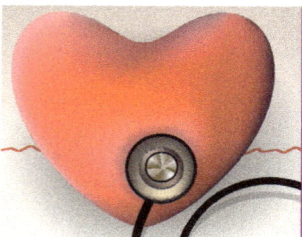

the instrument measuring blood pressure – blood pressure gauge, creative activities

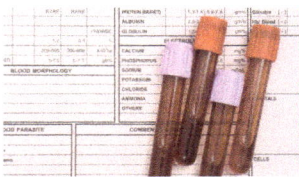

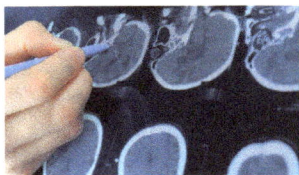

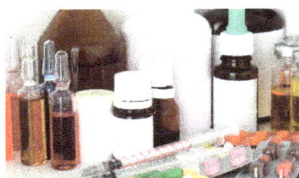

OUR IMMUNE SYSTEM IS OUR BODY'S DEFENSE SYSTEM

OUR IMMUNE SYSTEM

Did You Know?

To make sure that we stay healthy, our body has a sophisticated, efficient system of cells and organs that operates round the clock. This system is our:

Immune system

Why Our Immune System is so Sophisticated and so Efficient

Our immune system can tell the difference between cells that make up the tissue and organs in our body, and between cells such as germs, viruses and parasites that invade our body and can make us sick. When our immune system discovers these invaders, it launches a defensive response intended to ward them off and destroy them.

The Roles of Our Immune System

The roles of our immune system are:

- To detect "invaders" such as germs, viruses, parasites, fungi and toxic substances, and to prevent them from entering our body and spreading.

- To protect the systems in our body against infections and, in this way, assure that they function properly.

- To mobilize a full-scale defense system to fight the invaders and destroy them.

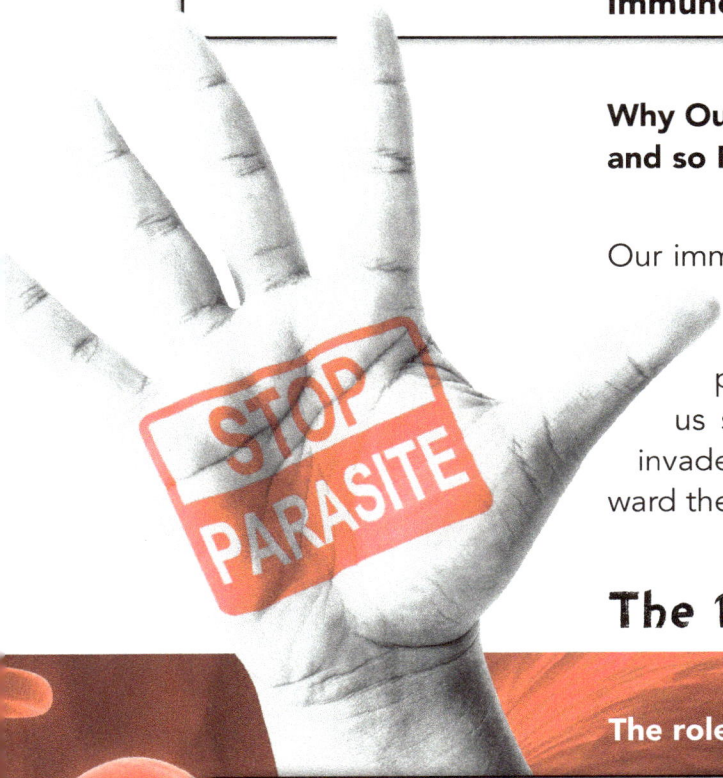

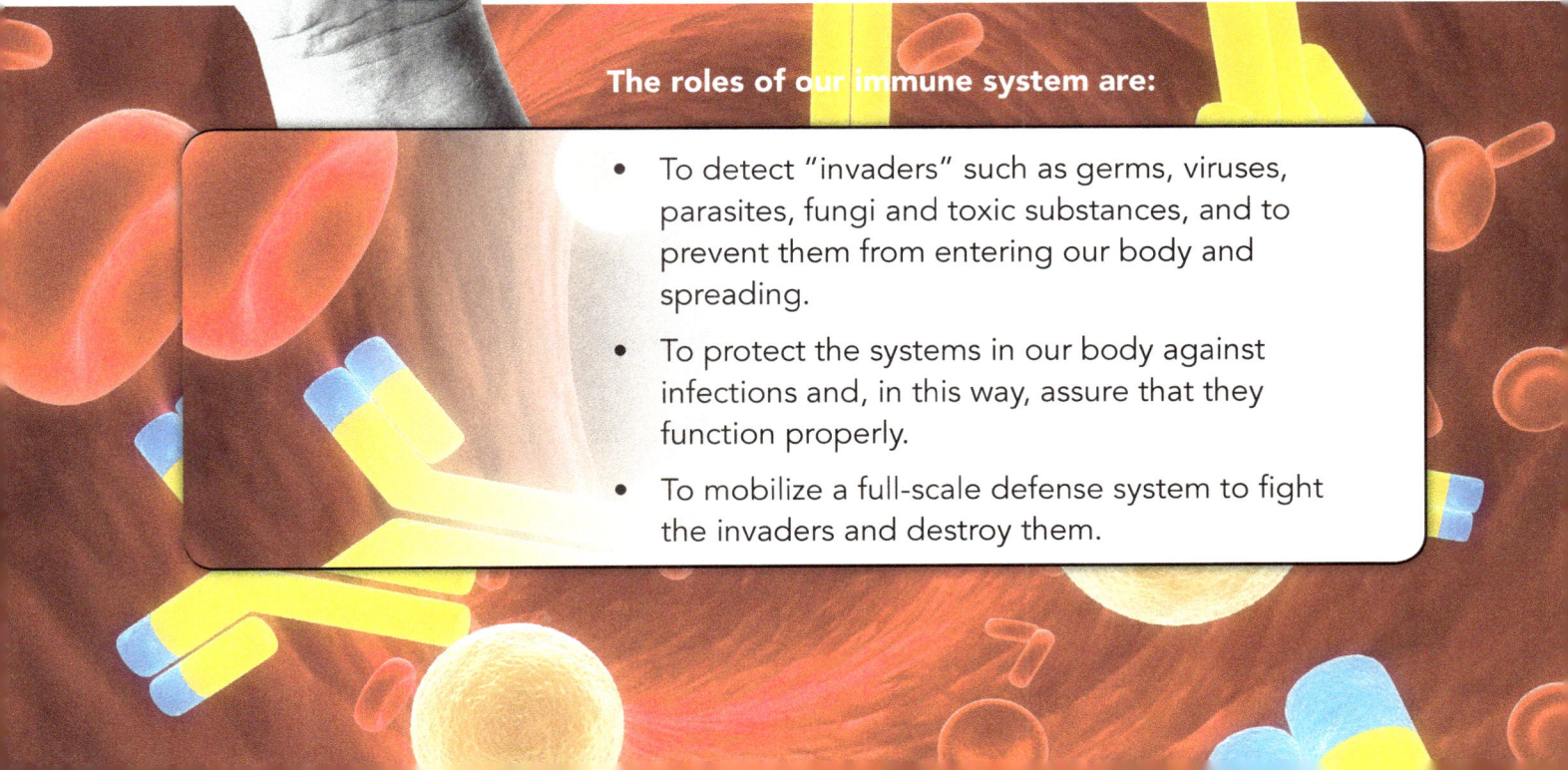

Important Facts:

> **Proteins are normally the building material of living cells.**

Proteins that are not the building material of living cells are perceived as foreign substances, and can provoke an immune reaction, and are called:

> **Antigens**

Antibody

Viruses, parasites, germs, fungi and poisonous substances can operate as antigens, triggering a defensive response by our immune system.

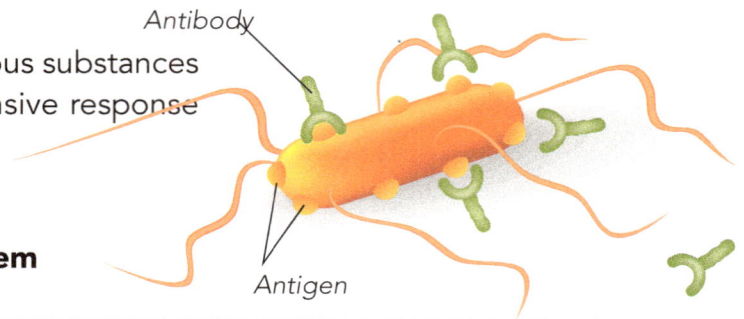

Antigen

Our Immune System is Our Defense System

> **Let's compare our immune system to a defense system.**

It has two lines of defense:

> **An external line of defense, consisting of our skin and of the tissue that covers the lumen of our respiratory and digestive tracts.**
>
> **An internal line of defense, consisting of our body's inner cells and organs. They function as "factories" that produce defense mechanisms against foreign invaders managing to penetrate our external line of defense.**

Human Skin Celles

Our Body's External Line of Defense

Our Body's External Line of Defense Consists of:

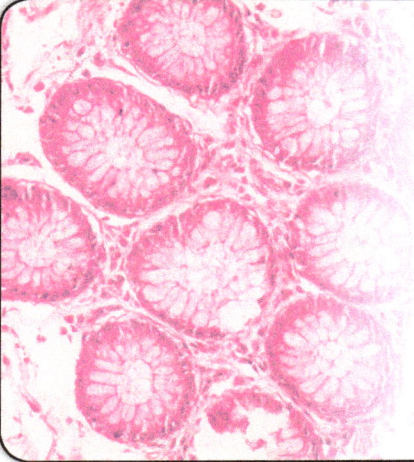

Tissue

1. Our skin, which is our body's largest organ. Our skin separates the inside of our body from the outside world. So, it is a kind of "protective shield" against invisible invaders.

2. The tissue that cover the lumen of our respiratory and digestive tracts. It is equipped with mechanisms that prevent foreign invaders from penetrating our body through it.

The thin skin tissue

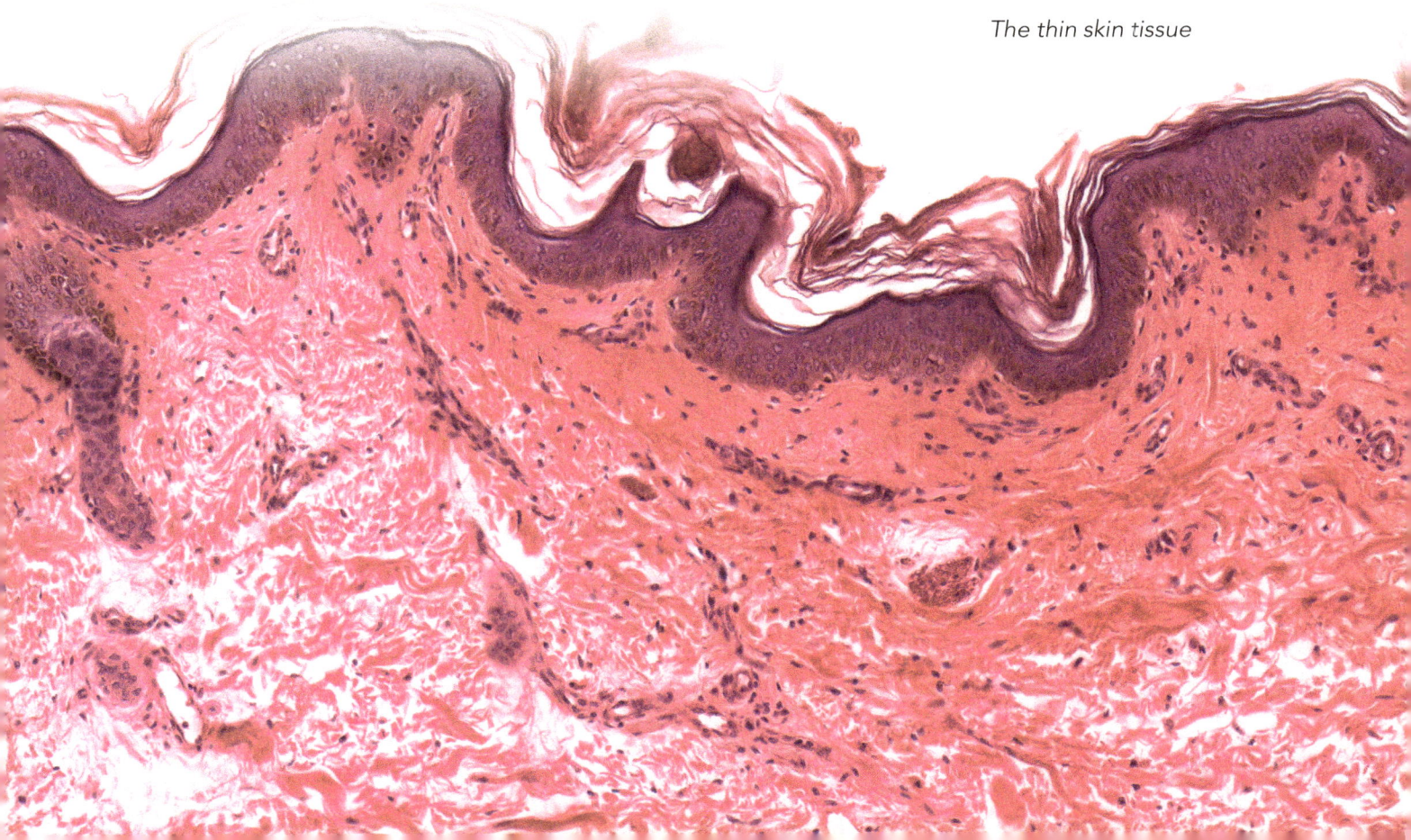

Our Body's Internal Line of Defense

Our body's internal line of defense is a kind of "factory" that produces defense mechanisms against foreign invaders. This "factory" has five platoons:

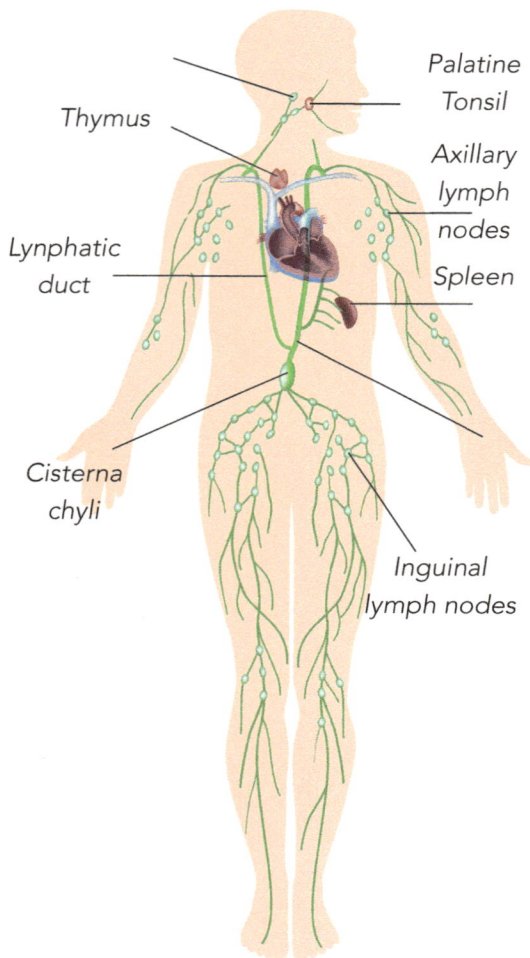

1 Marrow Platoon **2 Spleen Platoon** **3 Thymus Platoon** **4 Lymphatic System Platoon** **5 Lymph Nodes Platoon**

Thymus

Lynphatic duct

Cisterna chyli

Palatine Tonsil

Axillary lymph nodes

Spleen

Inguinal lymph nodes

The Five Platoons That Manufacture Our Body's Defense Mechanisms

1. Marrow Platoon

The Marrow Platoon is the tissue inside our bones that produces the cells of our blood system: red blood cells, platelets and leukocytes (which are different types of white blood cells).

2. Spleen Platoon

The Spleen Platoon is an internal organ that serves as a meeting place for different types of white blood cells.

3. Thymus Platoon

The Thymus Platoon is the organ through which part of our white blood cells pass. As they do so, they acquire special characteristics that enable them to fight invaders.

4. Lymphatic System Platoon

The Lymphatic System is made up of the lymphoid organs of the immune system, which are distributed throughout our body and linked to one another by lymphatic vessels.

The Lymphatic System Consists of:

- A network of capillaries and lymphatic vessels **is** draining to lymph nodes platoon**.**
- Lymph, or lymphatic fluid, which circulates throughout our lymphatic system until it reaches our bloodstream. It transports cells of our immune system to our body's tissues

How Interesting!

Our body movements and muscle contractions press on the lymphatic vessels carrying lymphatic fluid, causing it to move and to circulate throughout our body. In contrast, it is only the contractions of our heart that cause our blood to circulate throughout our body.

5. Lymph Nodes Platoon

Lymph Nodes consist of the immune system's "fighter" cells. Our lymphatic and blood vessels carry these cells, which gather in large quantities along the vessels, concentrating in particular in our groin, belly, under our armpit and round our neck. That is how node-like structures, called lymph nodes, are formed. These lymph nodes become a meeting place for different "fighter" immune cells.

Lymph Node

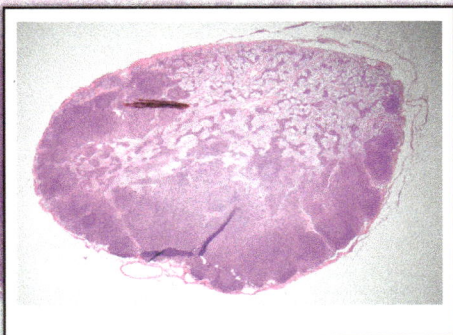

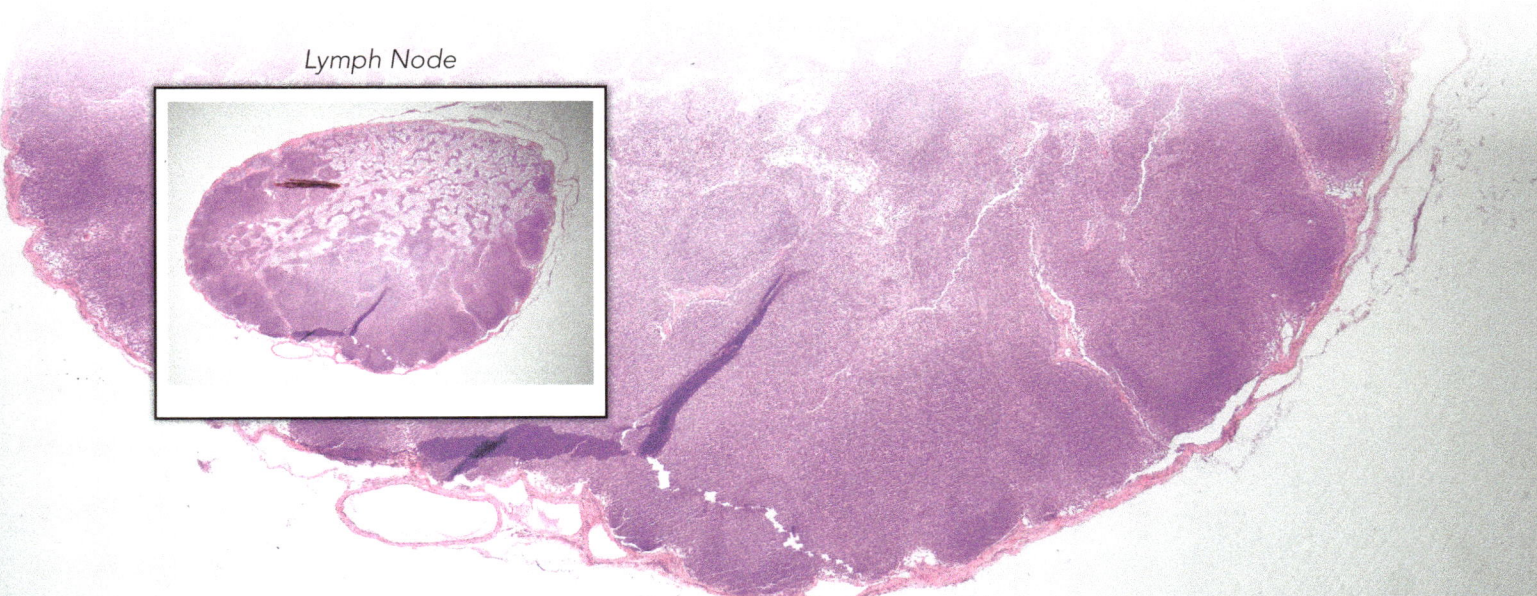

Important Information

Our immune system is made up of a group of organs and tissues functioning together as a unit and sharing a common goal: to protect our body against "invaders".

Useful Information

Sometimes, when we have a cold, we feel painful little lumps in our neck. These lumps are lymph nodes. They are swollen because the immune cells inside them just fought the invaders.

The Active Cells Platoon in Our Body's Internal Line of Defense Operates in This Way:

The defense cells, which are our immune cells, set out to protect our body.

⬇

They leave our bone marrow and thymus gland,

⬇

travel through our blood vessels,

⬇

and pass through our lymph vessel system,

⬇

reaching our lymph nodes and spleen.

⬇

From there, they wander with our bloodstream throughout our body, "on patrol".

⬇

Wherever they find an infection, as the result of the penetration of an invader,

⬇

they rush to locate it

⬇

and to carry out their duty.

Bone marrow

Trachea
Thymus
Lungs
Heart

Macrophage

The platoons on guard set out to take defensive action.

The first to set out to defend our body is the white blood cell platoon, which is made up of cells called macrophages. Their defense mechanism identifies the invader as a foreign protein, swallow it and present it, or parts of it, to the other white blood cells.

Neutrophils form another white blood cell platoon. They wander with our bloodstream, reach infected areas in our body, detect invaders, and kill the germs directly.

Neutrophil

Lymphocyte Blood Cell Platoon:

This is the main platoon that defends our body against invaders.

The Lymphocyte Blood Cell Platoon Is Divided into Two Parts:

Lymphocyte

T-Cell (T-Lymphocyte) Platoon

B-Cell (B-Lymphocyte) Platoon

The membranes of T-cells and B-cells have special molecules called receptors.

These receptors are the defense mechanisms of T-cells and B-cells, and they can detect invaders that have penetrated our body. Each receptor is adapted to the identity of a specific invader. They can be likened to field scouts, because their role is to find out what is going on in our body and who has invaded it.

What is a molecule?

A molecule is a tiny particle from which all material is built.

T-Cells and B-Cells Embark on Defensive Action Against the Invaders

T-Cells	B-Cells
When T-cells embark on defensive action, they have several roles:	When B-cells embark on defensive action, they have several roles:
They form contact with macrophages cells that have already met the foreign protein and swallowed it.	They detect the invaders and, following their familiarity with them, start to produce antibodies against them.
↓	↓
After familiarizing themselves with the foreign protein.	These antibodies, which are Y-shaped protein molecules, are released into our lymphatic system and bloodstream.
↓	↓
additional fighter T-cells directly kill various viruses and parasites with the help of cells called killer cells.	Each B-cell produces one type of "fighter" antibody that is specially adapted to a particular antigen, and against which it embarks on defensive action.
↓	↓
Other defender T-cells start to release substances that activate B-cells.	A small group of B-cells turn into memory B-cells.
↓	
Another small group of T-cells multiply rapidly, and remain in our bloodstream as memory T-cells.	

B-cell producing antibodies

What Do Memory Cells Remember?

T-Cells	B-Cells
If the same foreign protein penetrates our body again, our memory T-cells remember its chemical signal. They quickly detect it, and in this way can respond far more swiftly than the first time.	If the same invader penetrates our body a second time, memory B-cells remember it, based on its chemical signal, and swiftly detect it. At once, they accelerate antibody production to a much greater extent compared to their first encounter with the foreign protein.

What I Would Like To Know:

Can You Catch the Same Infection More than Once?

This is a very interesting question. For some insight, read this historical story:

A Story from the Past

The ancient Greeks realized that people who recovered from the plague did not catch this fatal disease again for the rest of their lives. Their body remembered the agent that caused it the first time, and was able to respond to its presence far more efficiently when it returned a second time.

How Is This Story from the Past Connected to Modern Medical Knowledge?

In the past, people did not know the causes of diseases. Today, medical science has shown that the immune system, whose role it is to keep our body safe, remembers every type of invader that ever infected us, thanks to memory T-cells and memory B-cells.

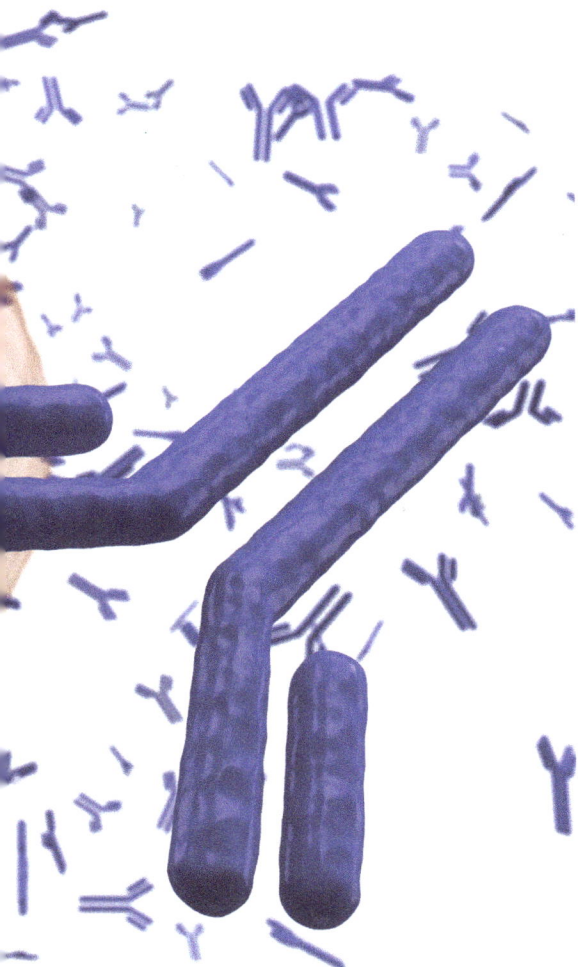

Important Information

Our body has different types of cells. Each cell is designed to perform duties specific to only it. All our cells cooperate by transmitting information by means of chemical signals produced by a variety of molecules.

This reciprocity between the different cells and organs in our body allows them: *(See the box below)*

> **to build a sophisticated, complex information network**

> **to respond swiftly and precisely to any invader penetrating our body.**

Think about This

Every B-cell produces antibodies, releasing them into our bloodstream at the astonishing rate of approximately 2,000 per second, or 120,000 per minute.

Calculate how many antibodies are released into our bloodstream in 10 minutes, in 60 minutes, and in as many minutes as you like.

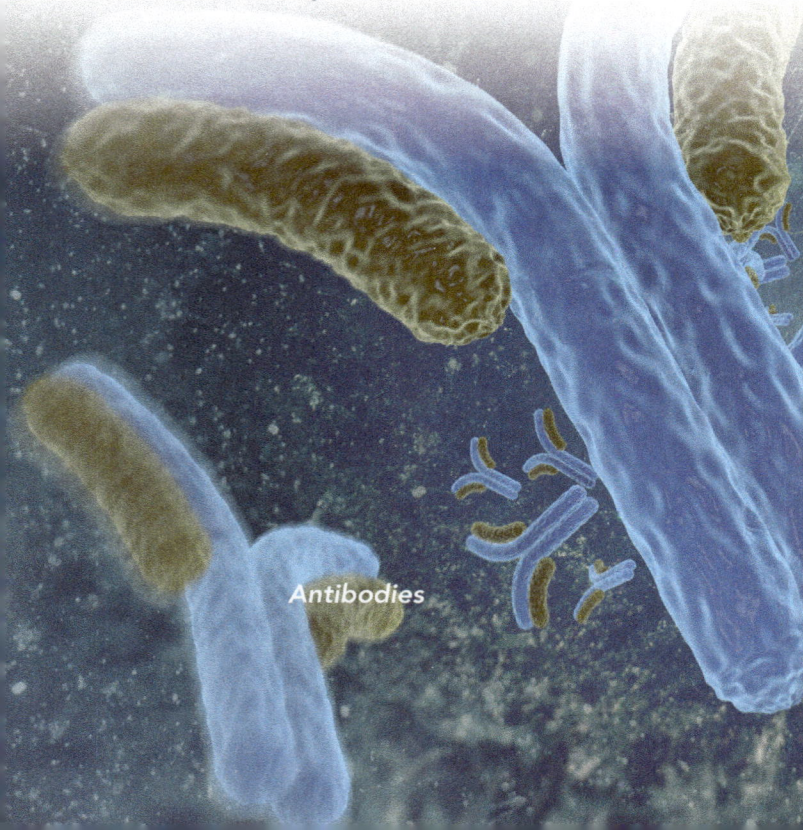

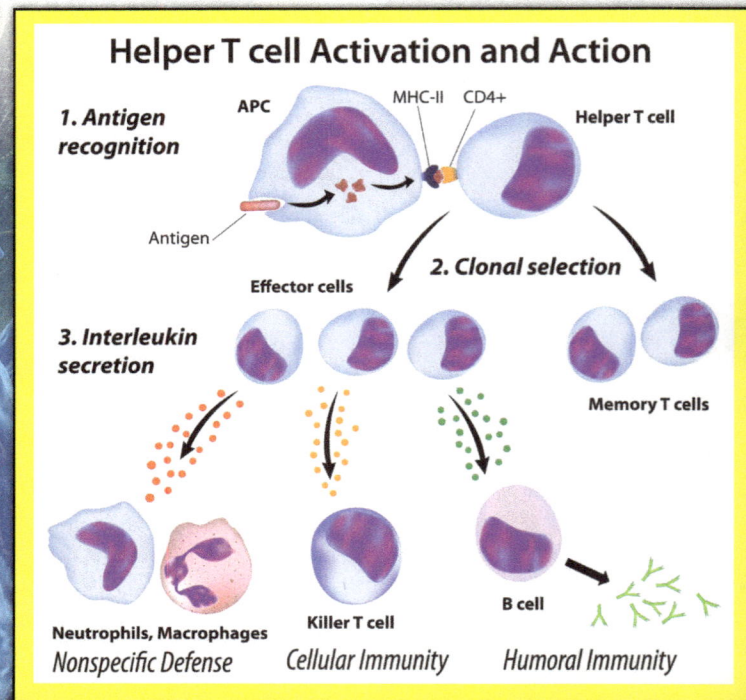

Antibodies

Helper T cell Activation and Action

1. Antigen recognition

APC   MHC-II   CD4+   Helper T cell

Antigen

2. Clonal selection

Effector cells

3. Interleukin secretion

Memory T cells

Neutrophils, Macrophages
Nonspecific Defense

Killer T cell
Cellular Immunity

B cell
Humoral Immunity

How is it possible that you got the flu or caught a cold once again this year?

Yes, there is a reason that you got the flu again this year even though you had it last year. It is because the flu virus you caught this year is a different kind. So, your body's memory T-cells and memory B-cells did not recognize it, and could not respond appropriately.

Similarly, if you caught a cold again this year, that is because the common cold is caused by many different types of viruses, and your memory T-cells and memory B-cells are unfamiliar with the particular type that invaded your body this time round.

Remember:

Sometimes, there are different types of pathogens that your memory cells are unacquainted with. That is why this year you may catch a different version of the very same illness that you came down with last year.

However, if you are ever exposed to the very same "invaders" again, it is more likely that you will not fall ill this time round, or that this time you will catch the mildest form of the illness.

Does Our Immune System Ever Fail To Perform its Duty?

When our body's "defense system", which is our immune system, fails to perform its duty and has difficulty responding to invaders, it is due to a condition called an:

Flu virus

Immunodeficiency Disorder

There are two kinds of immunodeficiency disorders:

- **Congenital Immunodeficiency:**

This condition appears in babies born with defects in their immune system.

- **Acquired Immunodeficiency:**

This condition appears when a person was born with a healthy immune system, but it was harmed in the course of life.

The severest form of acquired immunodeficiency appears in people who have contracted the human immunodeficiency virus (HIV) and now suffer from acquired immunodeficiency syndrome (AIDS).

How Do People Who Have AIDS Cope with Their Disease?

People who have AIDS cope with the help of medications. Before specific medications were developed, it was fatal. Today, research, focusing in several directions, has enabled the development of a range of effective medications. However, in spite of the fact that these medications **delay the multiplication of the HIV virus and halt the progress of AIDS in infected people they do not get rid of it entirely.**

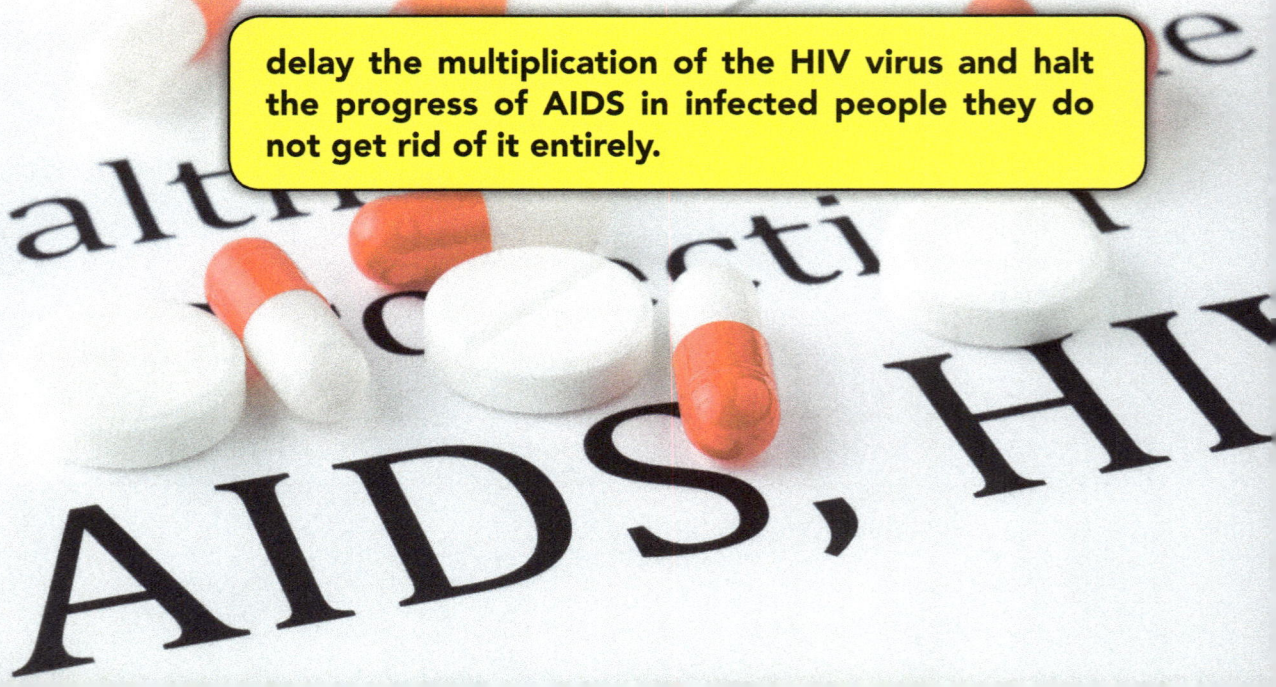

I Am Curious

Why Is it so Hard for Scientists To Develop a Vaccine against the HIV Virus?

It is difficult for scientists to develop a vaccine against the HIV virus because it is so different than all other known viruses.

The reason that the HIV virus is different from any other known virus is because it constantly changes its genetic features, that is, mutates, at an incredible speed. That is its special "trick".

More on the "Trick" that the HIV Virus Uses

The "trick" that the HIV virus uses in order to continue multiplying is to constantly change its protein shell (capsid), and at an incredible speed. The protein shell of all viruses is composed of antigens, which trigger the body's immune response. However, the shell of the HIV virus changes with such dizzying swiftness that even the body's T-cells and B-cells, whose receptors are the immune system's unique protective mechanism, cannot manage to adapt themselves quickly enough. As a result, the immune system fails in its duty to protect the body, and collapses.

The Challenge That Science Faces

The challenge that science faces is to develop a vaccine that will quell the incredibly swift, constant mutation of the HIV virus and, in so doing, immunize the body against it.

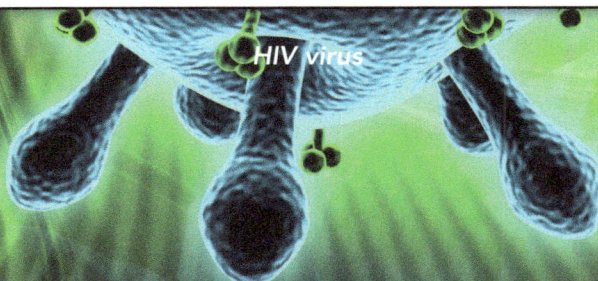

HIV virus

Important Information

Since the mid-1990s, significant progress has been made in the treatment of AIDS patients and of HIV carriers (people who have a dormant form of the HIV virus).

What Happens When the Immune System Overreacts to Environmental Antigens?

Did you ever start sneezing, and could not stop?

Do your eyes water at times?

Do your hands start itching the moment you touch grass or trees?

These are typical reactions of the immune system when something is wrong with it.

Sometimes, our immune system reacts very strongly to common substances in our environment that normally do not trigger an immune response.

This reaction is known as an allergic response.

Many people are allergic to some antigen or other in our environment.

Invaders that Trigger an Allergic Reaction by Our Immune System

- The pollen of various flowers, grass, weeds and trees, which fly in the air.

- Cigarette smoke, substances emitted into the air by industrial plants, sawdust, trees, flour, etc.

- Milk products, eggs, peanuts and nuts.

- Seasonal weather changes, transitional seasons (spring and autumn), winds and dampness.

- The hair, fur and feathers of animals such as cats, dogs, poultry, birds and horses.

- House dust mites, which are microscopic organisms found mainly in bedding.

Cancer and the Immune System

How does a Cancer develop?

Sometimes the control mechanisms of a cell are damaged. Something goes wrong with one cell.

If that cell starts to multiply uncontrollably, it causes the section of the tissue in which it is located to grow and to turn into what is known as a **tumor**.

In the first stage, when the tumor is benign, it does not damage the body.

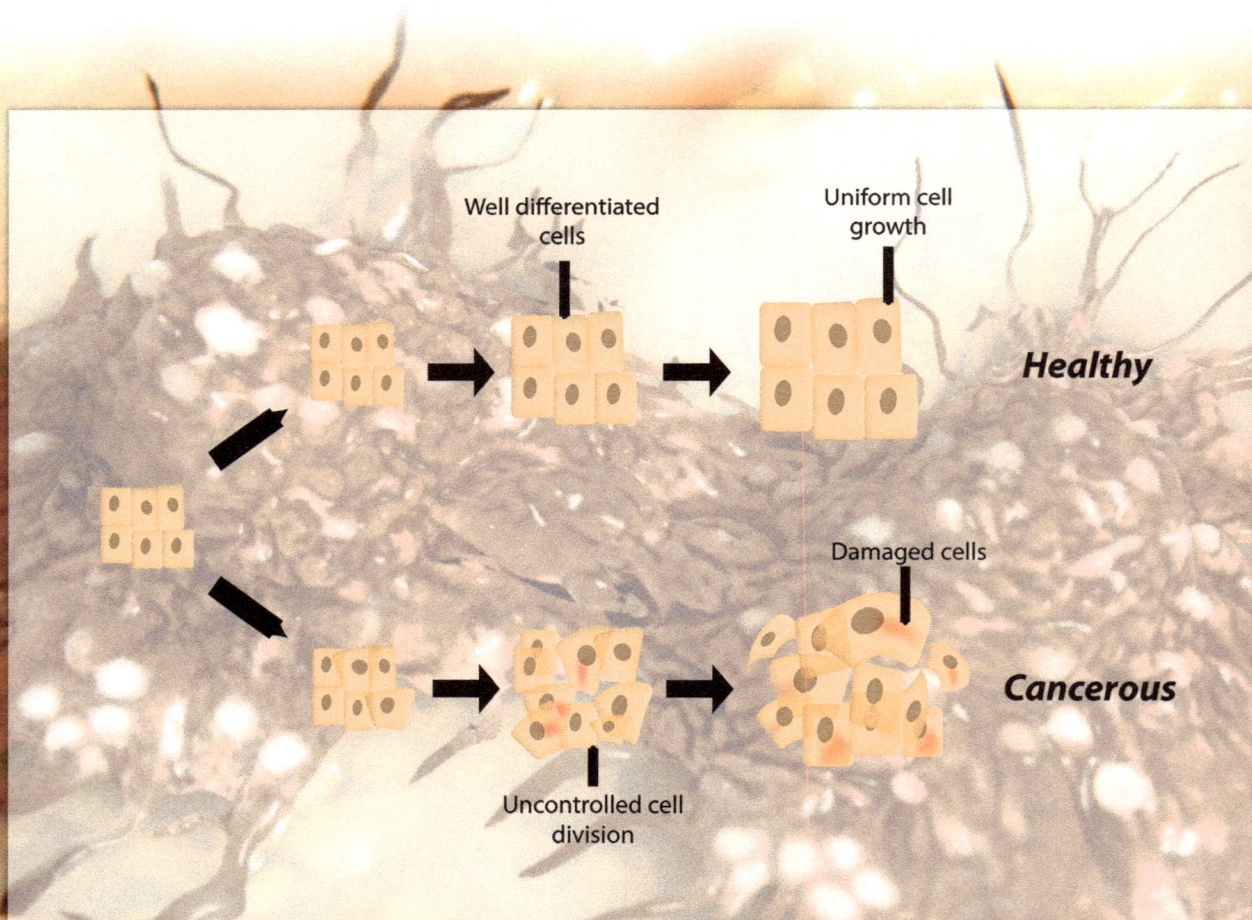

Well differentiated cells

Uniform cell growth

Healthy

Damaged cells

Cancerous

Uncontrolled cell division

Cancer progression

When Do Tumors Damage the Body?

Cancer cell squeezes through the wall of a blood capillary

> When the cells in which something went wrong not only create tumors locally, but also invade neighboring tissue.

> The tumor cells use the body's fluids to travel to other parts of the body, where they multiply and create additional tumors.

When Are these Tumors Called?

These tumors are called cancerous tumors.

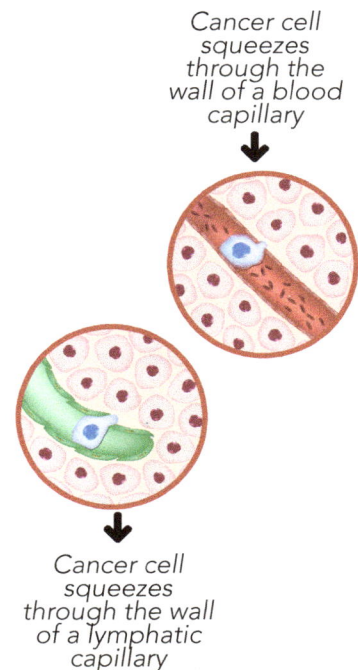

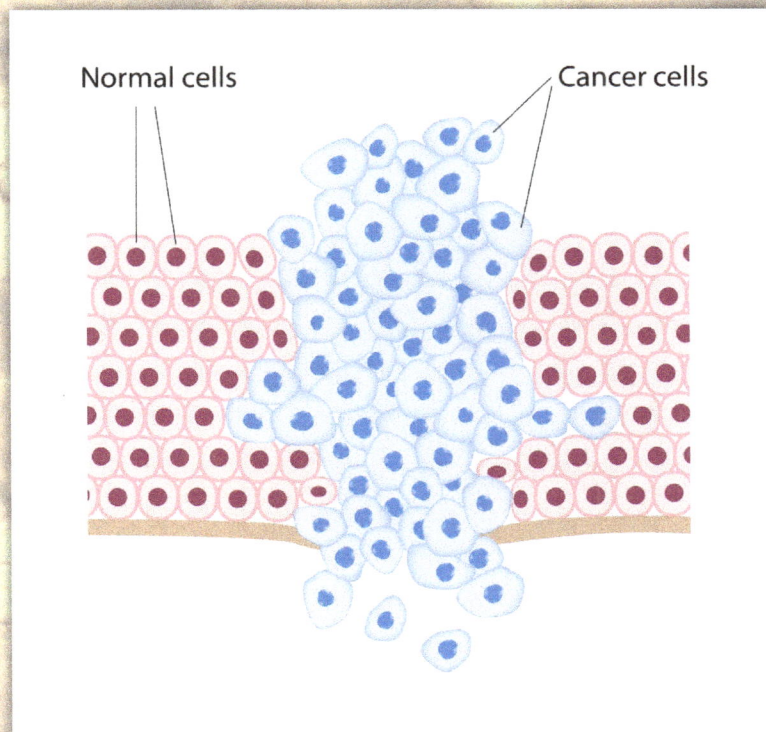

Cancer cell squeezes through the wall of a lymphatic capillary

Normal cells

Cancer cells

How the Immune System Copes with Cancer

The moment the immune system detects cancerous antigens, the immune cells embark on the offensive.

They set out to fight back.

↓

Macrophages cells surround the antigens on the surface of the cancerous cells.

↓

As a result,

↓

the T-cell system is activated:

↓

Some T-cells embark on direct action, and kill the cancerous cells.

↓

Cancer cells attacked by lymphocytes

Other T-cells activate the B-cell system: The B-cells produce antibodies against the antigens on the cancerous cells, and in this way help to destroy them.

Sometimes, the immune system has a hard time coping with cancer. In such cases, the medical profession comes to the rescue.

Cancer cells

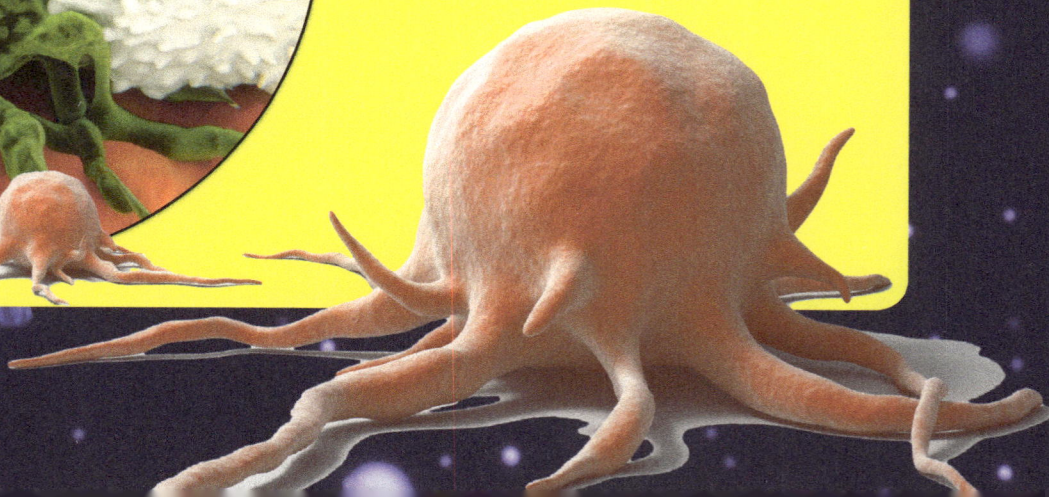

How the Medical Profession Helps Sick People Cope with Cancer

There are different kinds of medical treatments for malignant tumors. Their goal is:

The destruction of the malignant cells, and the restriction of damage to other tissue.

Cancer

The Advantages of Medical Treatment:

1. The number of people recovering from cancer increases.

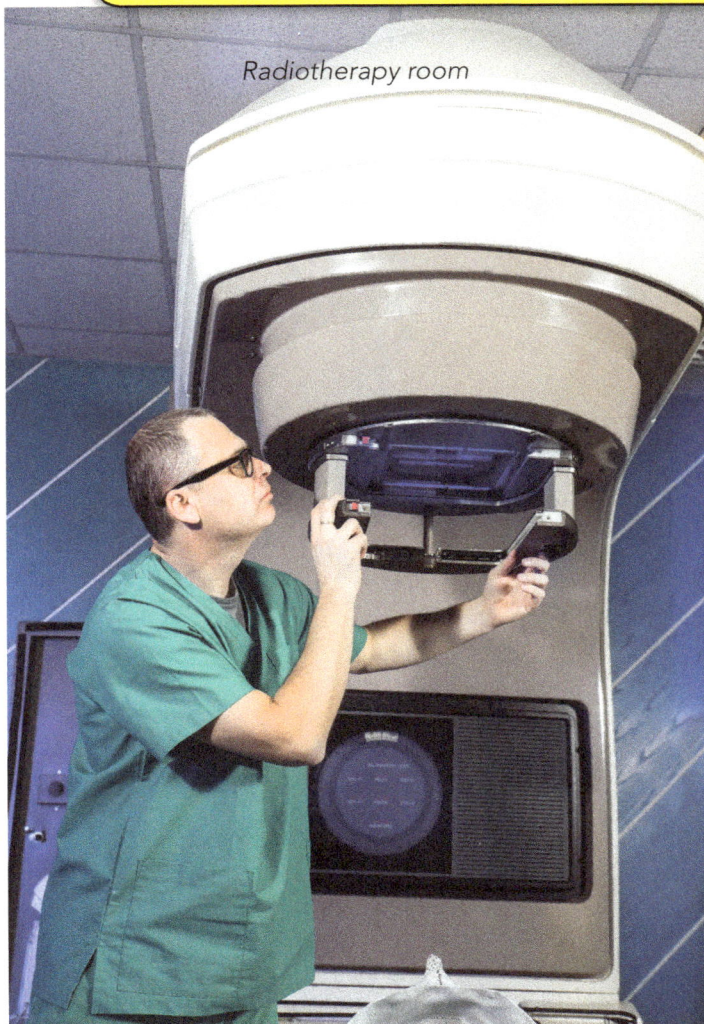

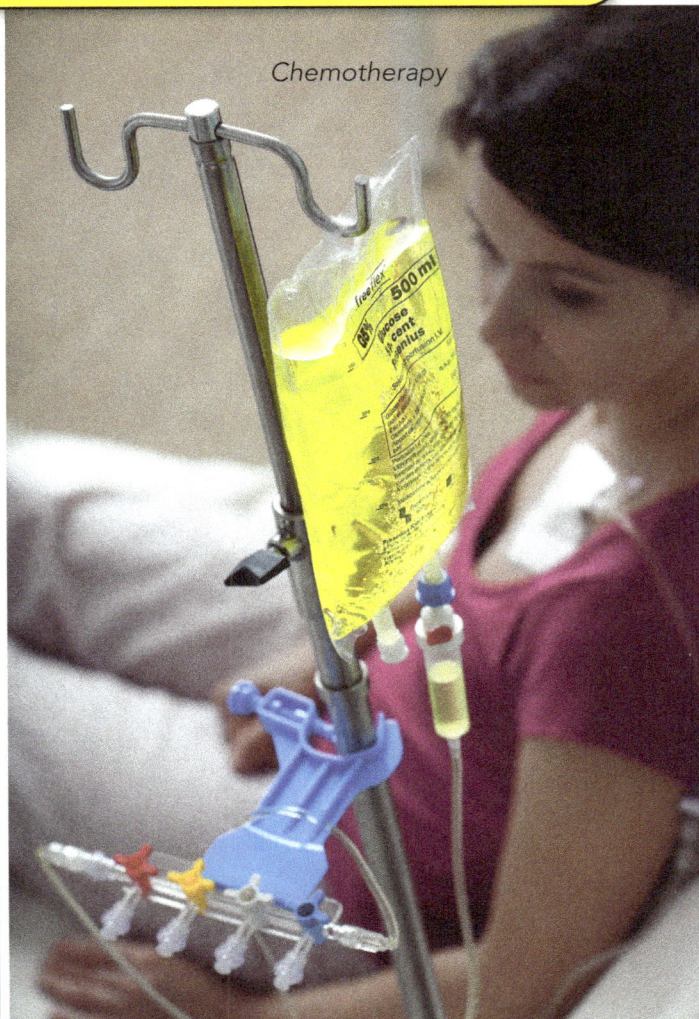

Radiotherapy room

Chemotherapy

2. The life expectancy of many sick people rises.

The Disadvantages of Medical Treatment:

1. When the malignant cells are destroyed, healthy tissue is damaged.

2. Sometimes, the malignant cells are totally destroyed, while at others only partly.

The medical profession has been conducting research on cancer for decades. It aspires to:

1. develop more focused, effective methods of destroying malignant cells that are multiplying, while restricting the damage to other tissue.

2. detect the basic fault causing healthy cells to become cancerous, and divide and multiply unceasingly.

This Is Very Important

The biggest challenge that cancer researchers face is to:

- outline ways to prevent the development of cancerous cells
- improve treatment methods
- improve the methods for early detection of cancer

Medical advice: Dr. Yael Levy

PATHOGENS

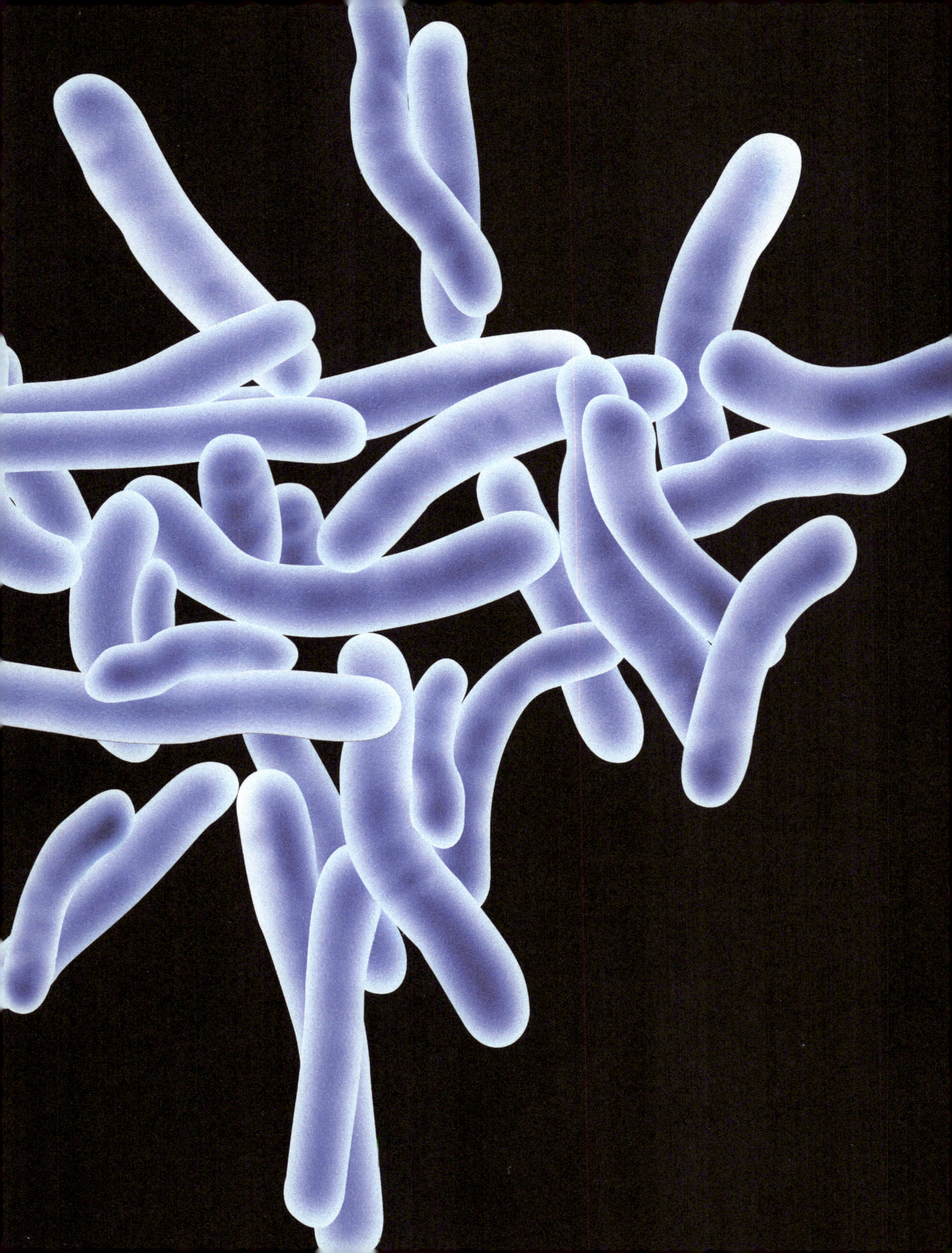

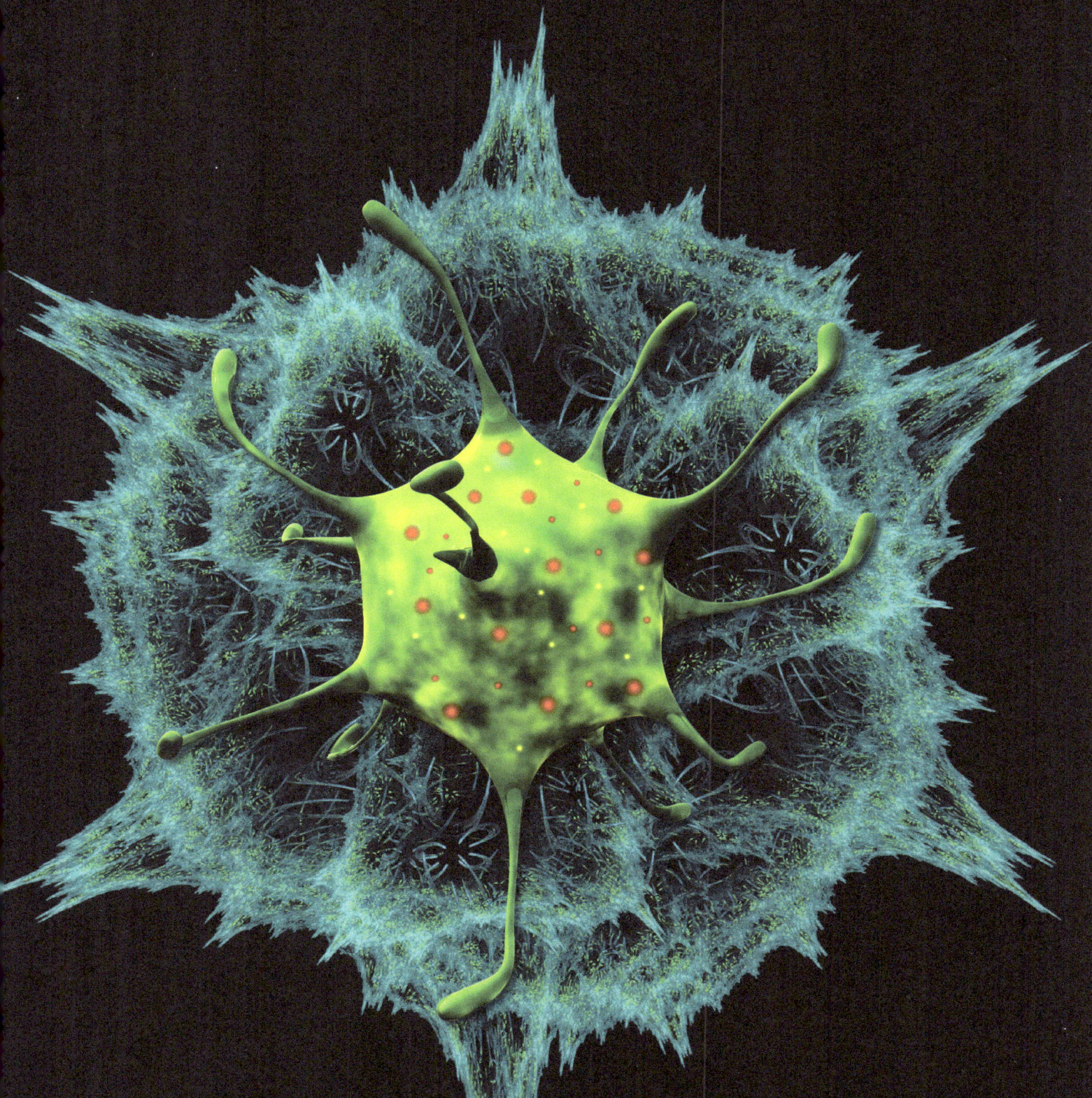

GERMS

Germs

What Are Germs?

Germs are living organisms created from a single cell. They exist everywhere: in the air, in the water and in the soil. They also develop in all living beings.

What Do Germs Look Like?

Because germs consist of only a single cell, you need a microscope to see them. Their scientific name is bacteria, which is Latin for staffs or canes. They were called bacteria because the first ones discovered were rod-shaped.

Different Germs Have Different Shapes

Germs Can Be Divided into Three Groups, Based on Their ShapeGroup 3

Group 1	Group 2	Group 3
The germs in this group are spiral-shaped and are called spirochetes	The germs in this group are shaped like little balls and are called cocci.	The germs in this group are rod-shaped and are called bacilli.

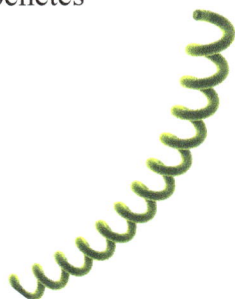

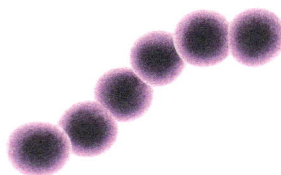

Types of pathogen

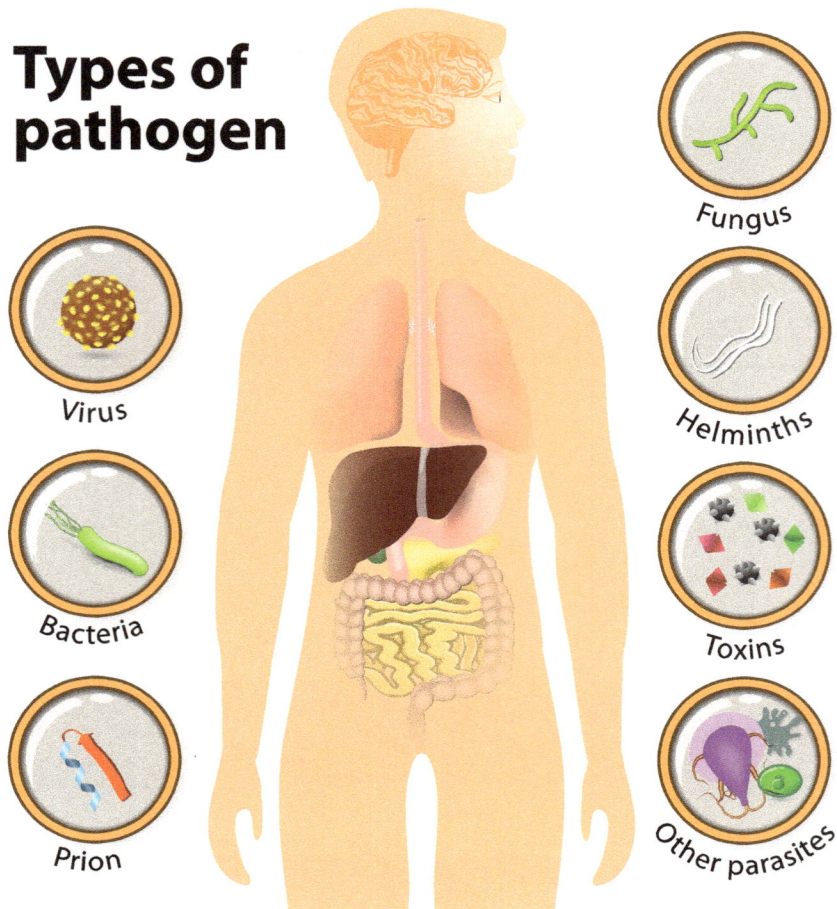

Types of Germs: Helpful Germs, Harmful Germs

There Are Two Types of Germs:

Helpful Germs

Helpful germs don't cause diseases and are called called:

non-pathogenic germs.

Harmful Germs

Harmful germs cause diseases and are called:

pathogenic germs.

You may be surprised to hear that most germs are, in fact, helpful and don't cause diseases.

Helpful germs exist in milk and in its products: cheese, yoghurt, and more.

Other germs live harmlessly in our body, inhabiting our skin, mouth, bowels, and so on.

Good germs have two roles:

1. To help break down the food we eat.

2. To help our immune system.

Of course, some germs are indeed harmful and cause diseases:

- **Some harmful germs only attack human beings.**
- **Some harmful germs only attack animals.**
- **Some harmful germs are transferred from animals to human beings.**

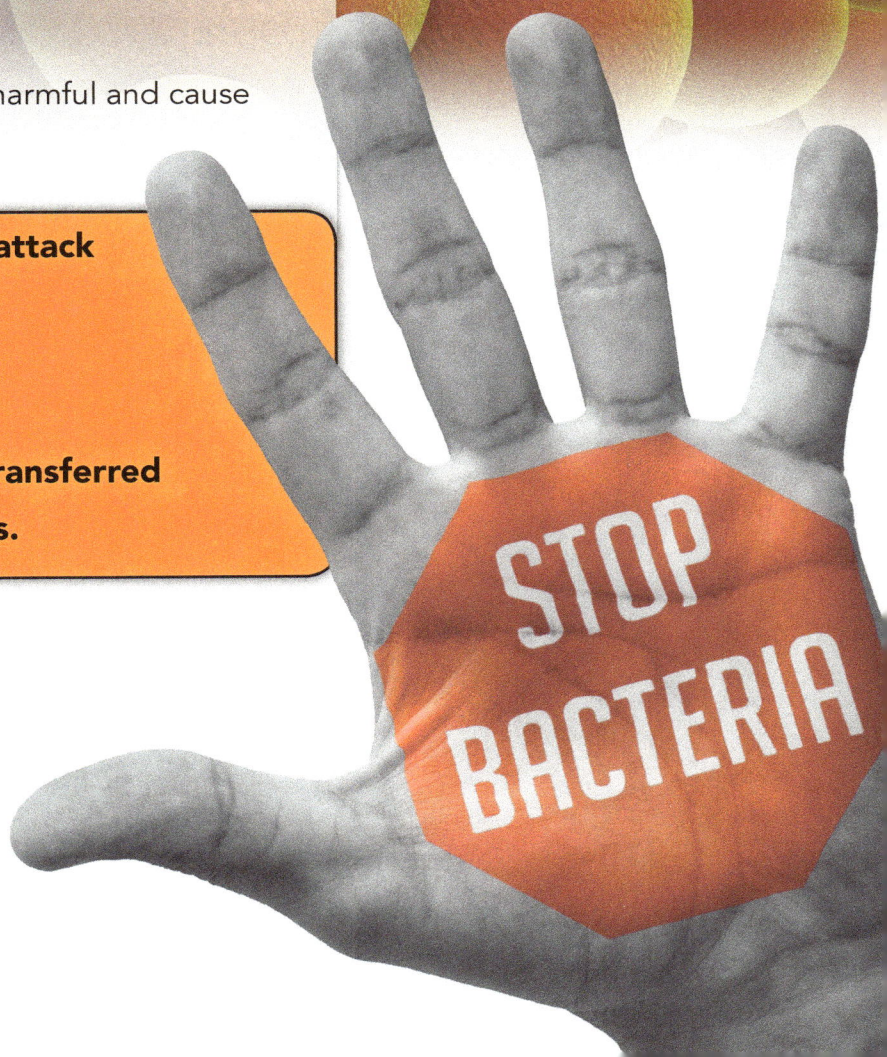

STOP BACTERIA

Where Do Germs Live?

There are germs in the air, in the water, in the soil, and in all the living organisms found all around us.

How Do Pathogens Get into Our Body?

Our skin is the first barrier that germs must face in order to enter our body. All the same, some find interesting ways to manage to get into our body.

Some germs attack food products. They turn milk sour, spoil butter and poison meat by excreting toxins. It is dangerous for our health to eat these food products.

Some germs manage to enter our mouth and upper respiratory tract, that is, our nose and throat. As we breathe air into our lungs, germs may enter our nose, ears, throat, mouth and pharynx, and under certain conditions make us sick.

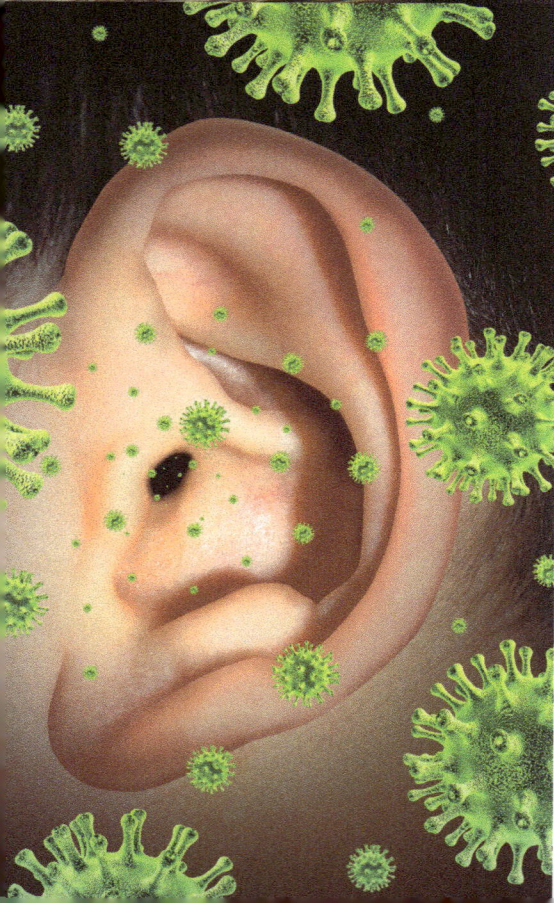

How Do We Know a Germ Has Got into Our Body?

When a germ manages to get into our body, it lets us know. For instance, if a germ gets into our lungs, they become inflamed, causing us to get a high temperature and to cough. That's how the lungs tell us they've fallen sick.

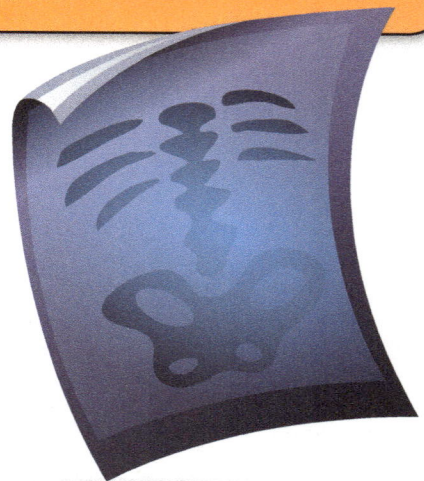

What Germs Do to Our Body

When germs get into our body, they multiply.

One germ splits into 2 germs. Then each of these 2 germs also splits into 2 germs. So, now there are 4 germs. Then each of these 4 germs also splits into another 2 germs. So, now there are 8 germs.

In this way, the germs continue to multiply in our body.

Germs multiply quickly. It takes one germ about 20 to 40 minutes to split into two germs. Each of these two germs in turn then also splits into two germs in another 20 to 40 minutes. This process can continue endlessly.

As a result, ten thousand million germs can be produced in just one day, making us sick.

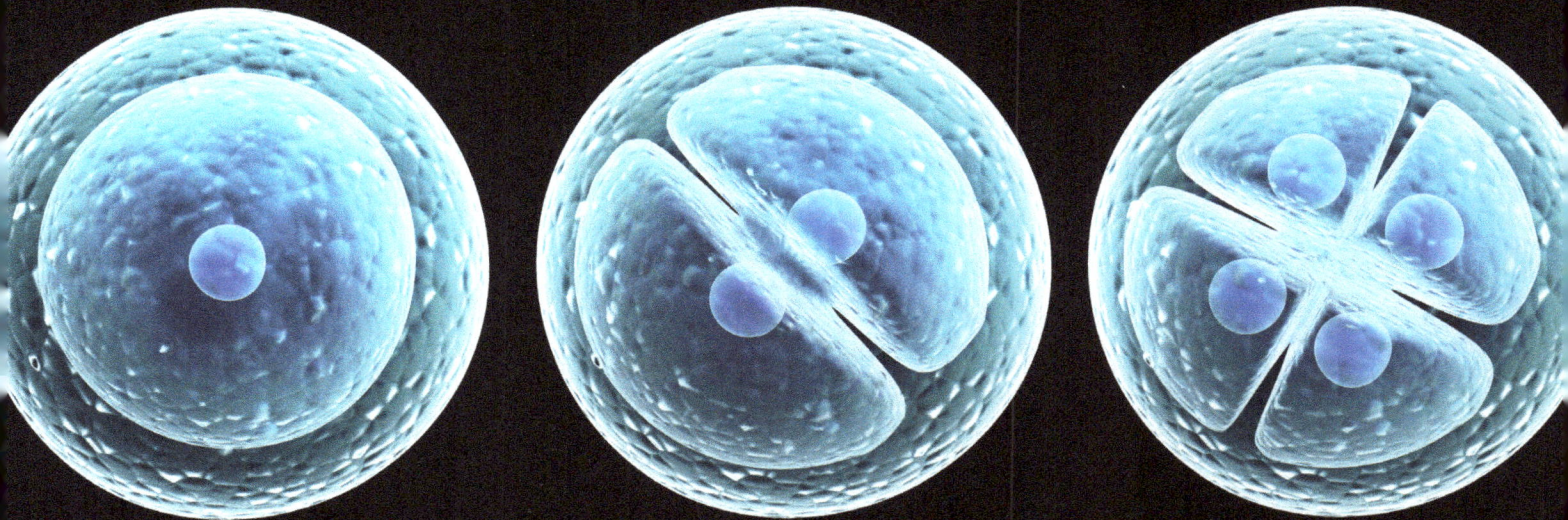

How Our Body Defends Itself against Germs

Leucocytes are divided into several groups. Our body's main defense against germs is the immune system, by means of white blood cells called leucocytes.

The first group of leucocytes is macrophages. Their means of defence against germs is ingestion. They identify the invader as a foreign protein, ingest it, and present it, or particles of it, to the other white blood cells

Another group of leucocytes is lymphocytes.

Our body creates two types of lymphocytes:

T-cells (T-lymphocytes)

Some T-cells are helpers. They release various substances into our blood and help B-cells in different ways. When they come into contact with "invaders" such as germs and viruses, they attach themselves to them and destroy them.

B-cells (B-lymphocytes)

B-cells, in contrast to T-cells, produce substances known as antibodies all the time. These antibodies exist in our blood, and are ready to attack and successfully fight off "invad ers" such as germs and viruses.

Important Facts

Each B-cell produces a special antibody for each different germ or virus, just as a locksmith makes a special key for each different lock.

B-cells are grouped according to the structure of the antibody they produce. Each group of B-cells has a special defense function.

T-cells and B-cells are two different groups. They work together for the same goal: the destruction of the germs in our body.

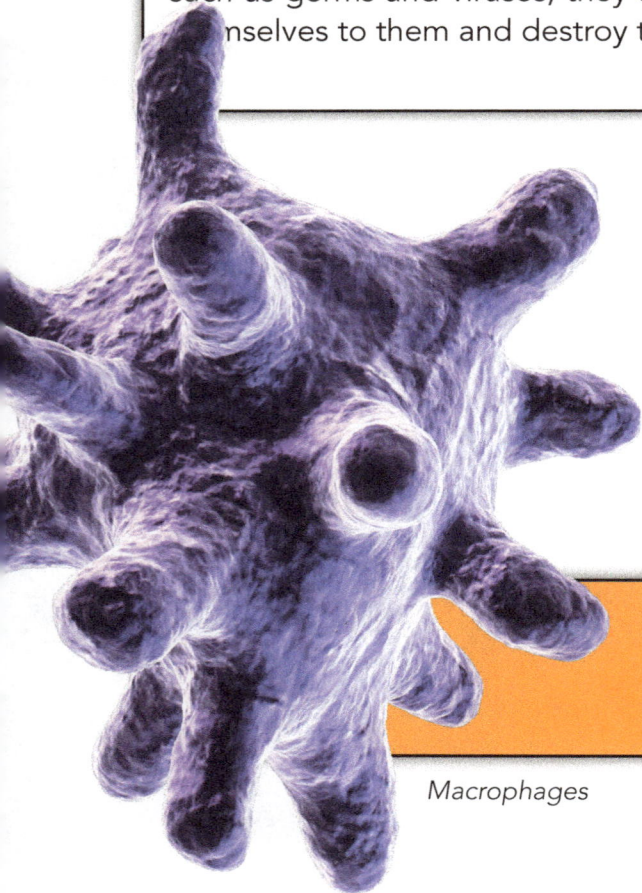

Macrophages

Fighting off Germs

Sometimes, our body is unable to fight off germs on its own. So, medicine was developed. Medicine helps us fight germs and destroy them.

Antibiotics are a medicine that fights germs.

Antibiotics

Antibiotics contain substances that are able to destroy germs or stop their development.

Certain types of germs are sensitive to certain antibiotics. That's why it's so important to identify the type of germ that's got into our body, and to find just the right antibiotic to destroy it.

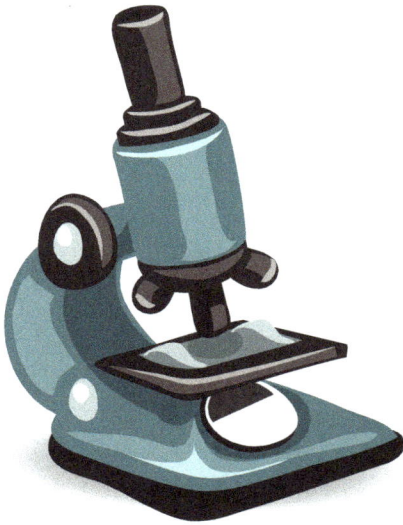

Identifying the Type of Germ

Like every living organism, germs also need "food" to thrive. In the laboratory, technicians experiment by putting "germ food", known by them as a "growth medium", on the surface of a special flat-bottomed shallow glass called a petri dish. They then place a sample that contains small amount of germs on top, and put the dish in an incubator with a temperature that enables them to multiply.

After several hours, a large group of germs is formed. You don't even need a microscope to see the large group of germs at the bottom of the petri dish, as it looks like a large stain.

Each stain, which is really a macroscopic cluster of germs, is called a "colony". This process of forming a "colony" is called "bacterial culture".

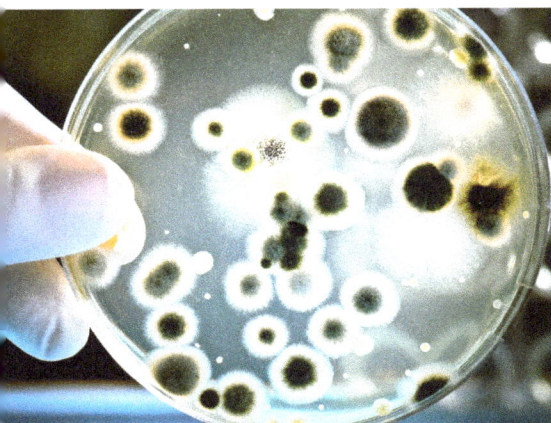

A Petri Dish

What Is the Purpose of a Bacterial Culture?

Bacterial cultures have two purposes:

> 1. **To identify the type of germ.**
>
> 2. **To determine the germ's sensitivity to a certain antibiotic, so it can be killed.**

How to Prevent Germs from Entering Your Body and Multiplying

Here are some things you can do:

- Always wash your hands before eating and after going to the toilet.

- Carefully wash any sores and scratches. Soap and water will usually wash off all the dirt and germs, and prevent germs from entering your body.

- Sometimes, however, soap and water do not get rid of all the germs. If they don't, use an antiseptic such as iodine.

- When you cough or sneeze, cover your mouth and nose with a tissue or with your hands. That way, you'll prevent harmful germs from spreading to other people.

- If you want to keep food, store it in the refrigerator or freezer.

- Water contains germs that can make babies sick. Boiling it kills the germs. So, always boil water before giving it to babies under one year old

Some particularly dangerous germs can make us come down with a serious disease such as:

Tetanus | Diphtheria | Meningitis | Pneumonia | Whooping Cough

Fortunately, vaccinations have been developed against these diseases.

Why Get Vaccinated?

Accination helps our body develop resistance to dangerous invaders without becoming sick.

How Does Our Body Develop Resistance?

Our body develops resistance with the help of a vaccination, that is, with the help of a special substance that deals solely with the invader that can cause a particular disease in our body.

This special substance is called a vaccine.

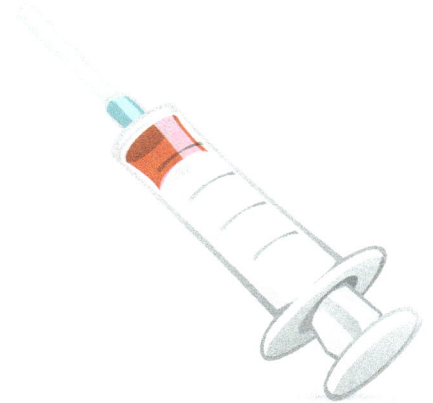

Childhood vaccines

✓ diphteria
✓ tetanus
✓ polio
☐ whooping cough
☐ meningitis C
☐ measles

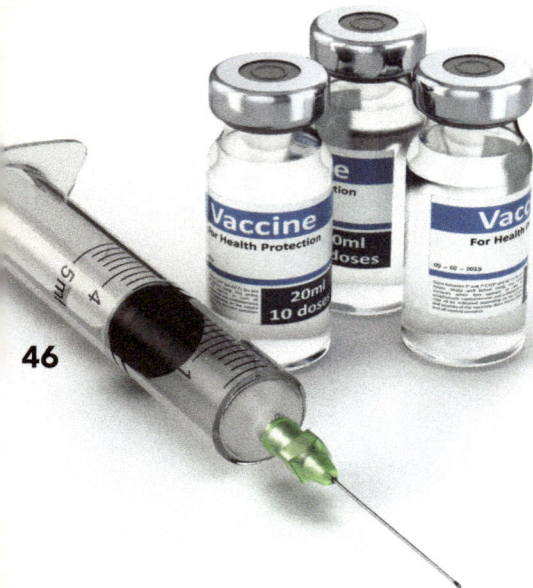

What Is a Vaccine?

A vaccine is a solution containing the weakened or dead form of the germ that causes a certain serious disease, or some of its components.

How Vaccines Work

Vaccines prepare our immune system to fight real pathogens, should they try to invade our body:

> **Vaccines cause the appropriate B-cells to multiply.**
>
> **Vaccines cause these B-cells to produce antibodies without making us sick.**

Then, when a real disease tries to attack our body, it is prepared for it and is able to defend itself.

Who Should Be Vaccinated?

The Ministry of Health recommends that all children be vaccinated. Where appropriate, adults are also vaccinated.

> **Babies receive vaccines according to a recommended schedule.**
>
> **They receive other vaccines when they are older. Adults also receive vaccines if necessary.**

How Are Vaccines Given?

Vaccines are given to us:

> **As an injection in our arm.**
> **As an injection in our thigh.**
> **As a liquid that we swallow.**

Some new vaccines are given us as a spray to our nose.

Some Interesting Facts

Anton van Leeuwenhoek was born in Holland in 1632. He invented the microscope. He discovered that tens of thousands of living organisms exist in the water, in the soil, in dust, and in many other substances.

Louis Pasteur was born in France in 1822. He discovered that infectious diseases were spread by germs, and were preventable. In 1860, he identified the germs causing silkworm diseases, and saved the French silk industry from ruin. He invented a method to kill harmful germs in milk without affecting its nutritious value. This procedure is called pasteurization. As a result, the lives of millions of babies were saved.

Joseph Lister was born in England, and worked as a surgeon in a Scottish hospital. He discovered that a substance called carbolic acid was an antiseptic, and introduced it to hospitals. This prevented infectious diseases from spreading from one patient to the other. He became world famous, and was appointed Chairman of Clinical Surgery at Kings College, London in 1877.

Robert Koch was born in Germany in 1843. He discovered that a particular germ caused a particular disease, and identified the germ that caused tuberculosis. He was awarded the Nobel Prize for Medicine in 1905.

How Germs Attack Our Teeth

It's important to understand the relationship between germs and our teeth:

> **1. Our teeth are protected by a layer of enamel, the hardest substance our body produces.**
>
> **2. There are always germs in our mouth and on our teeth.**
>
> **3. These germs can't get inside our teeth on their own and damage them.**
>
> **4. When these germs combine with other agents, such as sugar, they can get inside our teeth and damage them.**
>
> **5. Most food contains sugar. After we chew food and swallow it, some sugar is left on our teeth.**

The Connection between the Germs and Sugar Residues on our Teeth

Germs feed on sugar residues left on our teeth after we eat. They then produce acids capable of destroying the enamel coating of our teeth, causing:

1. Cavities   **2. Tooth decay**

When you get a cavity, go to your dentist at once for treatment. In that way, you'll prevent the development of tooth decay.

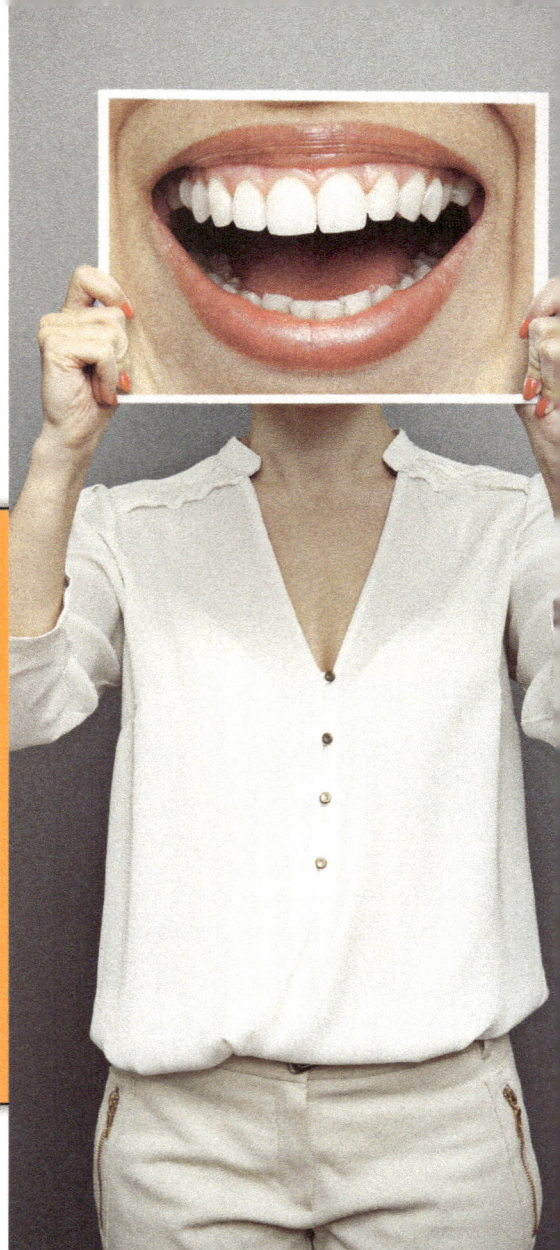

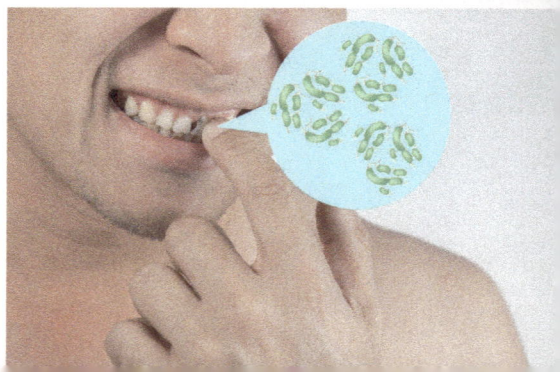

What Is Tooth Decay?

Tooth decay is a disease caused by:

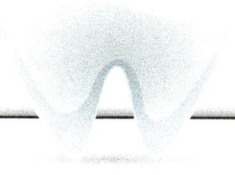

> **1. Germs accumulating on our teeth.**

> **2. Vitamin and mineral deficiency. Vitamins and minerals are food components essential for building our resistance. If we have a deficiency in vitamins and minerals, our teeth become soft and vulnerable, and the process of tooth decay sets in.**

How the Sugar in Our Food Causes Tooth Decay

Here's how the sugar in our food causes tooth decay:

It mixes with the germs on our teeth, ferments and creates an acid called lactic acid.

This lactic acid gradually dissolves the minerals in the hard outer enamel layer that protects our teeth.

It continues its march through our teeth. After reaching the dentin layer under the enamel coating, it continues on to the soft dental pulp inside, where tooth decay continues to progress.

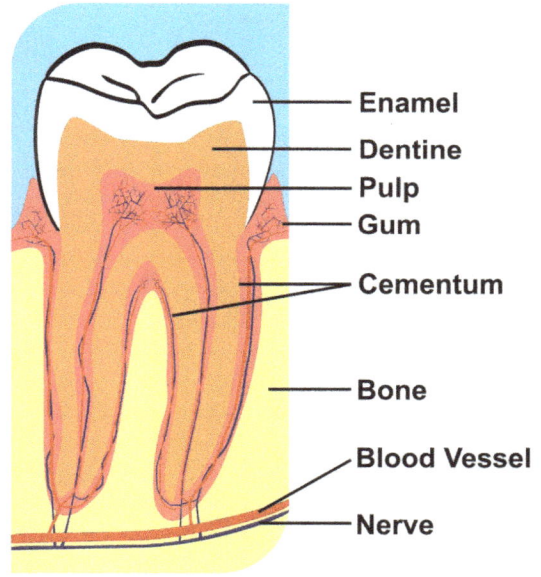

- Enamel
- Dentine
- Pulp
- Gum
- Cementum
- Bone
- Blood Vessel
- Nerve

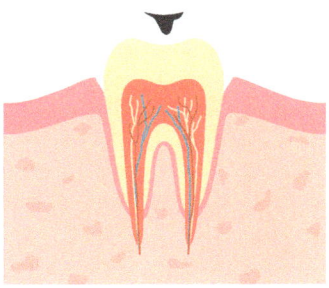

Enamel Decay

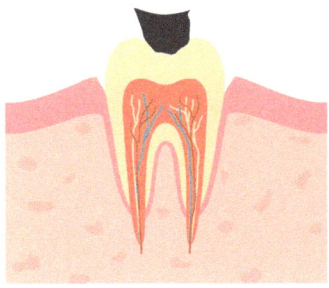

Dentin Decay

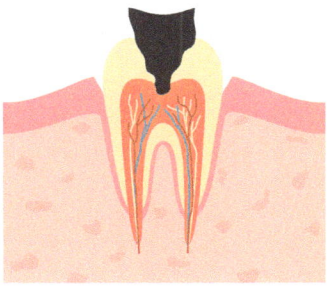

Pulp Decay

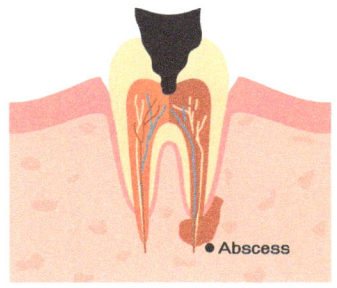

• Abscess

Infected Pulp

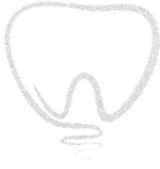

The Consequences of Tooth Decay

Tooth decay causes:

Discomfort | Swallowing and speech disorders | Aesthetic damage to our smile and face | Tooth loss | Gum, and even jawbone, infections | Pain

To Prevent Tooth Decay, Avoid Food with a Lot of Sugar that Lingers in Your Mouth

If you must have sweets, try to limit yourself to one a day. As soon as possible, brush your teeth well.

Food such as fruits and vegetables can be a tasty alternative to sweets.

What Else You Can Do To Prevent Tooth Decay

Keep your teeth and gums clean by brushing them well with toothpaste. Use a small toothbrush with nylon bristles, all the same height and with rounded tips.

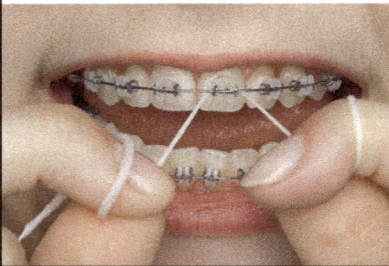

Your toothbrush cannot reach every area in your mouth. To reach those tricky areas, take a piece of dental floss and slide it between your teeth.

Visit your dentist at least once every six months to have your teeth checked.

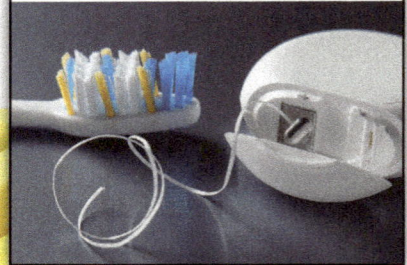

> **Our teeth are an important part of our body, and it's very important to look after them.**

Important Facts

- A low-sugar diet reduces the risk of tooth decay.
- Today, tooth decay is considered a preventable, and even mostly curable, disease.

Some Fun Things to Find Out and To Do

1. How many million people are there in the world?

2. Germs multiply quickly.

Read on to find out just how quickly, and to make your own calculations:

One germ multiplies in 20 to 40 minutes by splitting into two cells. Each of these two cells in turn splits into two cells in another 20 to 40 minutes. And so on, and so on. Based on this information, calculate how many germs there'll be in three hours from now, in five hours from now, and in nine hours from now.

3. Germs multiply very quickly indeed.

Draw dots, lines, shapes, curves, and use colors, or any other method you want, to show how quickly germs multiply.

4. Two germs have a date:

Germ A meets Germ B. Give each germ a name, then make up the conversation they have. It can be serious, funny, or however you like.

The author would like to thank Professor Itamar Shalit for his help and medical consultation.

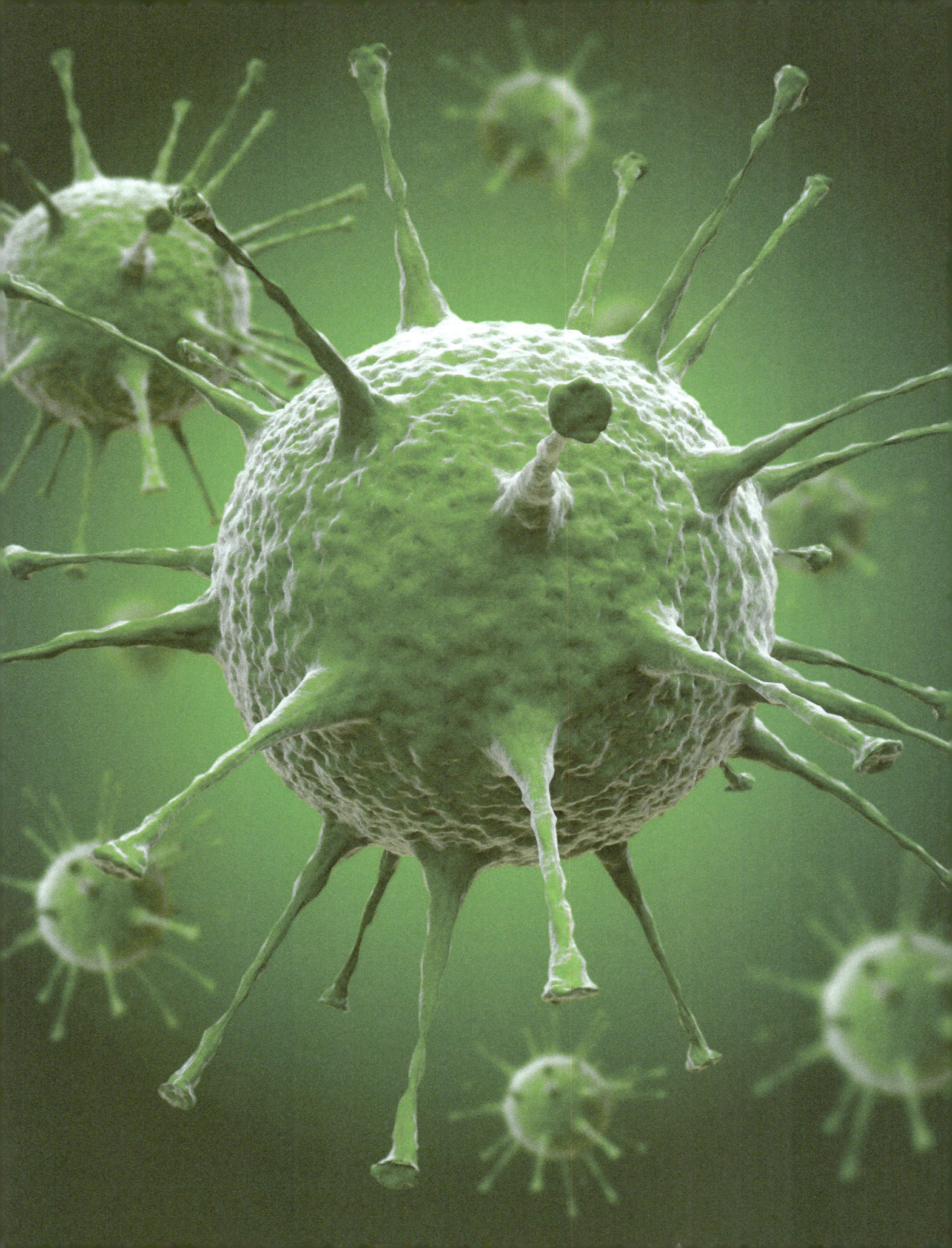

VIRUSES

Viruses

What Are Viruses?

Viruses are very tiny organisms. They are much smaller than germs.

Viruses contain genetic material that enables them to multiply in living cells and to make us sick.

Even the largest viruses can only be seen with the help of a microscope.

Some Old Breakthroughs

From 1935 to 1939, there were several breakthroughs in the research of viruses. In 1939, the first "photograph" of a virus, a simulation, was made using an electron microscope. This photograph revealed the structure of viruses, laying the ground for further research.

The Difference between Viruses and Germs

Germ	Viruses
Germs have all the mechanisms they need to multiply both outside and inside the cells of our body. As a result, they reproduce quickly in our body, usually outside cells, but also inside them.	Viruses lack many of the mechanisms needed to multiply. As a result, they must take over living cells and use their appropriate mechanisms in order to grow and multiply.

Smallpox Virues

How Viruses Multiply

Let's imagine the way a virus multiplies as an onslaught by a military vehicle bearing an armor-piercing implement. The military vehicle is the virus, intent on hitting the "command post": a living cell in our body.

56

Every virus

⬇

bears an "armor-piercing" implement: its protein shell.

⬇

Its protein shell identifies a specific receptor on the surface of a living cell, or "command post", in our body, and the virus instantly attaches itself to this receptor.

⬇

Once the virus settles down in the receptor,

⬇

it starts to penetrate the host cell's membrane,

⬇

and takes control of its raw materials: the "listening and communication devices" and the "supplies department".

⬇

The virus uses the host cell's materials and ability to make new proteins to create new viruses.

⬇

It rapidly produces multiple copies of itself in the "kidnapped" host cell. The new viruses burst out of the host cell one at a time, start to act, and invade new cells.

⬇

Sometimes, all the new viruses burst out simultaneously and destroy the "command station", the very host cell that gave them life.

Virus Replication

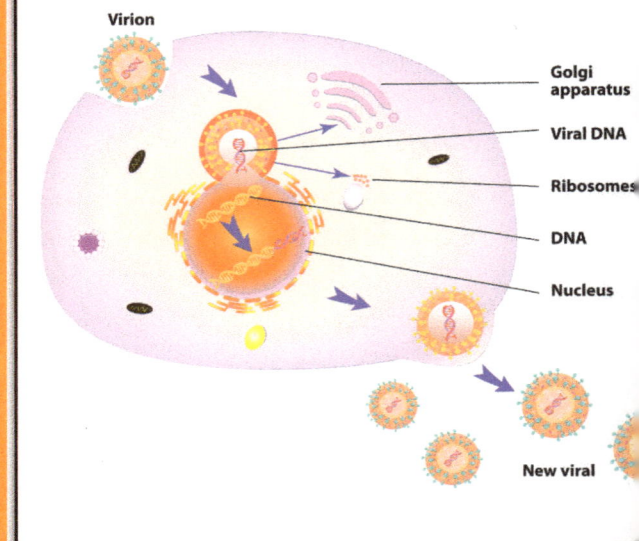

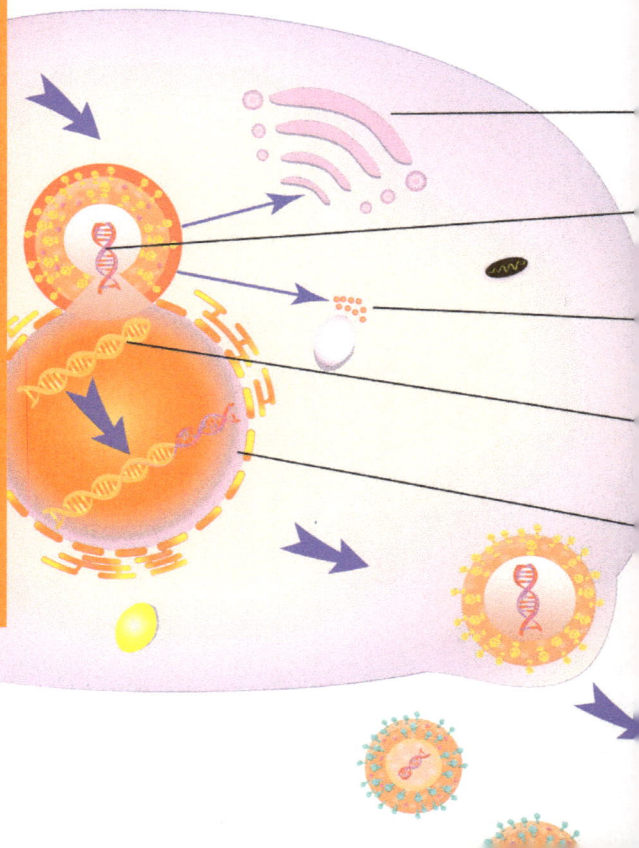

Virion

Golgi apparatus

Viral DNA

Ribosomes

DNA

Nucleus

New viral

By "kidnapping" their host cells and penetrating other cells, viruses are able to make us sick

Normally, our immune system manages to overcome viruses and to destroy them. However, sometimes a virus manages to invade our body and to make us sick.

When this happens, our body recruits all of its defense forces to fight the foreign invader.

How Our Immune System Fights Viruses

Our body recruits its whole defense system – the immune system – to fight viruses.

As with bacteria, the immune system fights viruses primarily with the help of **lymphocytes.**

There are two main types of lymphocytes:

T-cells (T-lymphocytes)	B-cells (B-lymphocytes)

Lets' imagine that T-cells and B-cells are two different platoons of soldiers, with complementary duties. When called upon to defend their "army base", our body, the two platoons of soldiers move into action.

Platoon 1: T-Cell Platoon

The main duty of the "soldiers" in **T-Cell Platoon** is:

to stop or to kill the "invading" virus before or after it manages to penetrate a living cell in our body.

Another duty of the "soldiers" in **T-Cell Platoon** is:

as helpers: to help create antibodies against the virus.

Platoon 2: B-Cell Platoon

The duty of the "soldiers" in **B-Cell Platoon** is

to create special antibodies that neutralize the virus when in contact with it.

Some Important Information

The two main types of "soldiers", T-cells and B-cells, fill the main role in the defense layout of our body. Other types of lymphocytes come to their help, and all of them together defend the "army base", our body, against a huge range of viruses.

Some More Important Information

Viruses that can't manage to penetrate a living cell can't multiply.

Vaccinations against Dangerous Viruses

Some viruses can make us severely ill. Others may cause life-threatening infections or undesirable complications.

Polio | Rabies | Rubella | Measles | Chicken Pox | Hepatitis B | Mumps Influenza

Vaccinations have been developed against these viruses.

The Purpose of Vaccination:

to help our body become immune to dangerous viruses without falling sick.

How Our Body Becomes Immune

Our body becomes immune with the help of a special substance that protects us against the particular virus causing the disease.

This special substance is called a vaccine.

What Is a Vaccine?

A vaccine is a solution that contains the weakened or dead form of the virus causing a particular serious disease, or some of its components.

In most countries, babies and toddlers are vaccinated against viruses that cause dangerous diseases. This has greatly reduced their incidence, which abounded before vaccinations against them were developed.

Did You Know?

Different types of viruses cause different types of colds and infections in our respiratory tract.

Signs of a Cold

Catarrh | Coughing | Sneezing

These may also be signs:

Fever | Headache | Tiredness and Weakness

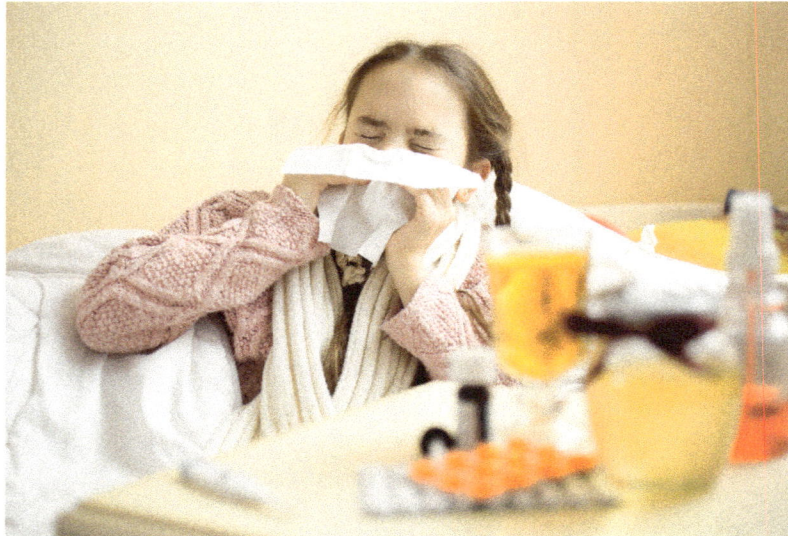

Important Facts

Antibiotics have no effect at all on viruses.

There still isn't any special medicine against the viruses that cause "the common cold".

Our immune system usually manages to overcome and destroy viruses.

Drugs against Viruses

Certain drugs indeed exist against viruses, including the viruses causing influenza (the flu). However, they cannot be compared in scope to antibiotics, which were specially developed to fight a large range of germs.

Fun activity

A host cell meets a virus.

Describe their meeting by writing a story or a poem, by making a drawing or a sculpture, by drawing lines or points, or in any other way you like.

Discoveries from the Past

Edward Jenner, an English village doctor, was born in 1749 and died in 1823. He was considered the inventor of vaccination. In 1796, he developed the vaccine against smallpox, a complicated and dangerous disease that, until then, the medical profession was unable to do anything about. Jenner developed the vaccine from material obtained from a cowpox lesion. He discovered that milkmaids who got sick with cowpox, which is a relatively mild disease, did not get sick with smallpox. The French laughed at Jenner, claiming that he was trying to turn people into cows. His successor, Louis Pasteur, further developed the vaccine, and by the 1980s smallpox was completely eradicated from the world.

Louis Pasteur was born in France in 1822. He developed a vaccine solution containing the agent that caused rabies, and used it to vaccinate dogs against this dangerous disease, as well as people who'd been bitten by dogs. Only after Pasteur's death was it discovered that the cause of rabies was in fact a virus, not a germ. By 1925, every dog and animal in danger of catching the disease was vaccinated.

STOP SMALLPOX

The author would like to thank Professor Itamar Shalit for his help and medical consultation.

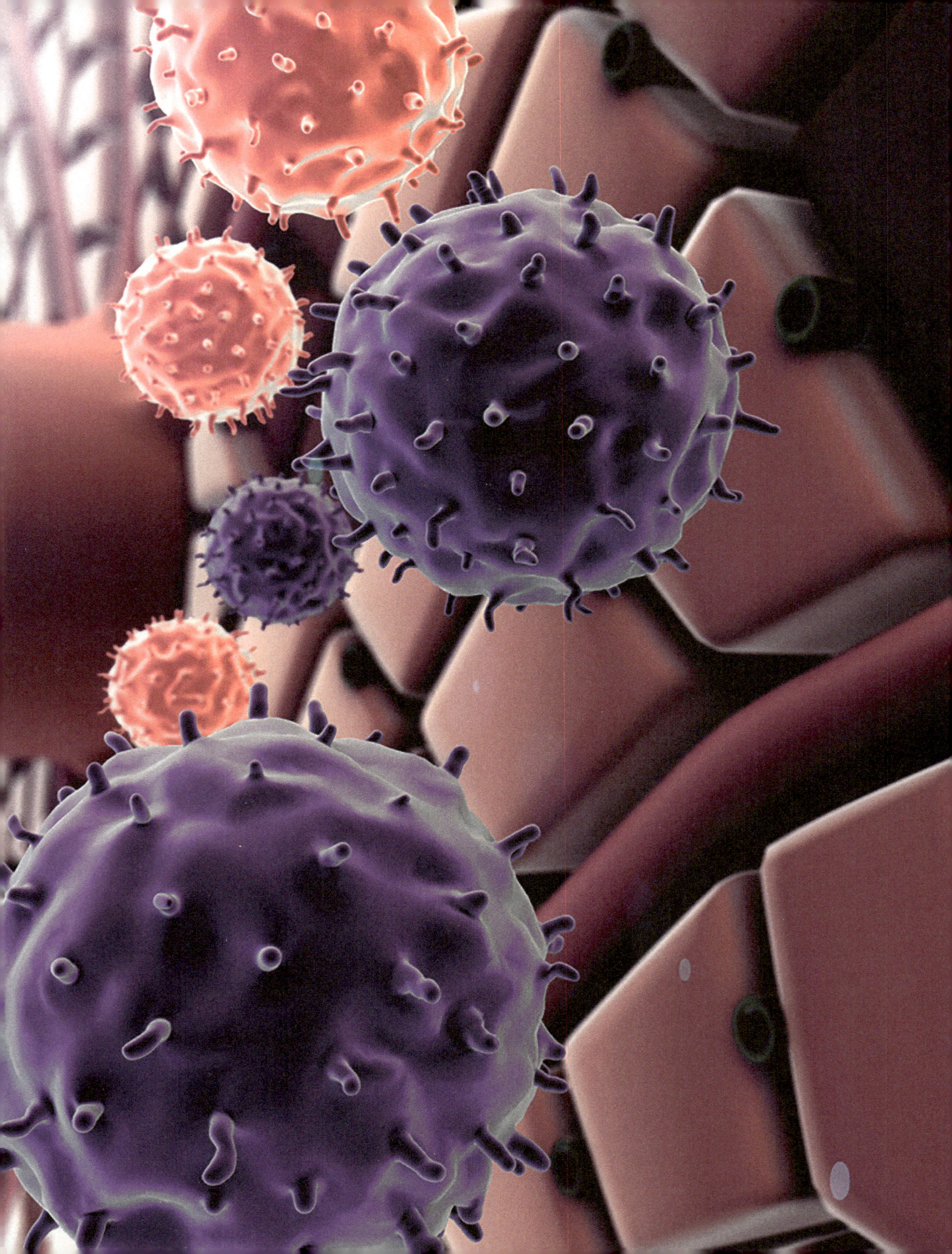

ON TEMPERATURES, FEVERS AND THERMOMETERS

Human Body Temperature

In medical language, the heat of the human body is called human body temperature.

The instrument used to measure human body temperature is called a thermometer.

Every living being has a characteristic body temperature.

Normal human body temperature ranges between:

36° C and 37° C or 97°F and 98° F.

A temperature in the range of 39-40° C or in the range of 102-104° F is considered to be high. It means you have a fever.

What Regulates our Body Temperature?

Our body's heat-regulating system maintains it at a constant temperature.

Getting To Know our Body's Heat-Regulating System

Our body's heat-regulating system consists of a small cluster of cells located in a tiny region in our brain called the hypothalamus gland.

The Role of the Body's Heat-Regulating System

1. It controls our body temperature.

2. It is designed to maintain our body at a constant temperature of 36-37° C or of 98.6° F.

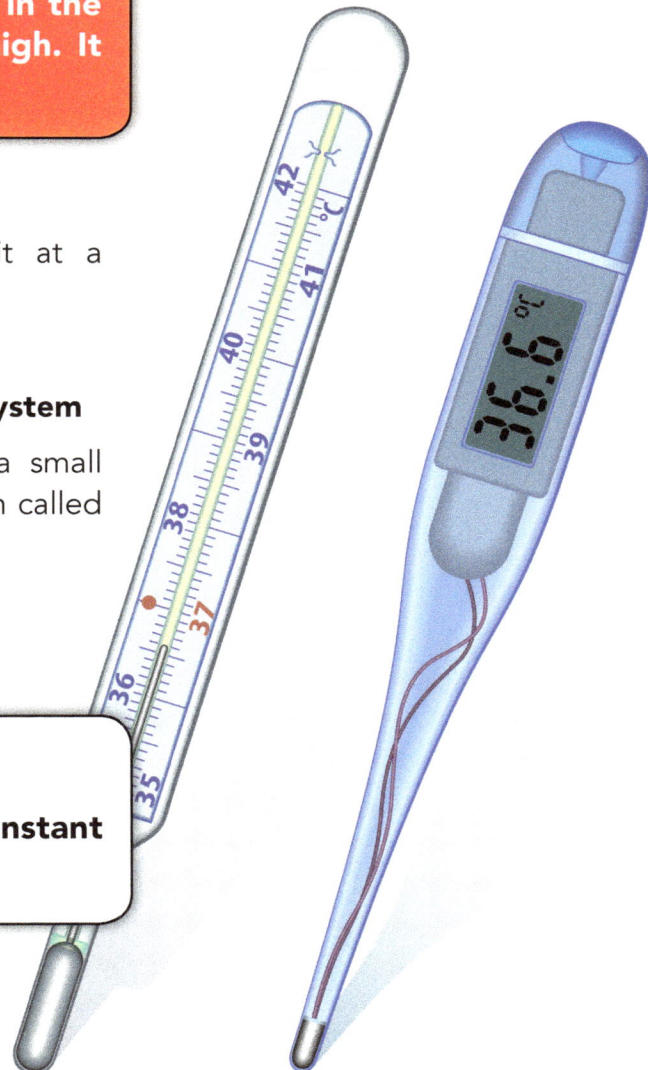

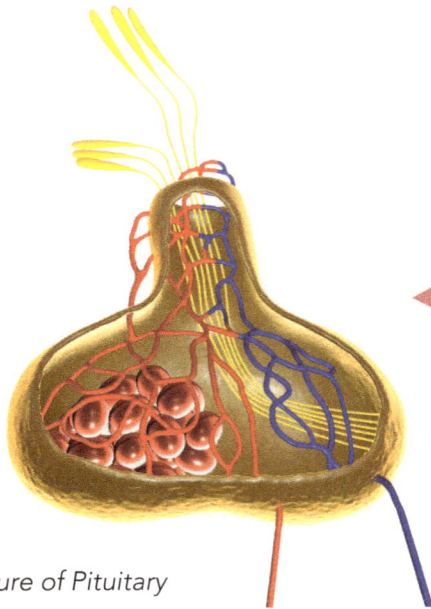
Structure of Pituitary

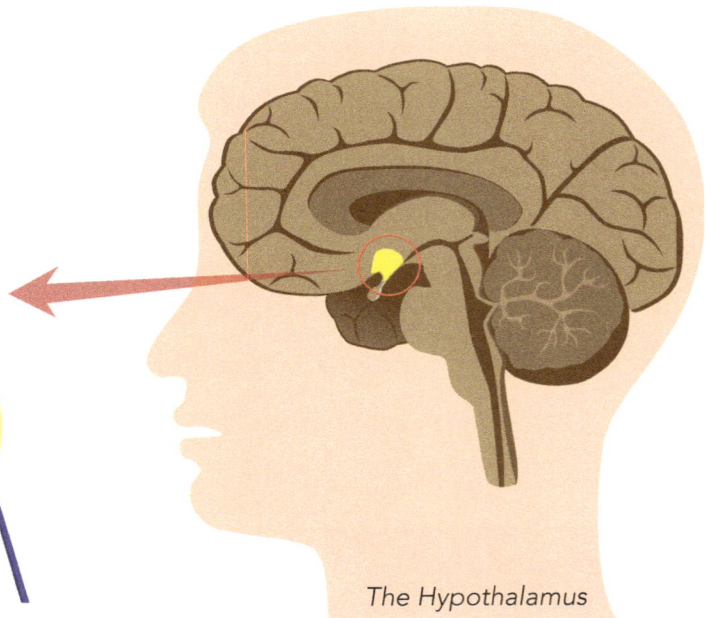
The Hypothalamus

Did You Know?

Our body's heat-regulating system can be compared to a thermostat, a device used for maintaining a constant temperature.

Electric devices such as boilers are usually equipped with thermostats, which work in exactly the same way as our body's heat-regulating system.

How Interesting!

You can get a high temperature, that is, a fever, in these cases:

If you have a bacterial or viral illness.

If you do physical activity in very hot weather.

If you are out too long in the sun.

If you do not drink enough water.

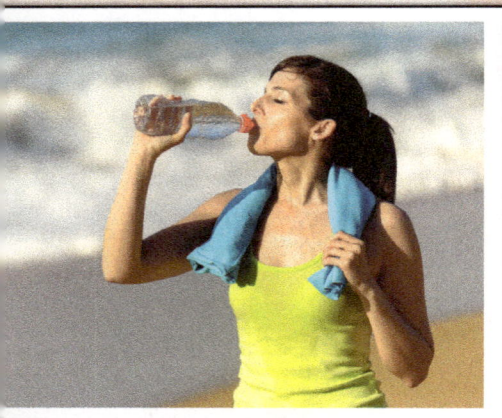

WHY DO WE GET A FEVER?

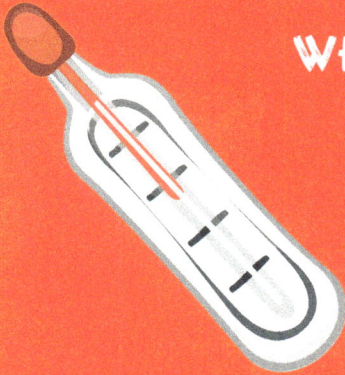

This is how we get a fever:

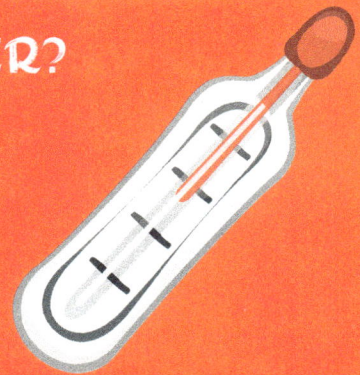

Macrophages

↓

surround the "invader" that penetrated our body into the infected area. They release chemicals that generate heat.

↓

These chemicals make their way in our bloodstream to our brain.

↓

Once there, they activate the tiny region of our brain forming our body's heat-regulating system, triggering it to cause our temperature to rise.

↓

Our body's heat-regulating system then sends signals that help our body generate heat and reach the new temperature.

If our body is unusually hot, that means we have a fever.

Did You Know?

A rise in the temperature of our body may curb the activity of bacteria and viruses that are sensitive to heat and, in that way, make it difficult for them to multiply.

How We Take Our Temperature

We use a medical thermometer to take our temperature.

How Interesting!

Medical thermometers only show temperatures ranging between 34° C and 42° C or between 98.6° F and 105.5° F. This is because that is the full temperature variability of the human body.

Types of Thermometers

There are several different kinds of medical thermometers. To better understand the invention and development of the medical thermometer, here's a tale from the past:

How the Thermometer Was Invented

At the end of the 16th century, the Italian inventor **Galileo Galilei** devised a thermometer for his own use. It was based on the expansion and contraction of air at different temperatures.

Over the centuries, changes and improvements were introduced in this first thermometer.

In the 18th century, the German physicist Daniel Fahrenheit developed a mercury-based thermometer, which became a household fixture until recent years.

Important Information

Mercury is a metal that exists in a liquid state at room temperature and expands when the temperature rises.

The functioning of the medical thermometer is based on this scientific principle.

Drop of Mercury

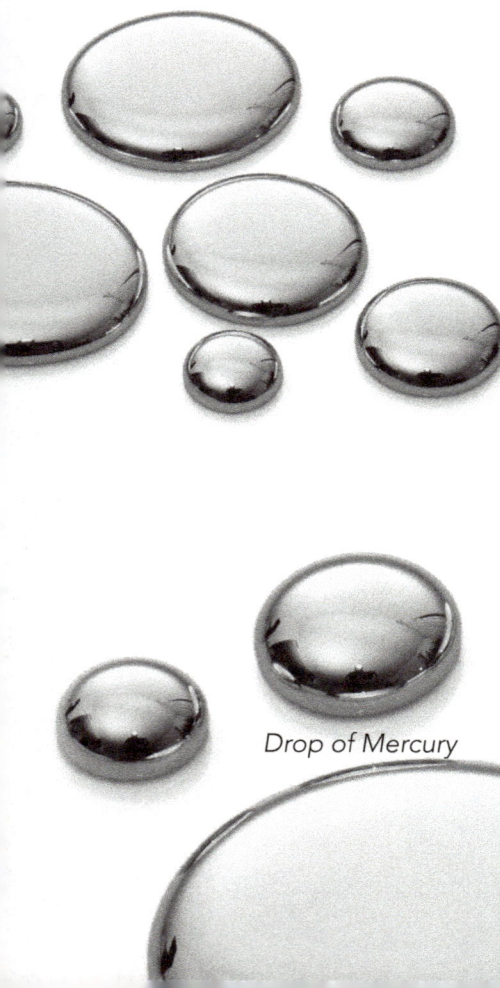

What Changes Occur in the Thermometer While It Is Measuring our Body Temperature?

Our body temperature heats the mercury in the thermometer bulb. This makes it expand and rise up the thermometer's long narrow glass tube.

The level that the mercury reaches on the graduations indicates our body temperature.

The Structure of the Mercury Thermometer:

- 1. The mercury thermometer consists of a long narrow glass tube.

- 2. The upper end of the tube is closed, while a bulb full of mercury is attached to the lower end.

- 3. The tube has gradation scale marks that indicate temperature measurements between 34 °C and 42 °C or between 98.6 °F and 105.5 °F.

- 4. When we place the thermometer in our mouth or under our armpit to take our temperature, the mercury rises in a thin column up the glass tube from the bulb at its lower end.

- 5. After we take our temperature, we shake the thermometer and the mercury returns back down to its original position in the bulb at its lower end.

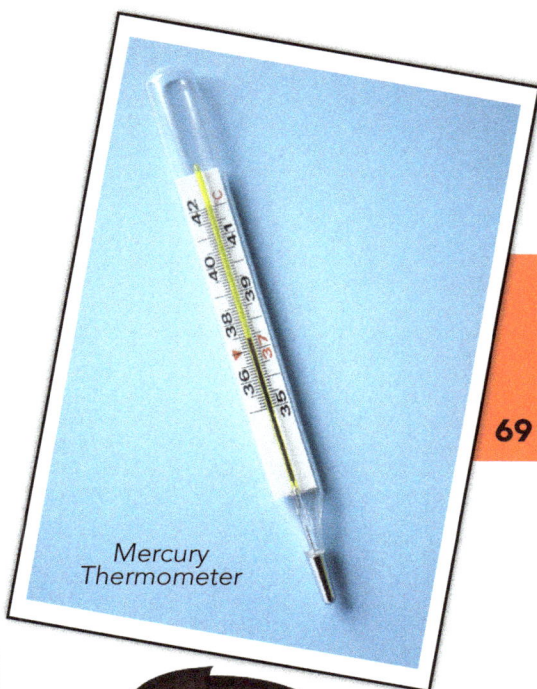

Mercury Thermometer

An Interesting Fact

The mercury thermometer is hardly used any more. Nowadays, most households and hospitals use digital thermometers.

The Digital Thermometer

The digital thermometer is an electronic device that is the same size as the mercury thermometer. Digital thermometers use special batteries in order to work.

What Do Digital Thermometers Measure?

Digital thermometers measure our body temperature.

They measure our temperature in either degrees Celsius (°C) or degrees Fahrenheit (°F).

The Structure of the Digital Thermometer

Digital thermometers consist of a long plastic tube with a small rectangular window in the middle that displays our body temperature. The On/Off button is next to the display window.

The digital thermometer has a temperature-sensitive electronic sensor in front. It records our body temperature and displays it digitally.

The battery compartment is in the back of the digital thermometer.

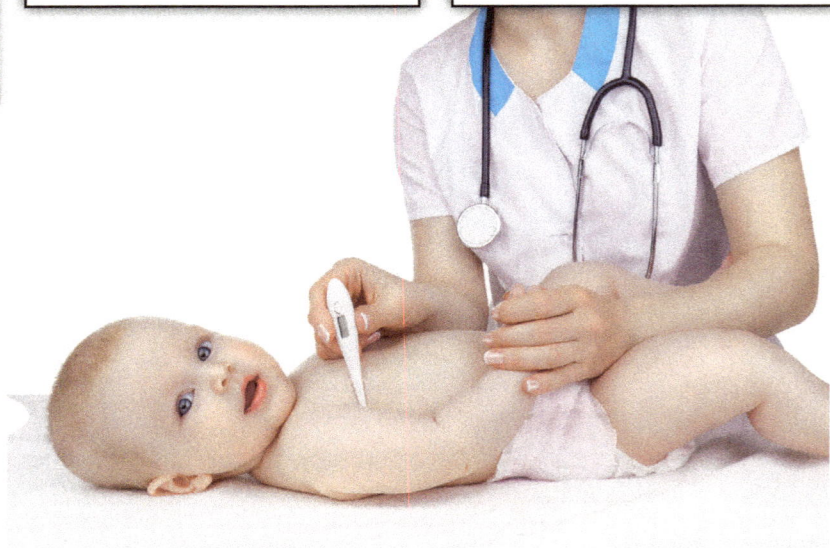

How To Use Digital Thermometers

1. To activate the thermometer, press the On/Off button. The number 188.8 will appear in the display window for 2-3 seconds, after which it will immediately switch to 31.9. The letter C or F will appear next to the number, telling us whether our temperature is being measured in degrees Celsius or in degrees Fahrenheit.

2. Place the thermometer in your mouth or under your armpit. When your peak body temperature is reached, a beep will sound. In many thermometers, a letter indicator will at once replace your temperature measurement. If you have a high temperature, that is, a fever the letter H, standing for the word "High", will appear on the side. If you have a low temperature, the letter L, standing for the word "Low", will appear on the side.

3. If you do not have a high or low temperature, most thermometers will automatically turn off in about 15 seconds.

There Are Several Kinds of Digital Thermometers:

- Ear thermometers : Ear thermometers use an infrared ray to read the temperature inside your ear canal. Digital ear thermometers are fast and can tell your temperature in less than two seconds.

- Forehead and ear thermometers.

- Fast-reading, animal-shaped, flexible-end infant thermometers.

- Flexible high-precision thermometers.

- Pacifier thermometers.

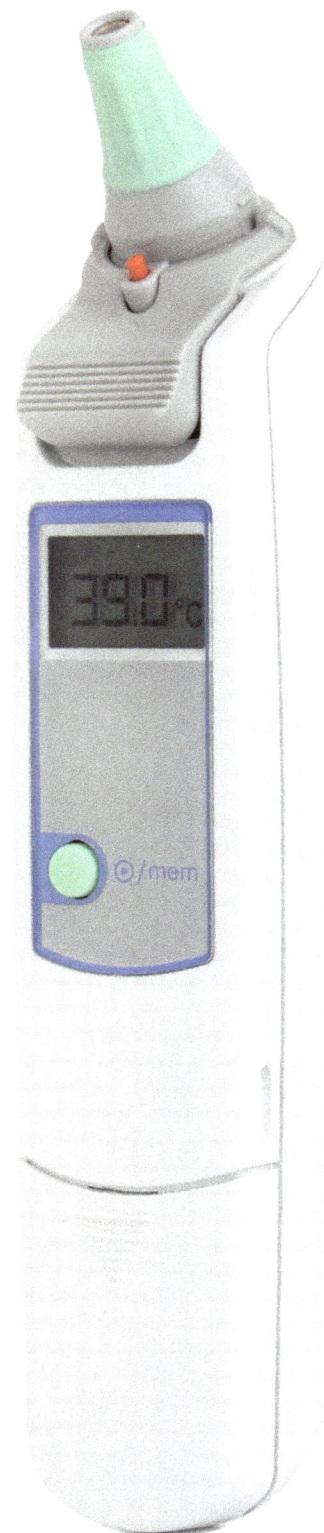

Ear Infrared Thermometer

Digital thermometers are cheap, in fact so cheap that some hospitals use disposable thermometers, that is, digital thermometers designed for one-time use.

72

> 40.0

39.0 - 39.9

37.5 - 38.9

36.3 - 37.4

< 35.0

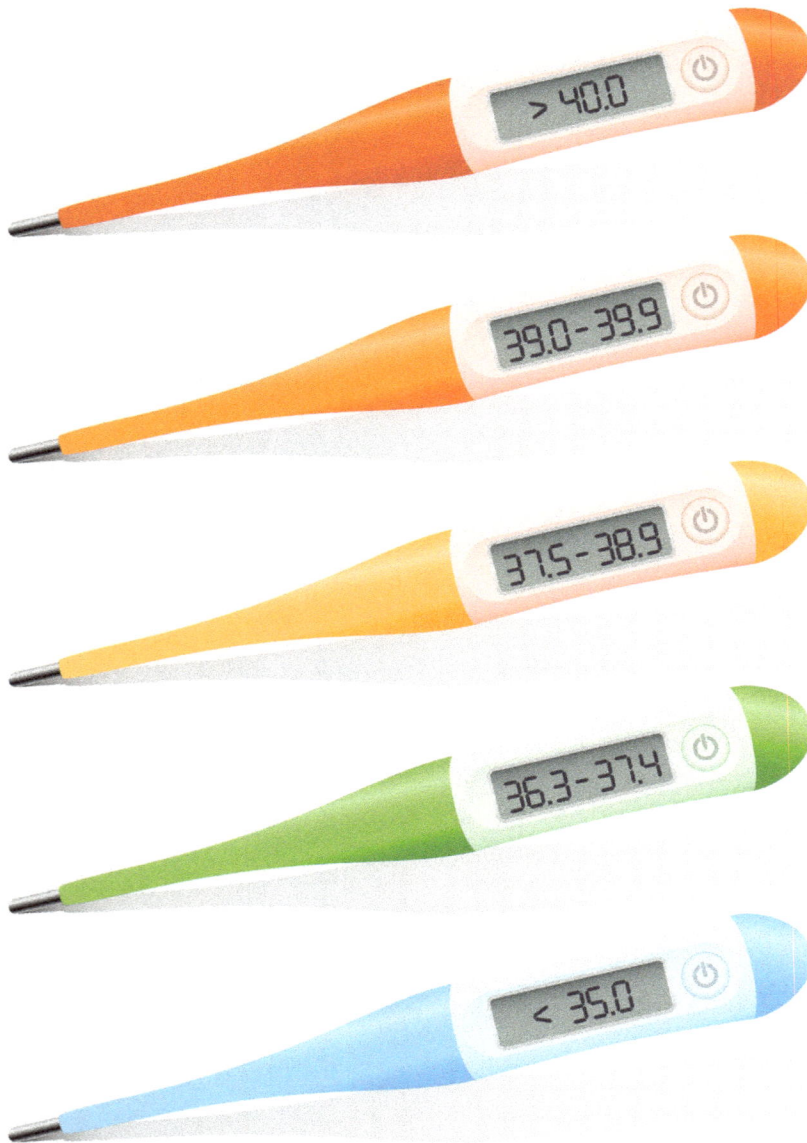

Advice: Prof. Yitzhak Varsano

THE STETHOSCOPE

The Stethoscope

What is the connection between the stethoscope and being sick?

A doctor uses a stethoscope to listen to the various sounds that our lungs and heart make. In this way, he or she determines whether they're working properly.

What are the different parts of the stethoscope?

Stethoscopes have two bendable metal ear tubes. At the top of each tube is a rubber earpiece, which is adaptable to our doctor's ears.

These two metal ear tubes merge towards the bottom of the stethoscope into a single rubber tube called the listening tube.

At the end of the listening tube is a smooth, flat, round metal plate known as a rotating head.

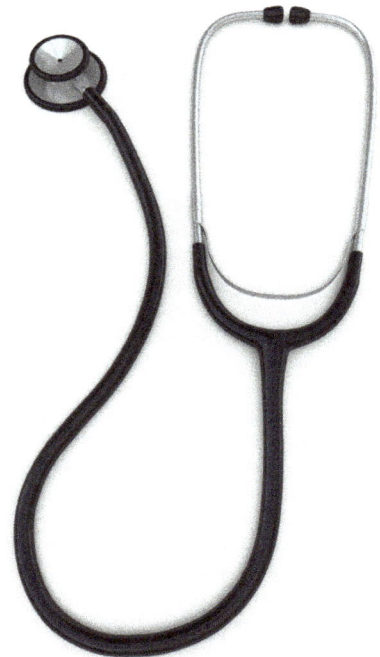

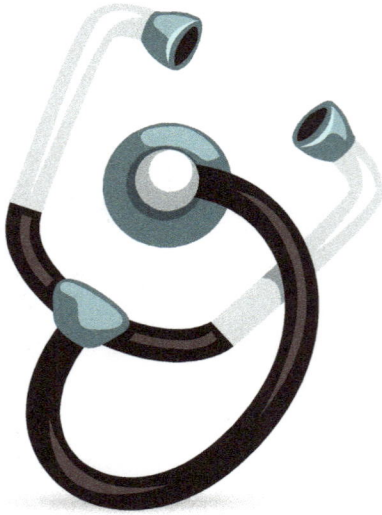

The Rotating Head at the End of the Listening Tube

The rotating head at the end of the listening tube is made up of two parts:

| On one side is a bell | On the other side is a diaphragm |

The Structure of the Bell

The bell has an open cavity that our doctor places on our body.

The Roles of the Bell

These are the roles of the bell:

To pick up the vibrations in our skin.
To enable our doctor to hear lower-pitch sounds.

What Is a Diaphragm?

A diaphragm is a thin sheet of material forming a partition. In stethoscopes, the diaphragm is a thin plastic layer stretched over the round metal plate of the rotating head at the end of the listening tube. It amplifies the sound waves it picks up from our lungs and heart. These amplified sound waves are carried through the sound-carrying tubes to the earpieces in our doctor's ears.

Bell

Diaphragm

The Roles of the Diaphragm

These are the roles of the diaphragm:

To pick up sound-wave vibrations and high-pitch sounds. To filter the vibrations in our skin and lower-pitch sounds.

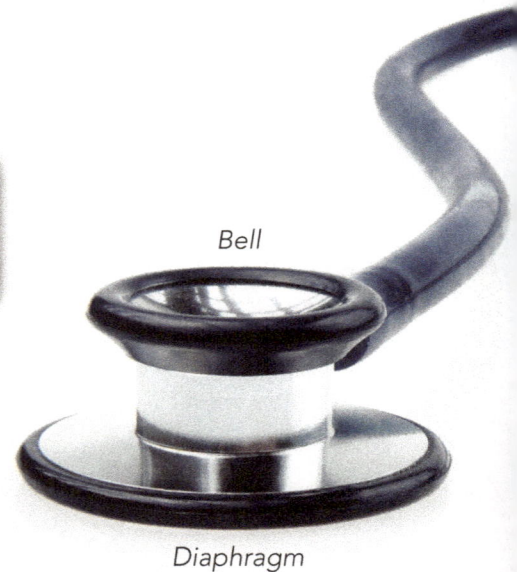

Depending on our condition, our doctor may use the bell or the diaphragm of the rotating head of his stethoscope to listen to the sounds that our lungs and heart make.

STETHOSCOPE IN THE SERVICE OF THE PULMONARY SYSTEM

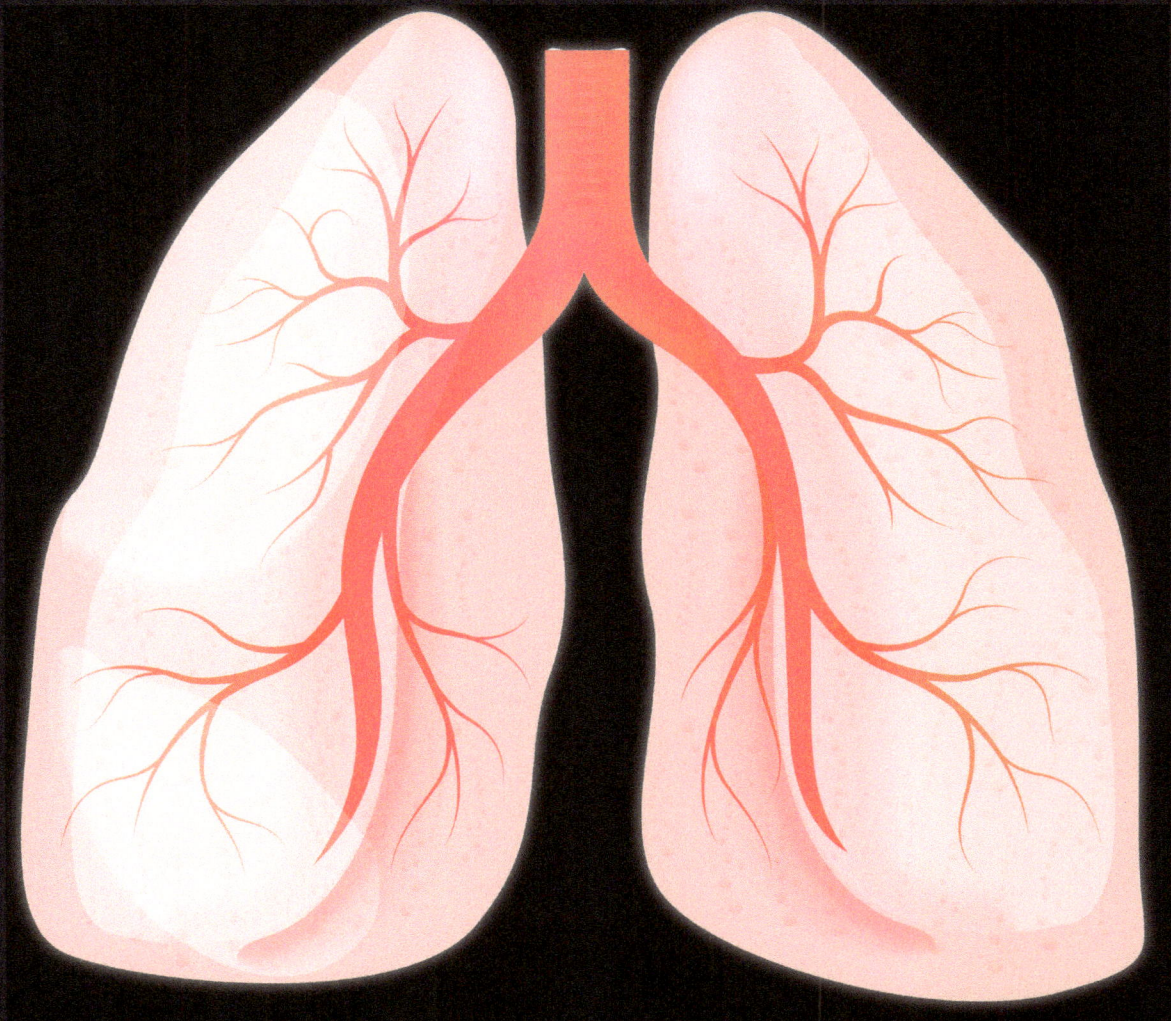

How our Doctor Examines Us with the Stethoscope

This is how our doctor examines us with a stethoscope:

To examine our heart and lungs, he puts the two earpieces at the tip of the stethoscope into his ears, and places the other end, the round metal plate, on our chest.

He moves the plate around on our chest to examine our lungs, and places it on our heart to examine our heart.

During the examination, the doctor listens very carefully to the sounds and reaches conclusions about our health.

To understand the connection between the stethoscope and our lungs, it is important to get to know the respiratory system.

The respiratory system consists of our nose, mouth, throat, windpipe, bronchi, alveoli, lungs, and tiny blood vessels, capillaries, that surround our alveoli and that are vital for gas exchange in our lungs.

The Structure of the Respiratory System

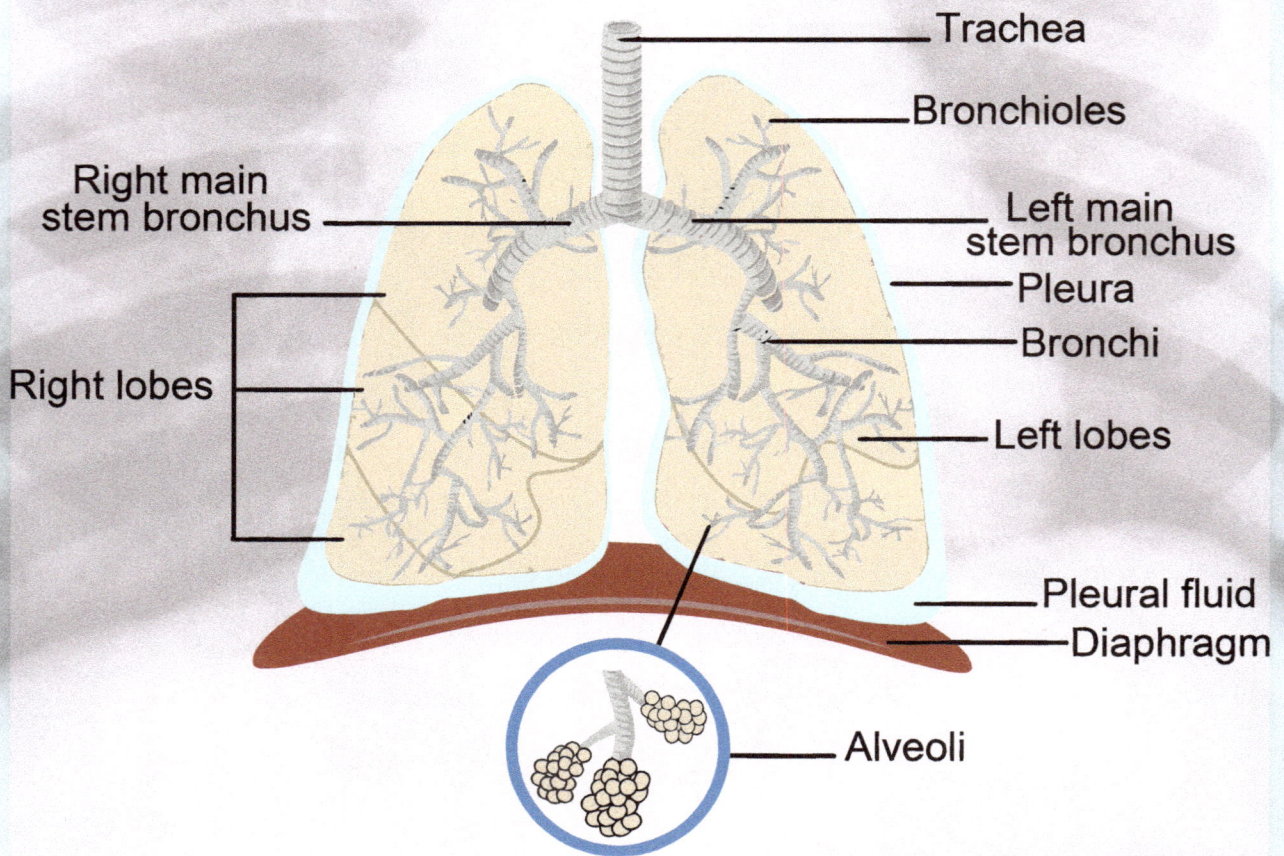

- Trachea
- Bronchioles
- Right main stem bronchus
- Left main stem bronchus
- Pleura
- Bronchi
- Right lobes
- Left lobes
- Pleural fluid
- Diaphragm
- Alveoli

How Air Flows into Our Lungs and Then Out Again

This is how air flows into our lungs:

- The air outside, which contains oxygen, enters our body through our nose or mouth. It passes through our throat, esophagus, and windpipe, to the bronchi of our lungs.

- From the bronchi of our lungs, the air reaches tiny round air sacs called alveoli.

- The oxygen penetrates our alveoli, enters our bloodstream, and joins our red blood cells that lead it to all the cells of our body.

- At the same time, the cells of our body release carbon dioxide into our blood.

- Some of the carbon dioxide enters our alveoli, from where we breathe it out into the air outside through our bronchi and our air passages.

Oxygen Transport Cycle

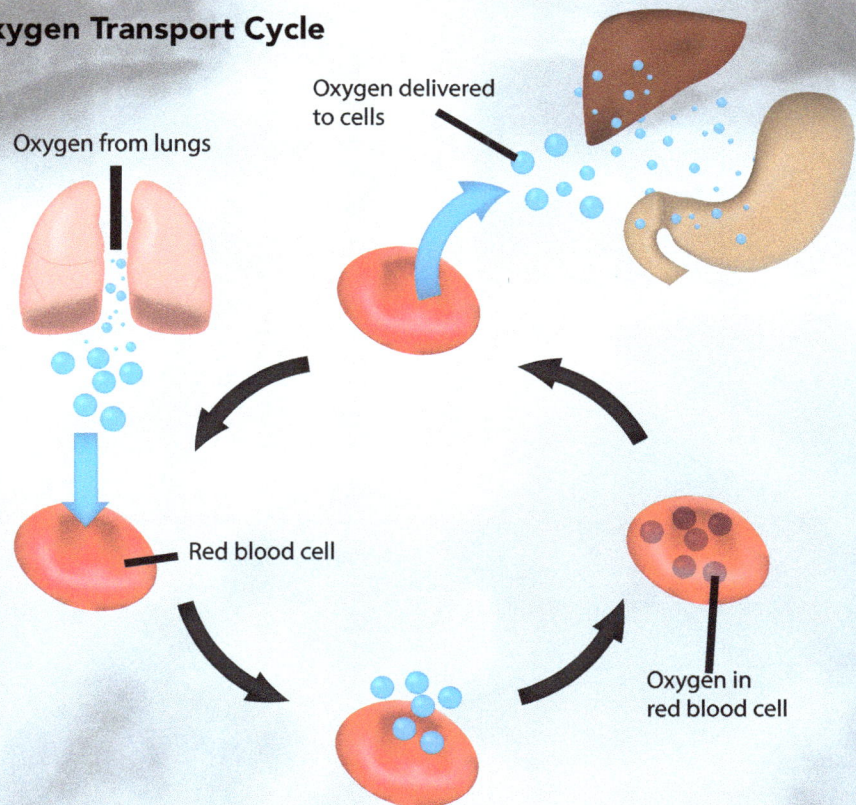

Oxygen from lungs

Oxygen delivered to cells

Red blood cell

Oxygen in red blood cell

Important Fact:

The structure of our alveoli allows oxygen to pass through them freely into our red blood cells. At the same time, carbon dioxide is able to pass freely in the opposite direction, to our alveoli.

↓

Remember!

Carbon dioxide:

Is produced in our blood in a fermentation process.

Is a poisonous gas that can harm our body.

Is a gas that must be removed from our body.

ALVEOLUS GAS EXCHANGE

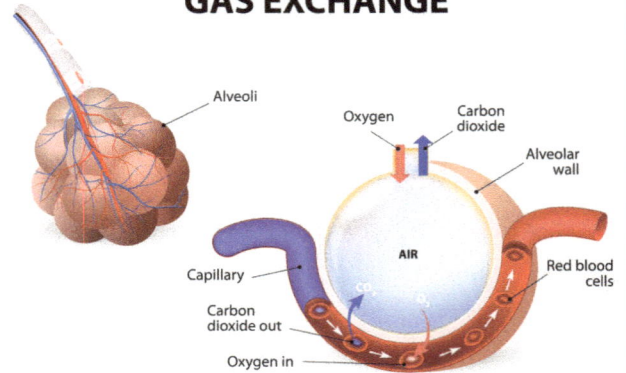

Alveoli

Oxygen

Carbon dioxide

Alveolar wall

Capillary

AIR

Red blood cells

Carbon dioxide out

Oxygen in

Gas Exchange in Humans

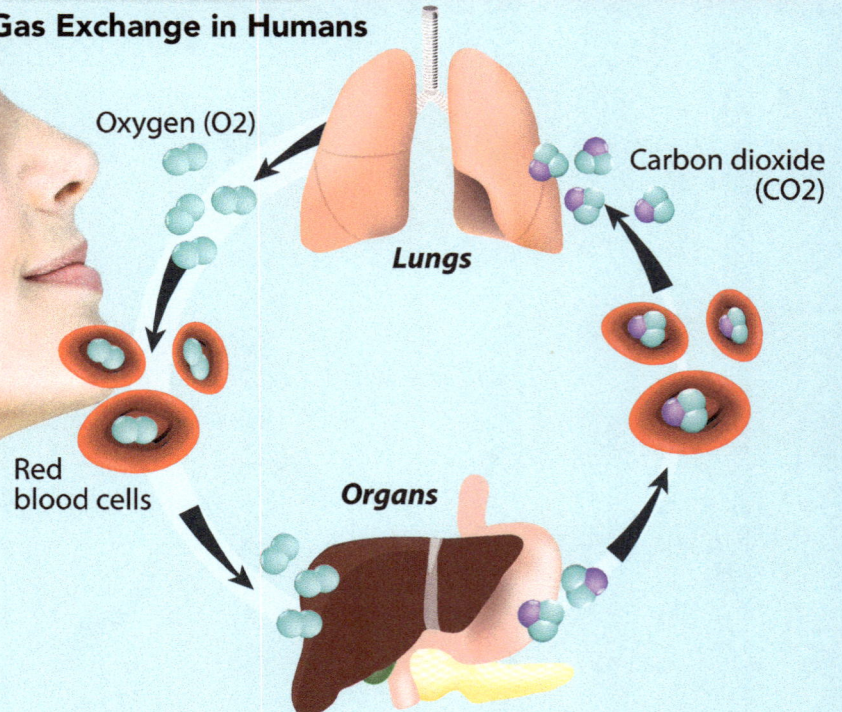

Oxygen (O2)

Carbon dioxide (CO2)

Lungs

Red blood cells

Organs

How Air Flows Through our Lungs

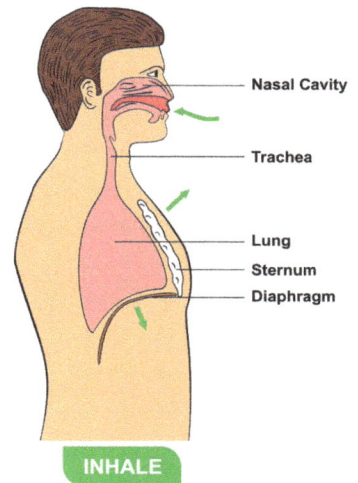

When we breathe air in, the process is called inhalation.

When we breathe air out, the process is called exhalation.

INHALE

This is the role of inhalation:

to transport a fresh supply of oxygen to our blood from the air outside.

This is the role of exhalation:

to expel air from our lungs and remove carbon dioxide from our body.

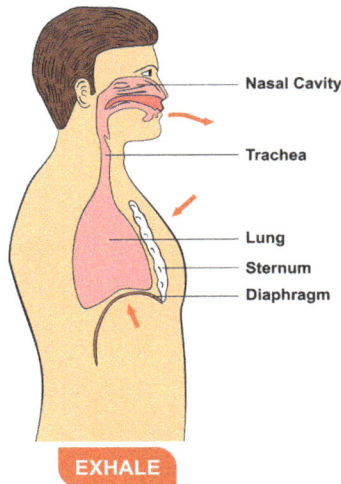

EXHALE

Important Information

The process of our lungs absorbing oxygen from the air outside into our body while at the same time removing carbon dioxide from our body is called:

GAS EXCHANGE

Each gas exchange cycle has two stages:

1. INHALATION
2. EXHALATION

Some Interesting Facts

A five-year-old child breathes about 26 breaths per minute.
A 15-year-old teen breathes about 20 breaths per minute.

Normally, we inhale and exhale about half a liter of air each time we breathe.

If we take a really deep breath, we can inhale and exhale about three liters of air.

The most our two lungs can hold is 4-4 ½ liters of air.

Clean air contains a vast number of antigens.

Isn't It Amazing?

Every day, we breathe into our body 10,000 liters of air, containing about 150,000 antigens.

What Our Doctor Hears Through His Stethoscope When He Examines Our Lungs

When our doctor examines our lungs when we are well, the air entering them sounds like a gentle wind through his stethoscope. But if we have an infection in our lungs, he hears other sounds.

How are other sounds created? | **What our doctor hears through his stethoscope.**

The Treatment of Lung Infections

Based on the noises our lungs make, our doctor diagnoses our illness and decides on an appropriate course of treatment and on what medicine we must take.

Other sounds are created when bacterial infection causes inflammatory mucous secretion in the respiratory track. This makes it hard for us to breathe.

When our doctor listens to the activity of our lungs as we inhale air, he may hear various sounds, such as fine wheezing or reduced air entry. These sounds indicate that we may have an infection in our lungs

The Connection between the Stethoscope, Our Lungs and Asthma

What is asthma?

Asthma is a chronic disease of the respiratory system. People with asthma find it hard to breathe air into and out of their lungs. This is because their breathing passages have narrowed, and thick phlegm has accumulated in them.

What the Doctor Hears Through his Stethoscope When He Examines a Child with Asthma

When the doctor listens with his stethoscope to a sick child's lungs, he hears different sounds.

1. Wheezing

2. Crackling

How are these sounds created?

- During an asthma attack, our bronchi, which are our breathing passages, contract.

- When the air passes through our contracted bronchi, it makes a wheezing sound.

- During an attack, thick phlegm is secreted into our bronchial lumen.

- When the air passes through our bronchi full of thick phlegm, it makes a rhonchi, or rattling, sound.

- The phlegm in our breathing passages makes us cough, and in this way our body ejects it

- When it is hard for air to pass through our narrowed, phlegm-packed bronchi, this leads to:

- breathing difficulties, that is, breathlessness.

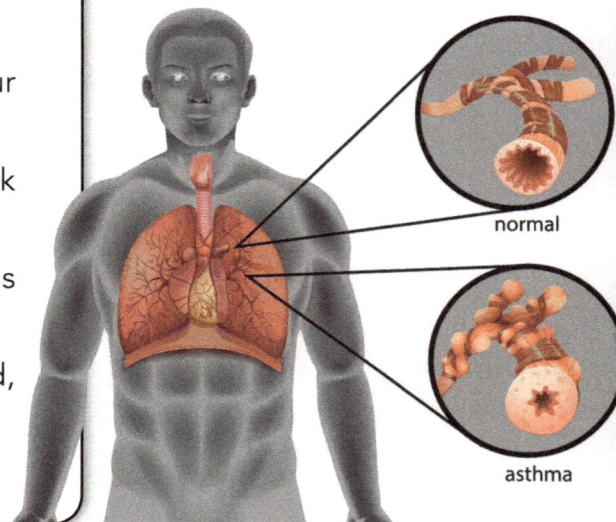

normal

asthma

Let us now compare the sounds made by our lungs to the notes that flutes produce.

This is how the flute works:

Flutes produce different notes when we alternatelyclose and uncover different finger holes.

When we blow into a flute whose finger holes are open, air enters it and produces low notes.

When we blow into a flute whose fingers holes are closed, air has difficulty passing through it, and it produces high discordant notes. These notes remind us of the wheezing and crackling sounds that the lungs of a sick child make.

Some Interesting Facts

The French physician, Dr. Laennec, invented the stethoscope in 1816. Stethoscope comes from two Greek words: stethos, which means "chest", and skopé, which means "examination".

The Future?

After 200 years, a new stethoscope has been invented.

Two American cardiologists, Prof. Jagat Narula and Dr. Brett Nelson, have reported on a new stethoscope. Our current stethoscope may be replaced by a hand-held ultrasound device called the Vscan. The Vscan is the size of a pack of playing cards, with the technology and screen quality of a smartphone.

It will enable the lungs and the heart to be scanned at a high level of precision. In fact, doctors will be able to see the patient's organs, instead of listening to them with the help of a stethoscope. Some specialists regard it as an advantage, while others oppose it. Nevertheless, Dr. Narula believes that the Vscan will soon become a device to be found everywhere, and medical schools will start teaching the use of this technology as a standard examination device.

An Interesting Experiment: The Sounds That Flutes Produce

Get out two flutes.

The first flute should be clean and dry.

The second flute should be still wet and full of saliva, because someone has just played it.

Play each of the two flutes.

Pay attention to the different notes that the two flutes produce.

You could record the notes in the recorder.

Which flute produces high notes?

Which flute produces low notes?

Medical advisor: Prof. Benzamine Volovitz

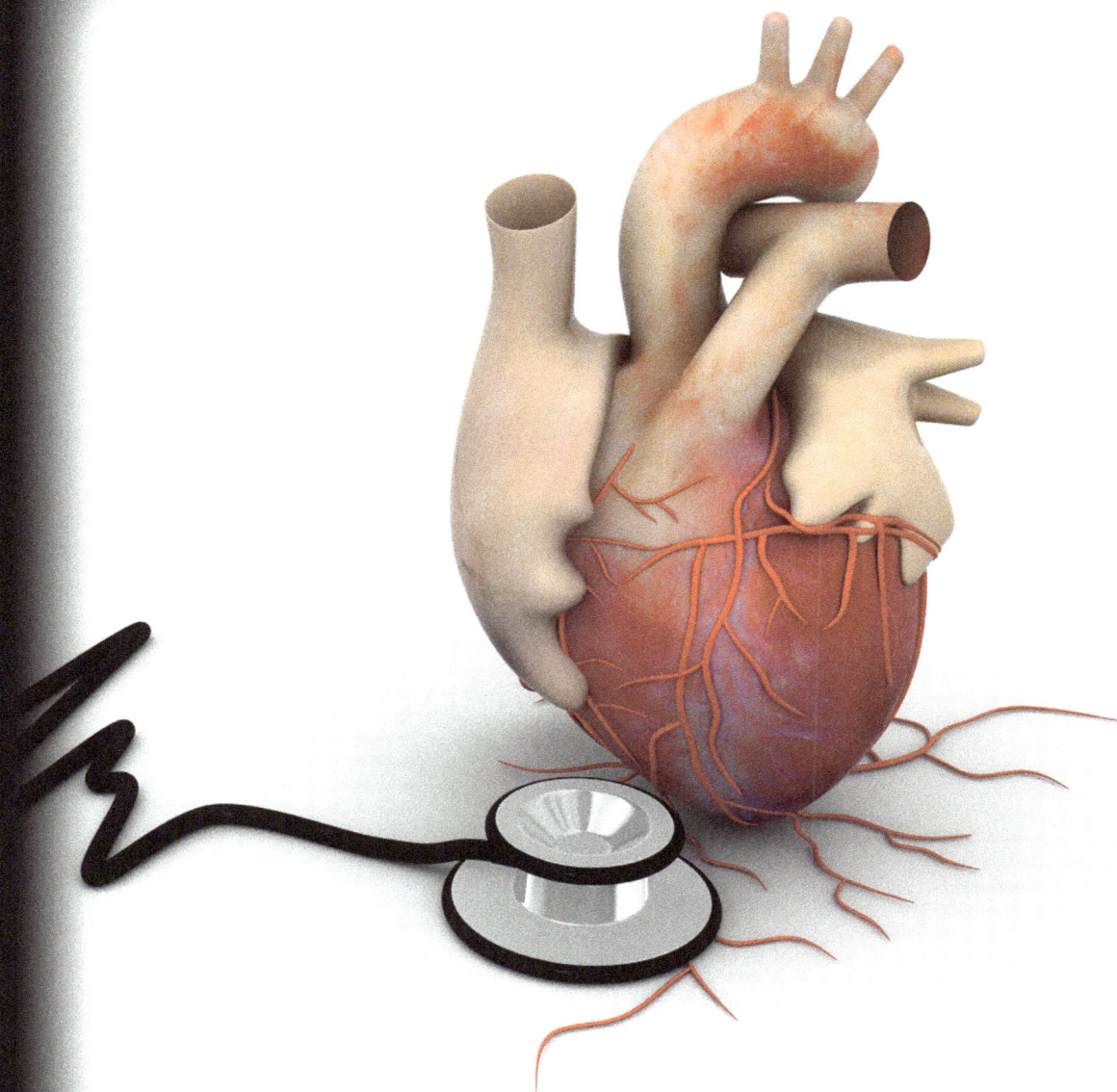

THE STETHOSCOPE IN THE SERVICE OF THE HEART

90

The Connection between the Stethoscope and Our Heart

To understand the connection between the stethoscope and our heart, it is important to get to know the structure and function of the heart.

Getting To Know Our Heart

The human heart is a hollow muscular organ.

It is about the same size as our fist, and is located in the middle of our chest.

Blood flows to and from our heart through a system of tubes called blood vessels. There are three major types of blood vessels: arteries, veins, and capillaries.

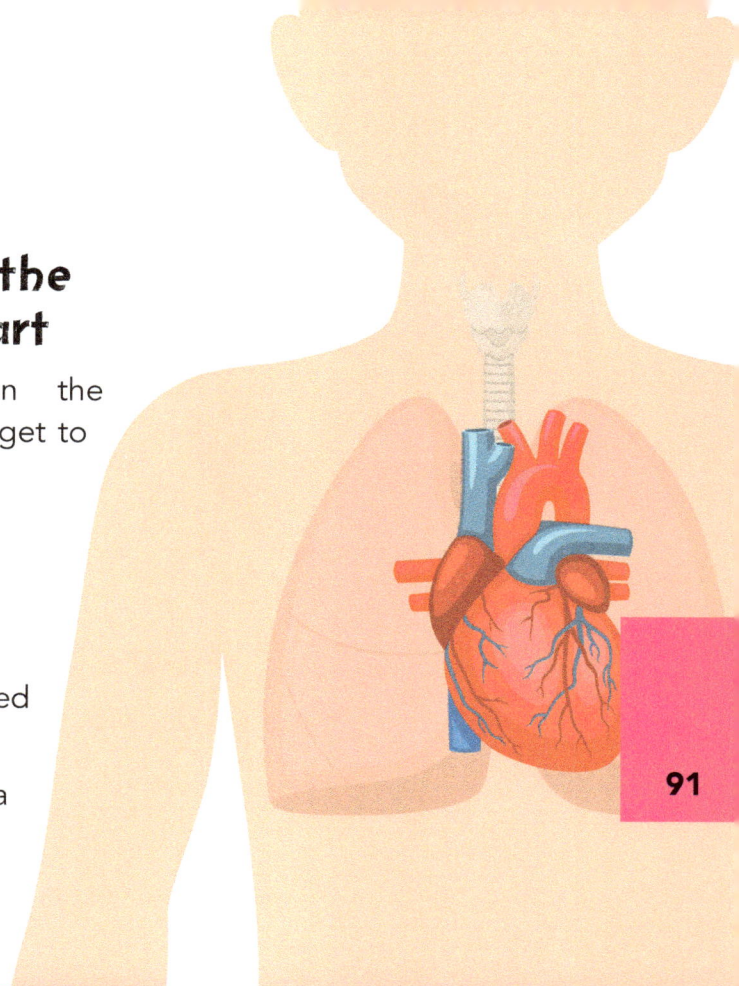

Some More Interesting Facts

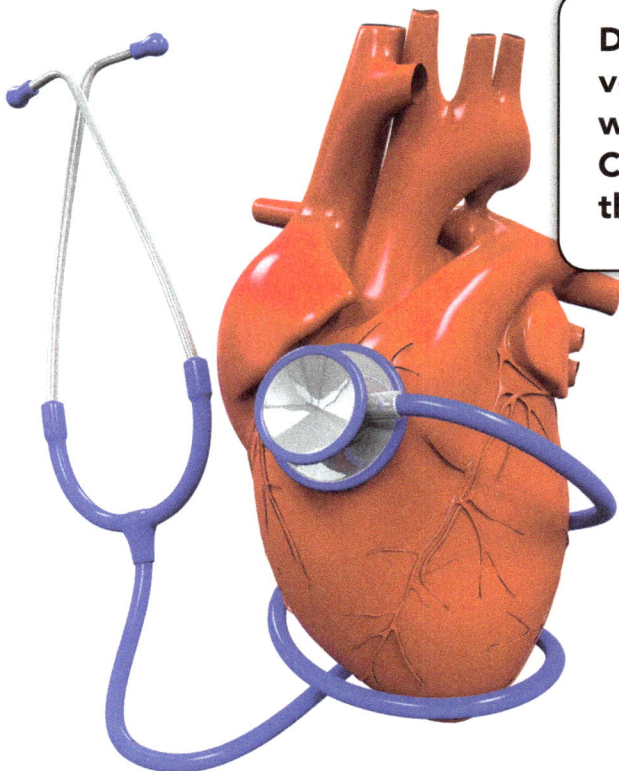

Doctors knew about arteries and veins in ancient times but capillaries were only discovered in the mid-17th Century following the invention of the microscope.

The Function of Our Heart:

The main function of our heart is to pump blood to every part of our body through our arteries, veins, and capillaries.

92

How Blood Flows Through Our Body's Highways: Our Arteries, Veins, and Capillaries

Blood flows from our heart,

⬇

and reaches every part of our body,

⬇

by means of our arteries.

⬇

Blood flows from different parts of our body to our heart

⬇

by means of our veins.

⬇

Substances such as oxygen and carbon dioxide pass

⬇

from our blood to the cells of our body, and from the cells of our body to our heart.

⬇

by means of our capillaries.

⬇

In this way, our lungs release carbon dioxide into the air outside,

⬇

and take in a new supply of oxygen for our blood from the air outside.

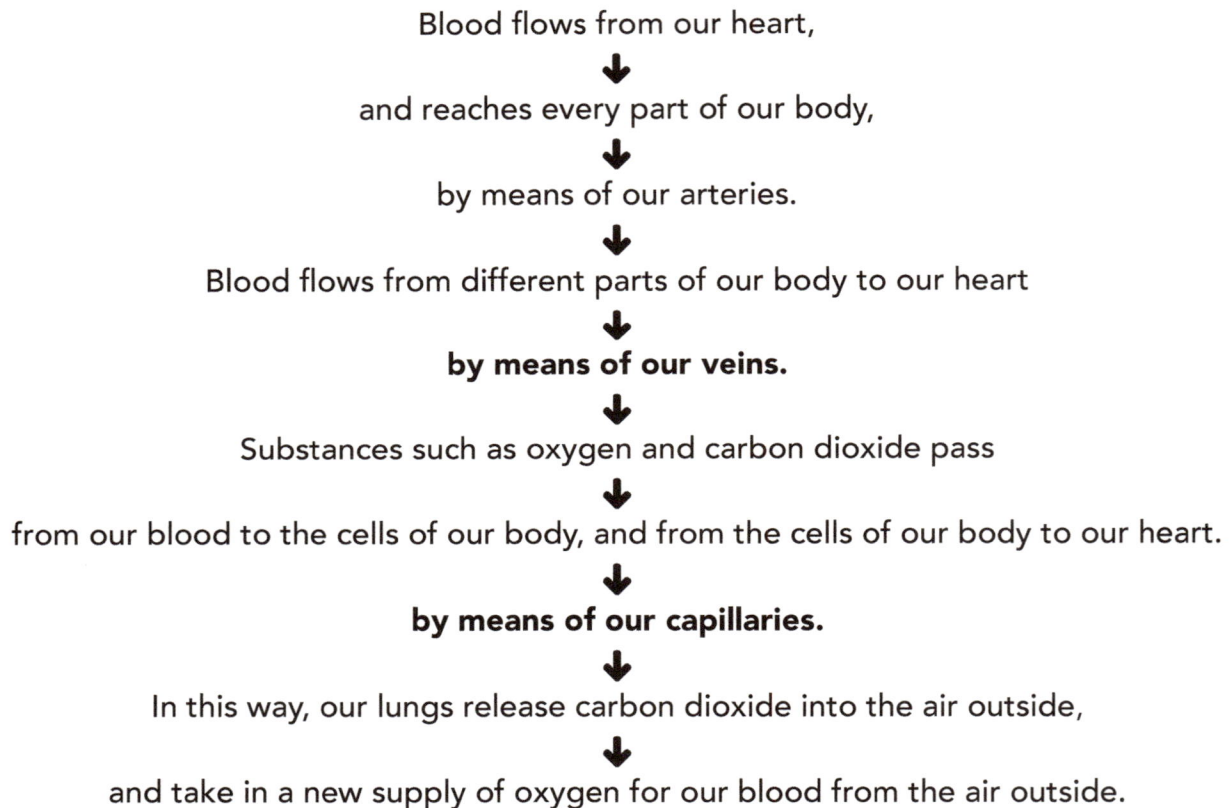

Approximately one hundred liters of blood pass through our heart each hour.

We could lift a 70-kg weight 20 meters high with the strength that our heart uses to pump our blood during one hour.

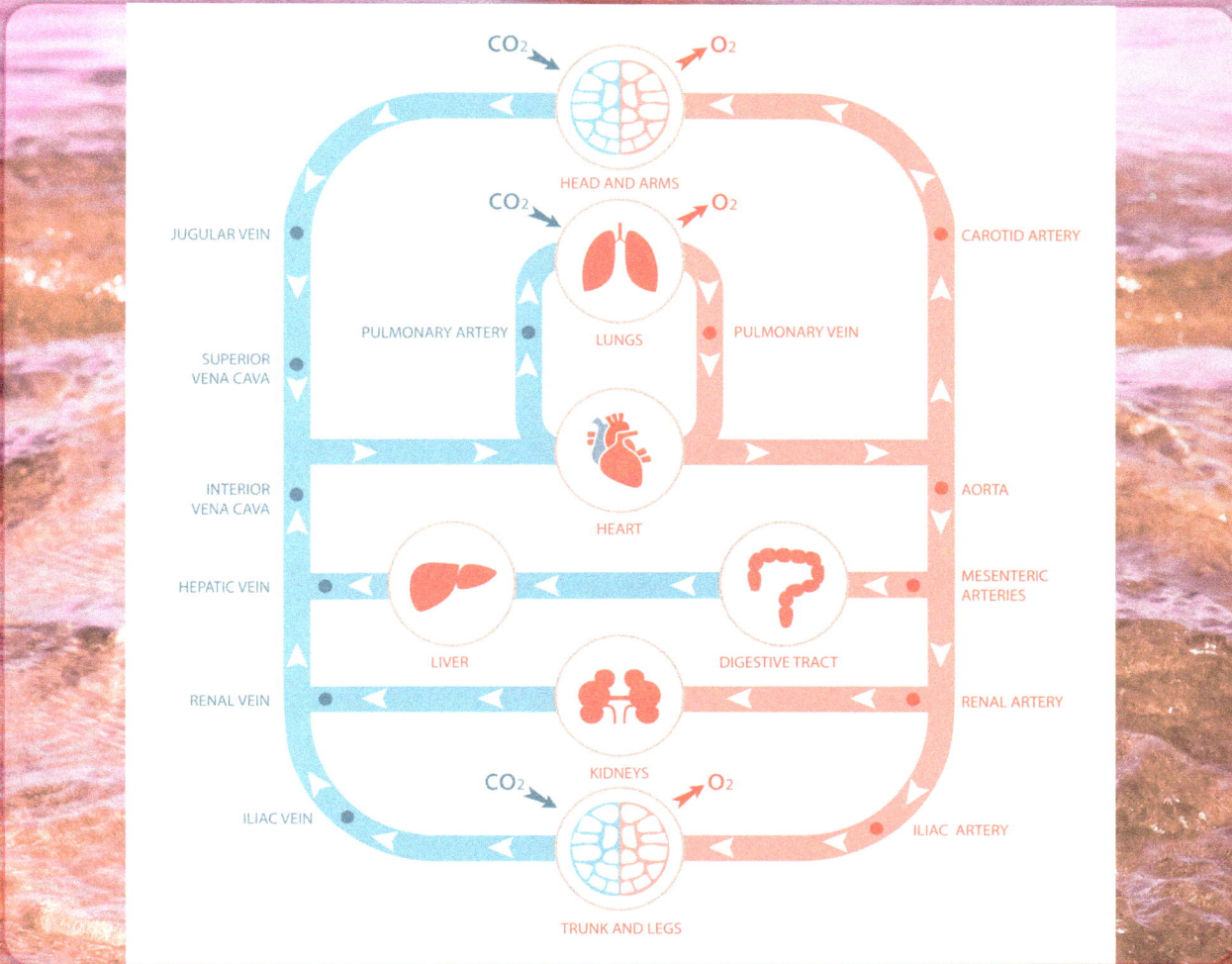

CO₂ → ←
HEAD AND ARMS

CO₂ → O₂

JUGULAR VEIN — CAROTID ARTERY

LUNGS

PULMONARY ARTERY — PULMONARY VEIN

SUPERIOR VENA CAVA

HEART

INTERIOR VENA CAVA — AORTA

HEPATIC VEIN — MESENTERIC ARTERIES

LIVER — DIGESTIVE TRACT

RENAL VEIN — RENAL ARTERY

KIDNEYS

CO₂ → O₂

ILIAC VEIN — ILIAC ARTERY

TRUNK AND LEGS

More Interesting Facts

The path of our blood in our body is very long and complex. But that same wonderful pump that we call our heart works so powerfully that every two or three minutes all the blood in our body passes through it and our blood vessels.

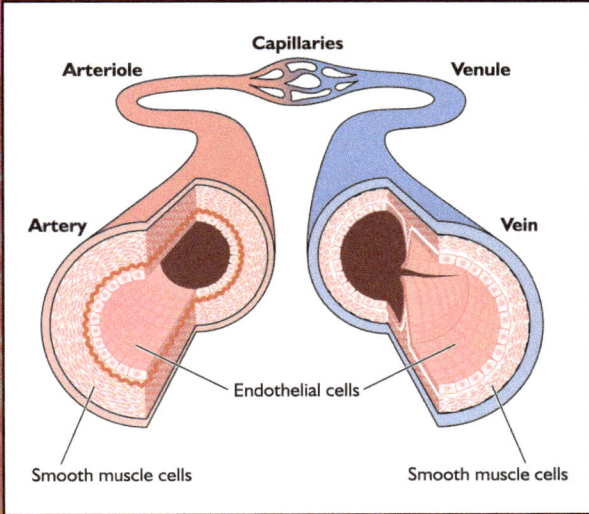

Capillaries

Arteriole   Venule

Artery   Vein

Endothelial cells

Smooth muscle cells   Smooth muscle cells

How Is Our Heart Built?

Our heart is divided into four hollow chambers, and has two pairs of valves.

The chambers of our heart consist of two superior atria and two inferior ventricles.

One atrium is on the right, and beneath it is the right ventricle. The other atrium is on the left, with left ventricle beneath it.

There are two heart valves that separate each atrium from each ventricle – the mitral valve and the tricuspid valve. There are also heart valves at the openings of the two major arteries leaving our heart – the aortic valve and the pulmonary valve.

A thick impenetrable wall separates the right side of our heart from the left side.

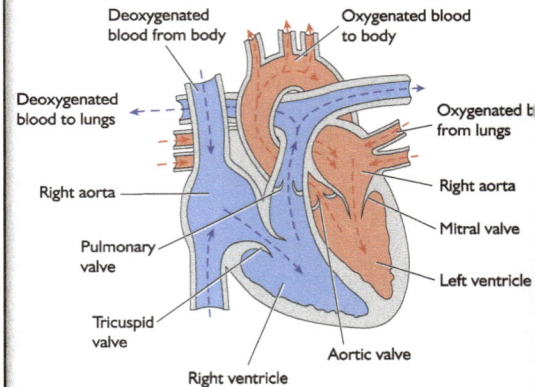

Deoxygenated blood from body

Oxygenated blood to body

Deoxygenated blood to lungs

Oxygenated b from lungs

Right aorta

Right aorta

Pulmonary valve

Mitral valve

Tricuspid valve

Left ventricle

Right ventricle

Aortic valve

What is a Heart Valve?

A heart valve is a membranous flap formed from folds of the innermost layer of a blood vessel wall.

What is the Role of the Heart Valves?

The role of the heart valves is to regulate the flow of blood in one direction only, from the atrium to the ventricles for example, and to prevent the backflow of blood.

There are two types of heart valves:

One type of heart valve is located at the opening between the atria and the ventricles. When these heart valves are open, they allow blood to flow in one direction, from atrium to the ventricles.

The two other heart valves are of a different type. They are located between the chambers of our heart and the openings of the two major arteries leaving our heart. The role of this type of heart valve is to prevent blood from backflowing into it from the two major arteries leaving it.

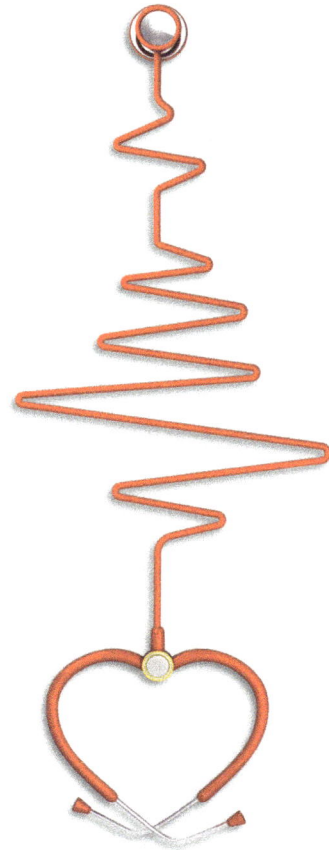

More Interesting Facts   Isn't It Amazing?

Our heart fills with blood and pumps out blood in a rhythmic cycle of relaxation and contraction. Each rhythmic cycle takes our heart about one second and is called a heartbeat.

During a lifespan of 75 years, a person has a total of over two and half milliard heartbeats.

Two distinct sounds are created with each heartbeat:

1. First heart sound
2. Second heart sound.

First Heart Sound

Second Heart Sound

The first heart sound is fainter. It is the sound of the heart valves between the atria and the ventricles closing.

The second heart sound is of the valves closing between the chambers of our heart and between the two major arteries leaving it.

These sounds are produced by our heart valves closing.

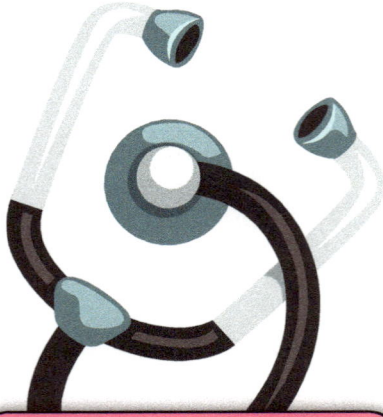

The Stethoscope and Our Heart

When our doctor places his stethoscope on our chest, he hears these two normal heart sounds.

But sometimes, he may hear a soft whisper accompanied by flowing sounds, a kind of rustle in between these two normal heart sounds.

Doctors call this "rustle" a heart murmur.

How Are Heart Murmurs Caused?

Heart murmurs are caused by abnormalities in the heart valves functioning.

The Reasons for Heart Murmurs:

1. The heart valves have become narrower, because they are damaged.

2. The valves of the superior atria do not close properly.

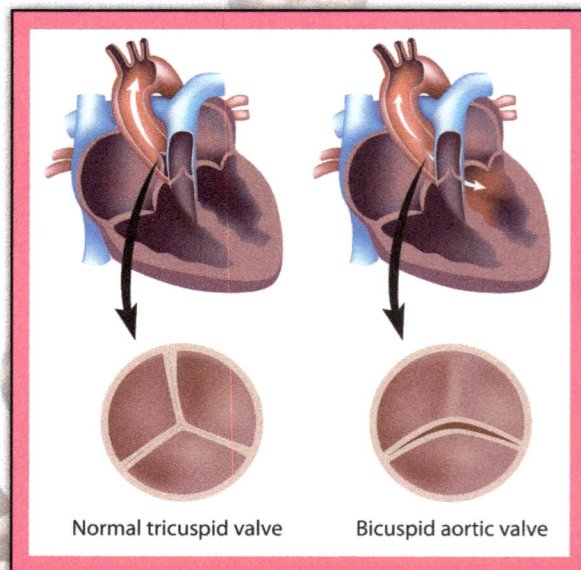

Try This!

You can "hear" and feel the second heart sound when you engage in strenuous activity, such as running or riding your bike fast, or when you're very excited. Notice how you feel in these and similar situations.

96

Normal tricuspid valve · Bicuspid aortic valve

Important Information

Not all heart murmurs indicate that we have a medical problem. Indeed, heart murmurs are frequent in childhood, and disappear during adolescence. Such murmurs are not an illness.

Be Adventurous

Try to conduct the first heart sound and the second heart sound in musical notes, playing a musical instrument, making a drawing, beating on the sink with cutlery, or in any other way.

Medical advisor Dr. Boaz Geva.

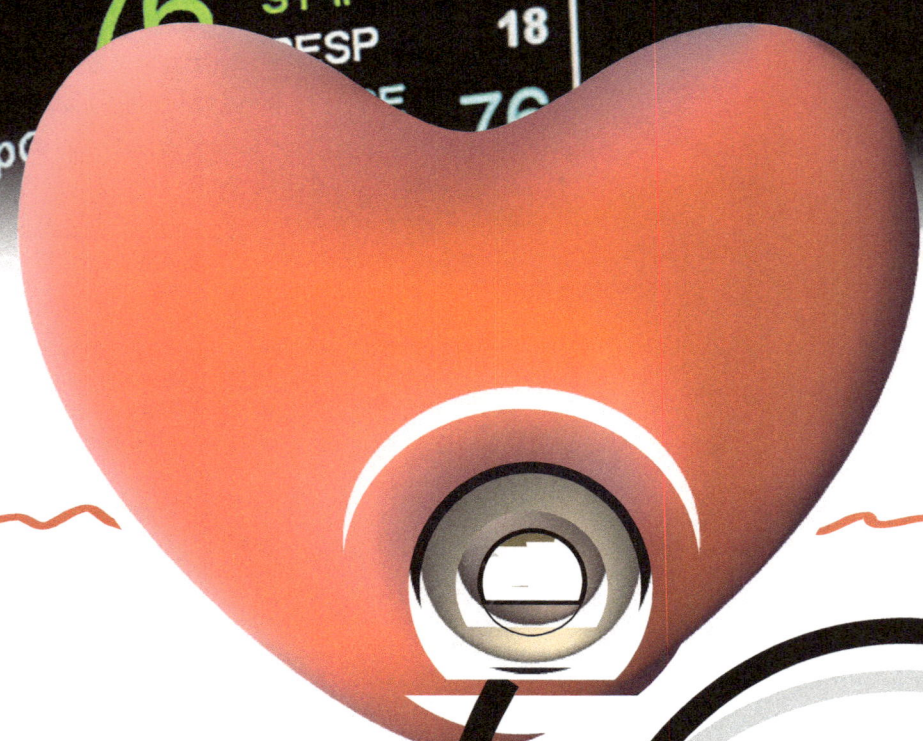

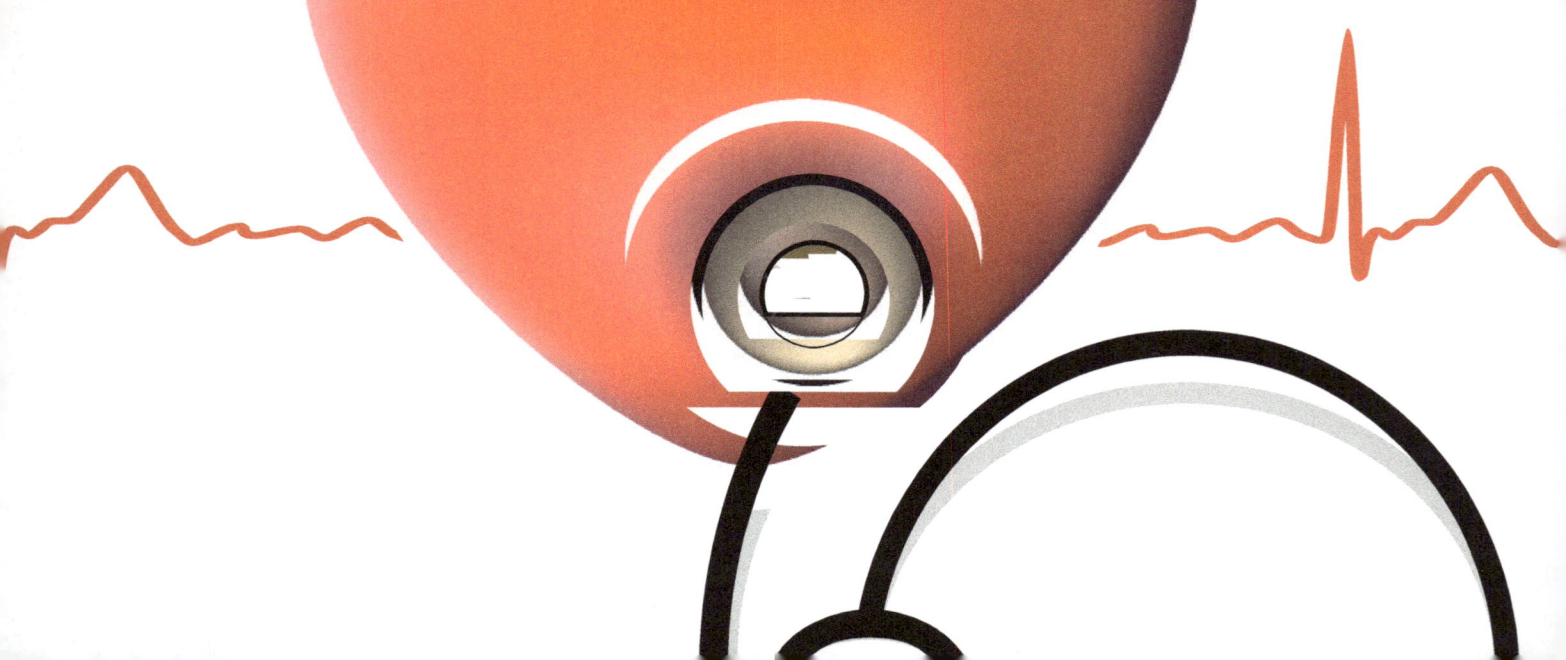

THE MONITORS OF OUR VITAL SIGNS

OUR PULSE

What is our Pulse?

When our heart chambers contract,

↓

a large quantity of blood is pumped with great force, like a wave, out of our left heart chamber and into our aorta,from which it flows into our body.

↓

The force of this wave of pumped blood causes the walls of our arteries to constrict and expand.

↓

The whole process takes under a second. Immediately upon its completion, another wave of blood is pumped with great force out of our left heart chamber. And another wave. And another wave.

↓

The repetitive process of our arteries constricting and expanding each second that these waves of blood are pumped with great force out of your left ventricle and into our aorta is called our

↓

pulse

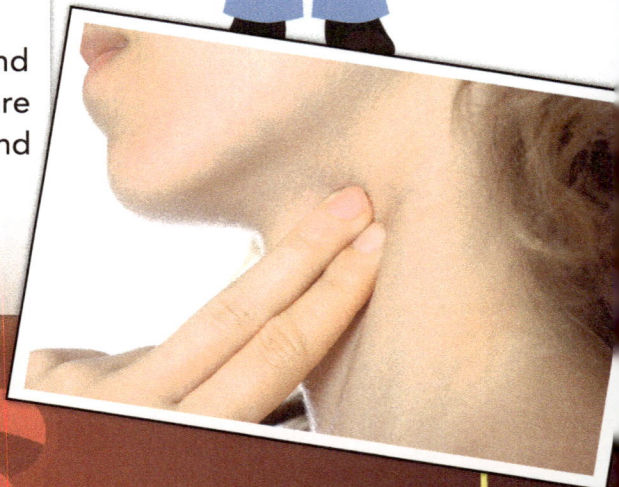

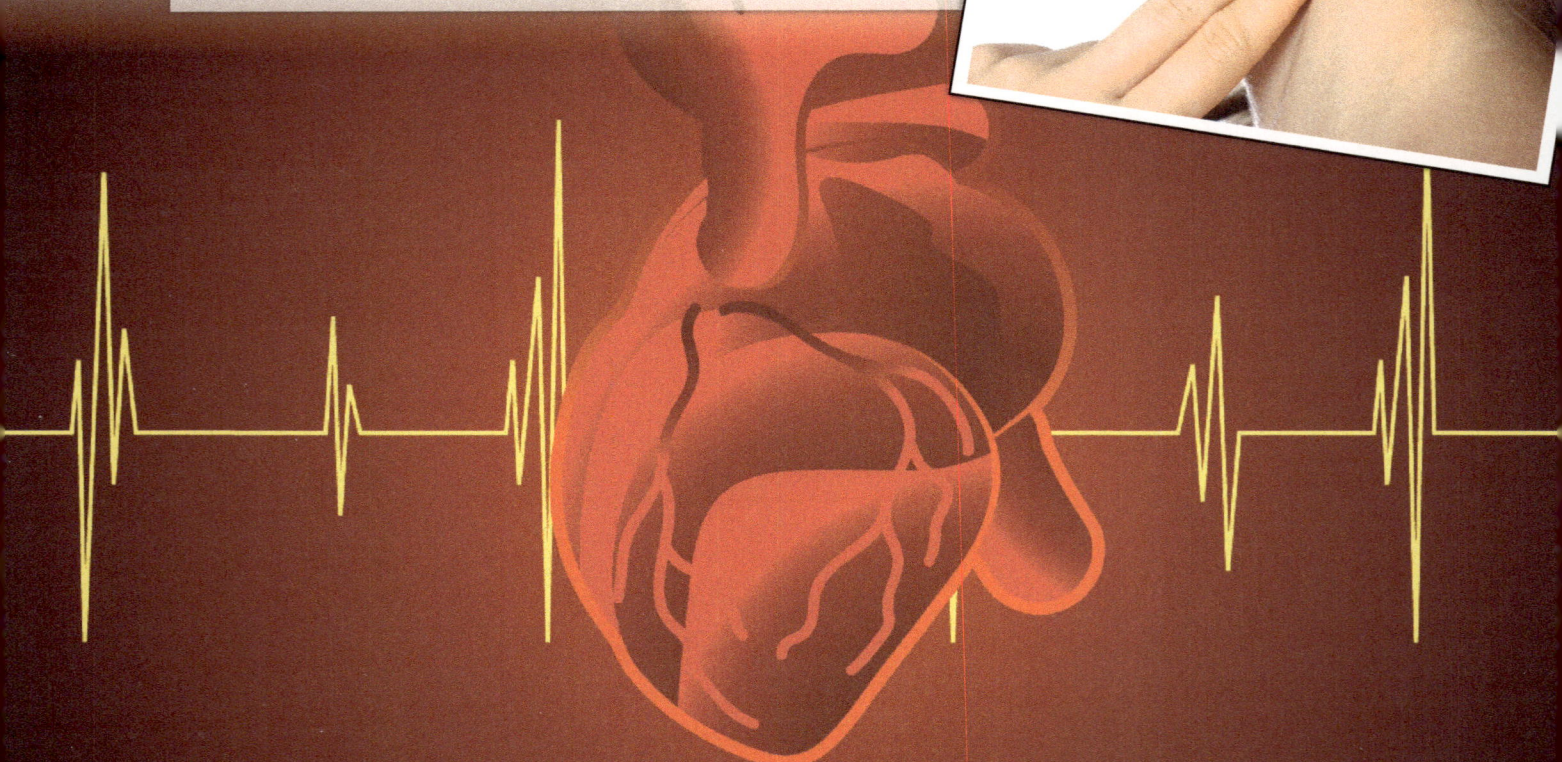

There are two kinds of pulses:

1. **Our tangible (venous) pulse:** Our tangible pulse is the rhythmic expansion and contraction of our arteries with each beat of our heart. We can feel it with our finger on different areas on our skin.

2. **Our arterial pulse:** Our arterial pulse is the vibration of each wave of blood going through our arteries with each beat of our heart. It equals a heartbeat, and our doctor can hear it with her stethoscope.

Why we check our pulse and where we can feel it on our skin:

We check our pulse in order to obtain information on the flow of blood in various places in our body. We can feel our pulse in any place where one of our arteries is close to the surface of our skin.

The usual places for checking our pulse are:

On the inside of our wrist, near our thumb.

On our neck.

On either side of our breathing tube.

On the inside of our elbow.

In our groin.

How do we check our pulse?

We can check our pulse by feeling one of the arteries close to the surface of our skin:

Place two fingers on your skin at a place where an artery passes close under it.

Press gently until you feel your pulse.

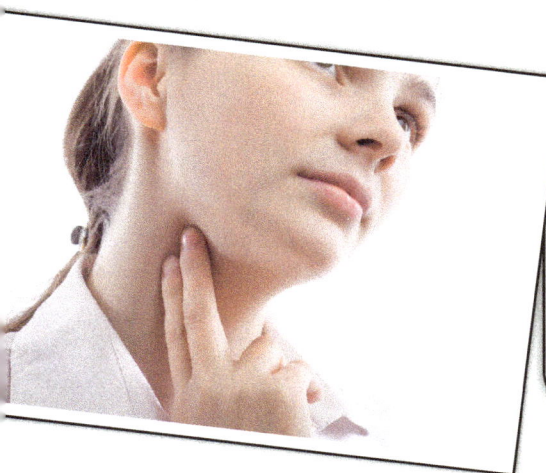

Remember:

Our pulse rate is exactly equal to our heartbeat rate.

We take our pulse to check how often our heart beats in a minute, that is, our heart rate.

If our pulse is regular in rhythm and force, this means that there is a good blood flow to the areas in our body that the artery reaches.

104

What our doctor checks when she takes our pulse:

Our heart rate	The regularity of our heartbeat	The force of our blood flow

What is a normal pulse?

We can take our pulse by feeling one of the arteries close to the surface of our skin.

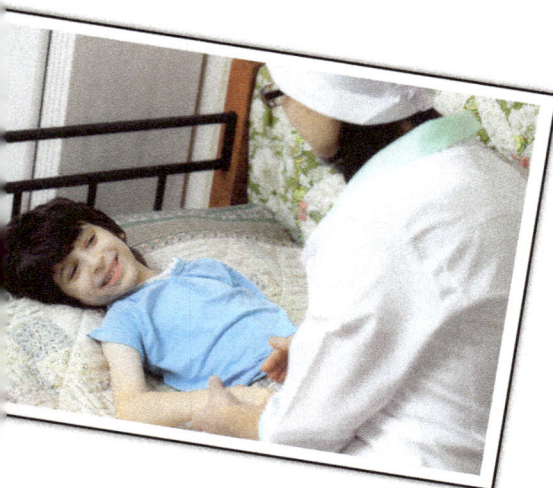

The resting pulse rate of healthy adults normally ranges from 60 to 100 beats a minute.	The resting pulse rate of healthy babies and children normally ranges from 80 to 120 beats a minute.

Under what conditions may our pulse rate vary?

Our pulse rate may vary under the influence of these factors:

Physical activity.

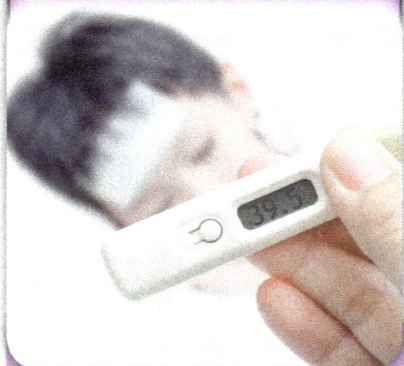

Mental activity.

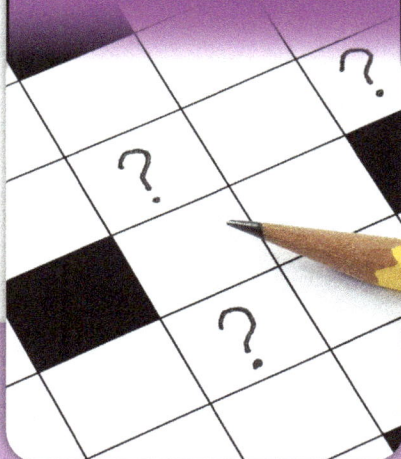

Illnesses that are accompanied by fever.

Try this!

You probably have seen your nurse or doctor checking the pulse of a sick person. She feels his pulse on the inside of his wrist, and counts the beats.

Try to find this place with your index and middle fingers.

When you find your pulse, look at your watch and count the number of beats you hear during a minute.

How many times did your pulse beat in that minute? Write the number down.

Do you think your pulse is faster than normal?

Did it sound calm and quiet?

What does your pulse tell you about your health at the moment?

Exercise, and then take your pulse:

- Walk in place for a number of minutes and check your pulse the instant you stop.

- Go out for an easy run near home. The moment you return, take your pulse.

- Compare your pulse under different conditions.

How Interesting!

Our heart doesn't "know" or realize it when we change our level of activity. The information on the effort and changes taking place in our body reaches the control centers in our brain from our muscles, through our blood. Our brain processes the information it receives at once, and gives an order to our heart to change its rate.

Medical advice: Prof. Obdi Dagan

OUR BLOOD PRESSURE

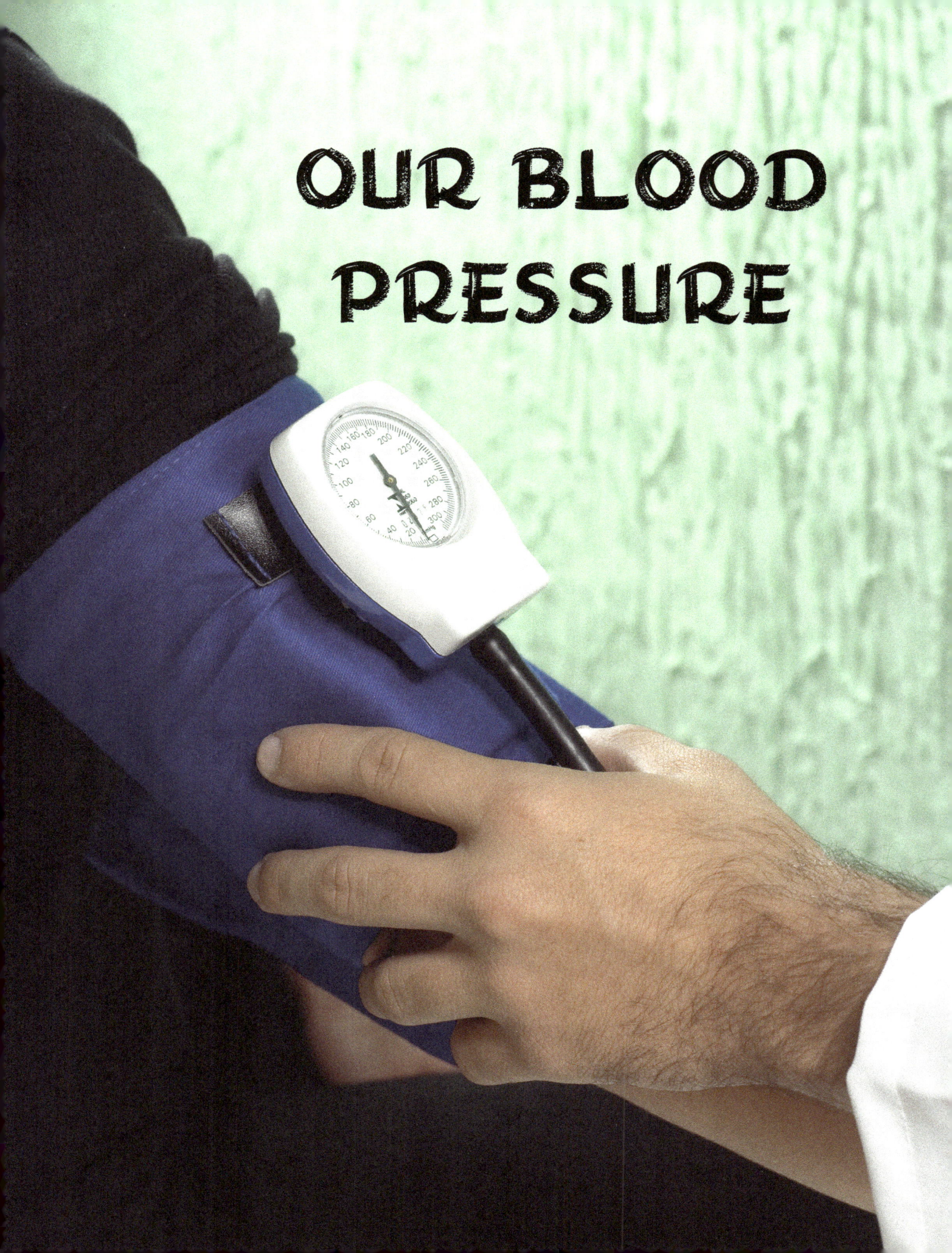

What Is Blood Pressure?

Blood pressure is the pressure exerted upon the walls of our arteries as our blood circulates through our body.

How is blood pressure caused?

Our heart works ceaselessly, pumping blood around the arteries located everywhere in our body.

↓

Our heart pumps blood out of its lower right chamber (ventricle) into the pulmonary artery, from where it flows into our lungs.

↓

This blood flows back into our heart, then out again through the aorta in the left ventricle, and into our body. It is pushed forcefully into our arteries, with whose walls it collides.

↓

The walls of our arteries are relatively small in diameter, and this leads to two outcomes:

↓

1. Intense resistance by our arteries to this blood flow, and

2. Pressure exerted against the walls of our arteries.

↓

This pressure is called "blood pressure".

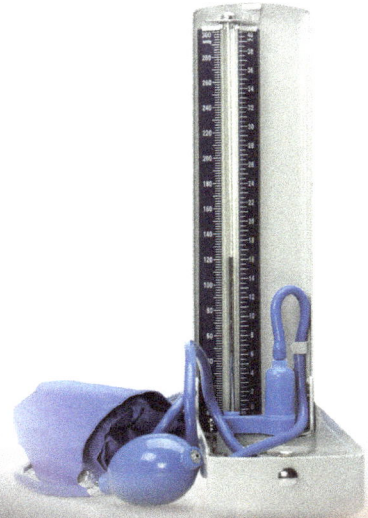

- The blood pressure in our arteries is much higher than in our veins.

- Our blood pressure rises and drops in rhythm with the beats of our heart.

- Two different types of blood pressure can develop:
- 1. High blood pressure, or systolic blood pressure.
- 2. Low blood pressure, or diastolic blood pressure.

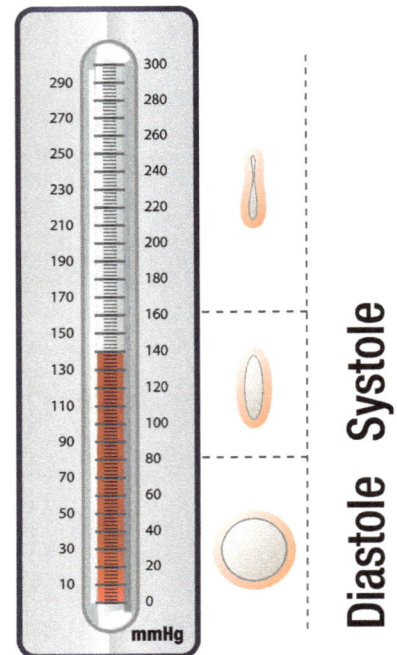

Diastole Systole

110

How are the two different types of blood pressure caused?

Our heart can be compared to a pump that pushes blood into our body. However, this pumping activity is not continuous, and takes place in rhythmic time intervals: Our heart beats, and then rests in between beats. Each beat of our heart creates a wave of pressure, reaching a peak when our left ventricle contracts and blood is pumped with great force out of it and into our arteries.

Systolic blood pressure is the maximum pressure exerted in our arteries as our blood flows through them.

The pressure in our arteries is at its lowest point when our heart relaxes to refill with blood. When our heart relaxes, blood flows into the two atria (upper heart chambers), fills them, and descends into the two ventricles (lower heart chambers), which refill at low pressure.

Diastolic blood pressure is the minimum pressure exerted in our arteries as our blood flows through them.

Diastole and Systole of human Heart

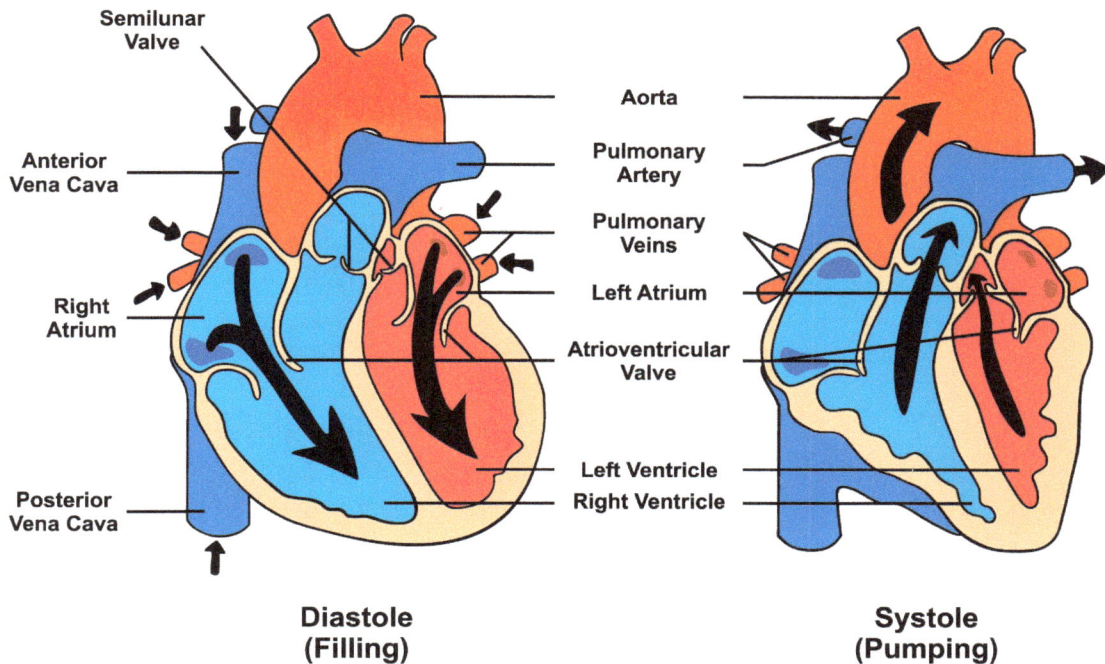

Labels (left): Semilunar Valve, Anterior Vena Cava, Right Atrium, Posterior Vena Cava

Labels (center): Aorta, Pulmonary Artery, Pulmonary Veins, Left Atrium, Atrioventricular Valve, Left Ventricle, Right Ventricle

Diastole (Filling)

Systole (Pumping)

Normally, both phases together last only about one second. Our heart contracts for about one third of a second every second, then relaxes for about two-thirds of a second immediately afterwards. So, the contraction phase is about half as long as the relaxation phase.

Important

Blood flows fairly continuously through our blood vessels. However, its pressure varies.

Our blood pressure can be compared to the pressure created inside a water hose attached to a tap. The more fully we open the tap, the stronger will be the pressure against its walls. The same will happen when we block the other end of the hose.

What influences our blood pressure?

Three main factors influence our blood pressure:

1. The volume of blood that our heart pumps with each beat.	2. The diameter of our blood vessels enormously affects the frictional resistance of their walls as our blood flows through them.	3. Increased activity, anger, physical exercise and excitement temporarily increase our blood pressure and heart rate.

When the pumping force of our heart exceeds that needed for the normal continuous flow of blood through our body, higher blood pressure is exerted against the walls of our arteries. This puts a heavy strain on our circulatory system.

High blood pressure forces our heart to increase its exertions, and is liable to harm our blood vessels.

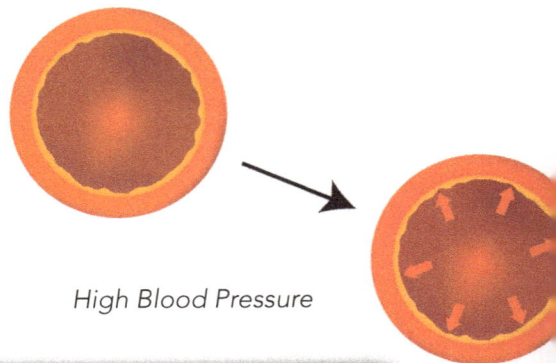

High Blood Pressure

That is why it is so important to maintain a healthy blood pressure.

systolic blood pressure   diastolic blood pressure

both are measurable

Measuring blood pressure

During each heartbeat, our blood pressure varies between the two different forces, systolic and diastolic. Because of this, both forces are measured when taking our blood pressure.

Our blood pressure is measured using an instrument called a:

Sphygmomanometer

Types of sphygmomanometers

There are several types of sphygmomanometers.

A. Digital sphygmomanometers:

Digital sphygmomanometers are electronic devices for measuring blood pressure.

They use:

Sensors sensitive to changes in blood pressure.

Electronic components. These include a microprocessor that detects changes in our blood pressure by the signals it receives. It then interprets them for display in digital form.

Because digital sphygmomanometers are so easy to operate, they are convenient for home use.

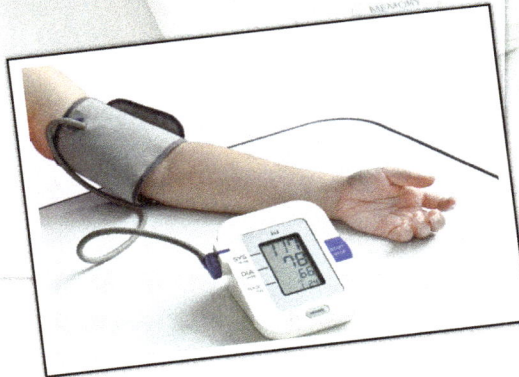

How interesting!

Nowadays, digital sphygmomanometers are in far wider use than manual ones, and are used by doctors and nurses when the situation calls for it.

B. Manual sphygmomanometers:

Manual sphygmomanometers were used until digital sphygmomanometers were developed and largely replaced them.

Manual sphygmomanometers are still used at times by health professionals such as doctors and nurses.

The parts of the manual sphygmomanometer:

- 1. An inflatable blood pressure cuff
- 2. A circular dial.
- 3. An air tube.
- 4. A hand pump.
- 5. A stethoscope.

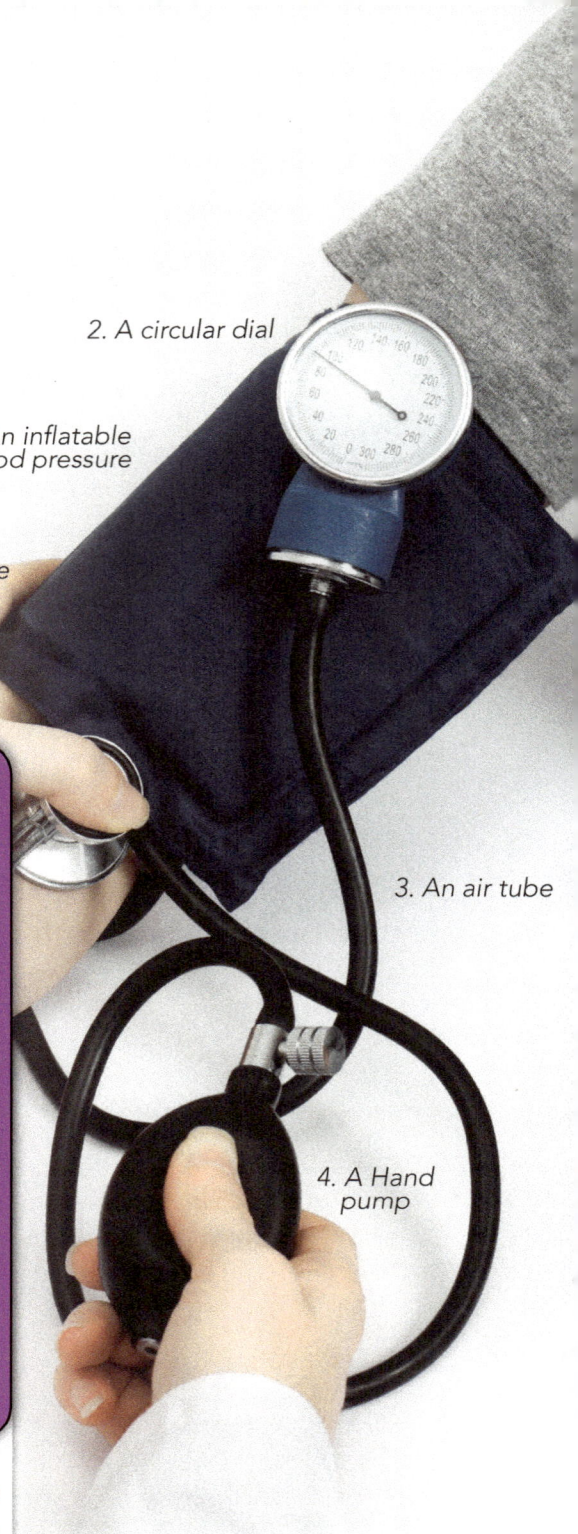

2. A circular dial

1. An inflatable blood pressure

5. A stethoscoepe

3. An air tube

4. A Hand pump

How health professionals measure our blood pressure with a manual sphygmomanometer:

1. Our health professional wraps the inflatable blood pressure cuff around our left or right upper arm.

2. Using a small hand pump, she inflates it until the blood flow in our arm is cut off.

3. She then gradually lets the air out of the cuff, and it loosens.

4. As our blood starts to flow again, she listens to our heartbeat. She does so using a stethoscope whose diaphragm is placed under the bottom edge of the cuff, over the artery running through the hollow of our elbow.

5. Our blood pressure is displayed on a circular dial in numbers.

114

When our health professional hears our blood start to flow again as she gradually lets the air out of the cuff, she writes down our maximum blood pressure as our heart contracts. This is our systolic blood pressure.

When she lets more air out of the cuff, our heart relaxes. She listens to our blood flowing freely through our arteries until our pulse can no longer be heard, and now writes down our minimum blood pressure. This is our diastolic blood pressure.

Mercury sphygmomanometers

The mercury sphygmomanometer is considered to be the most exact blood pressure measuring device available. It uses a measuring tube containing mercury, and gives precise blood pressure readings.

What are normal blood pressure values for children and adolescents?

Here are normal blood pressure values for children and adolescents:

A systolic blood pressure of 120	A diastolic blood pressure of 70

Blood pressure is typically recorded as two values, written as a ratio in this manner:

120/70

This is really important!

It only takes a few minutes to measure our blood pressure. It does not hurt at all, as the procedure is non-invasive.

Medical advice: Prof. Ovdi Dagan

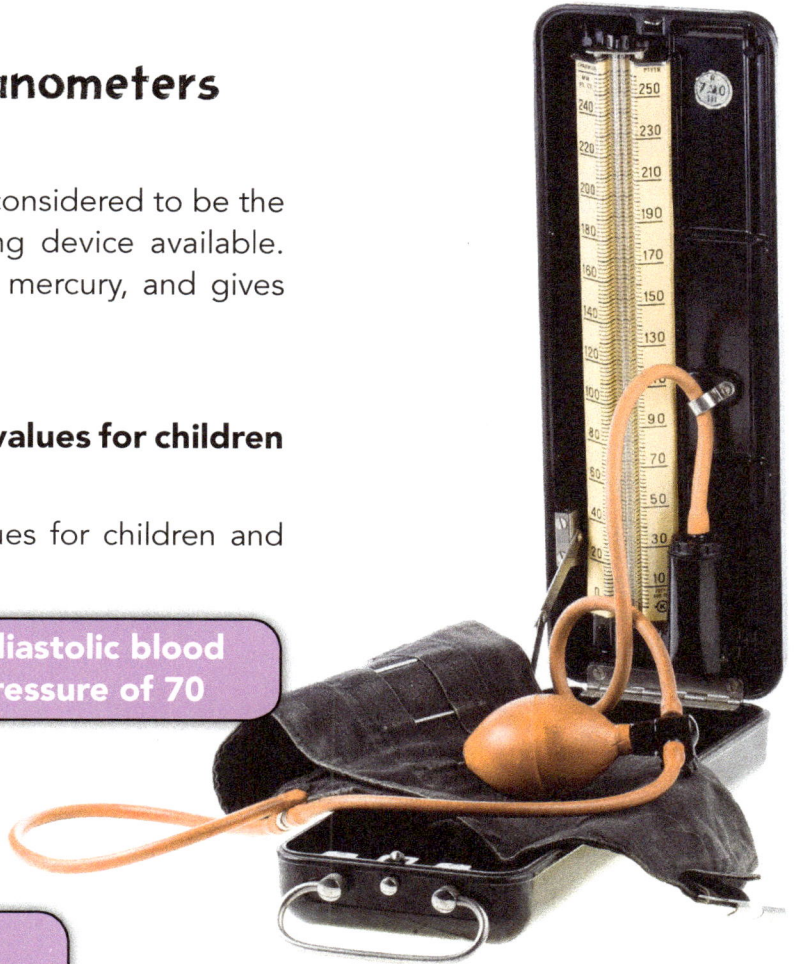

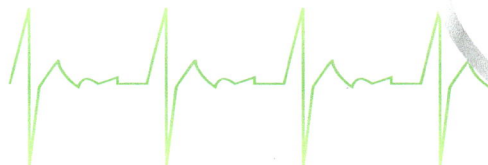

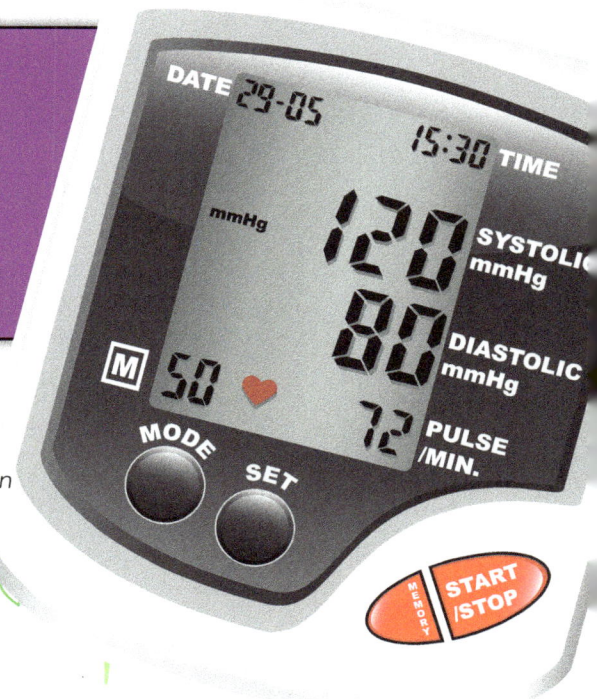

Vintage Manometer

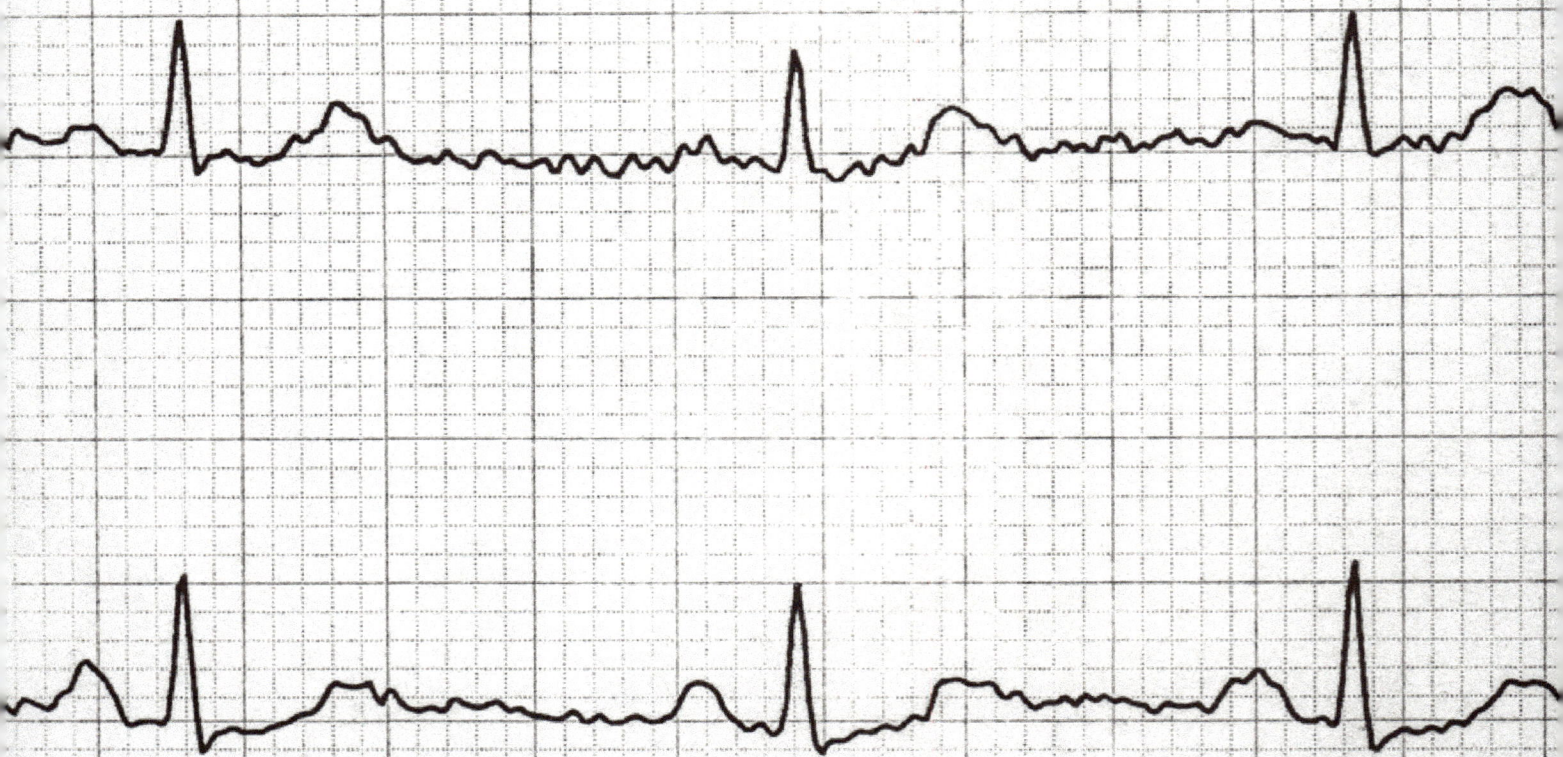

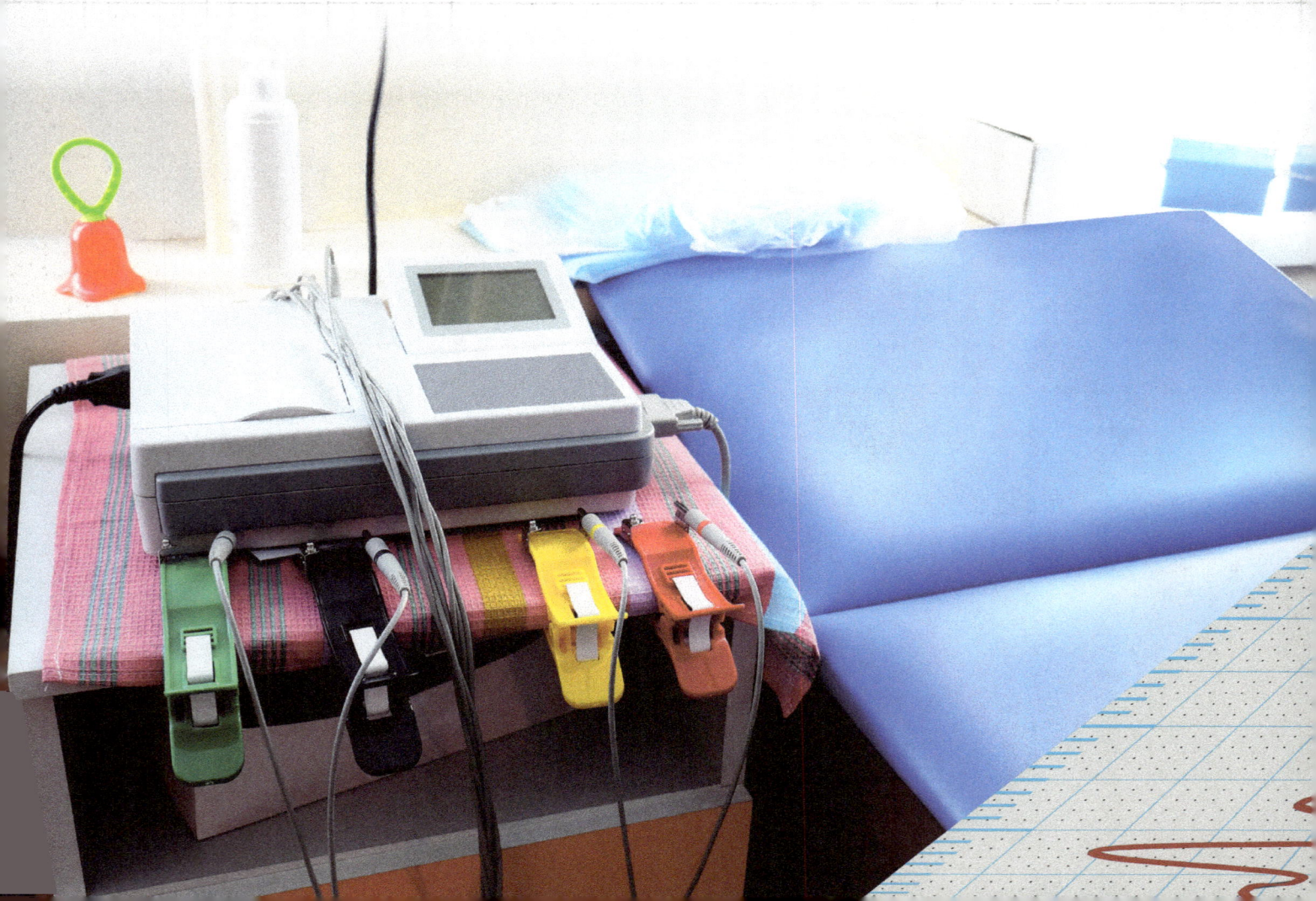

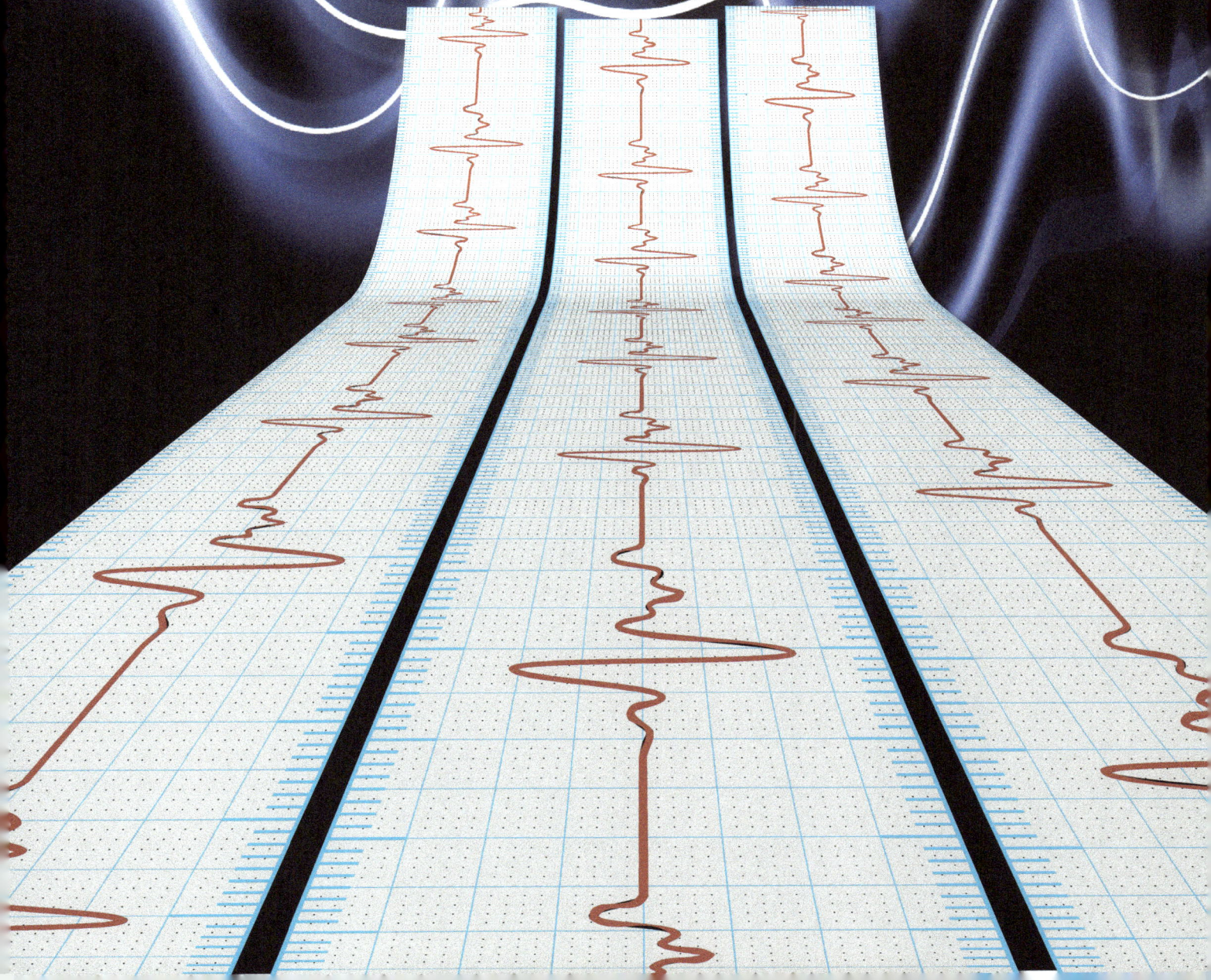

THE ECG

The ECG

The electrical waves that make our heart beat

A little bundle of conduction cells, called the SA node (sinoatrial node), is located in the upper part of our right atrium. These specialized cells differ from the other cells of our heart.

The SA node generates electrical nerve impulses and serves as a natural pacemaker, causing our heart to beat at a steady, even rhythm during our whole life.

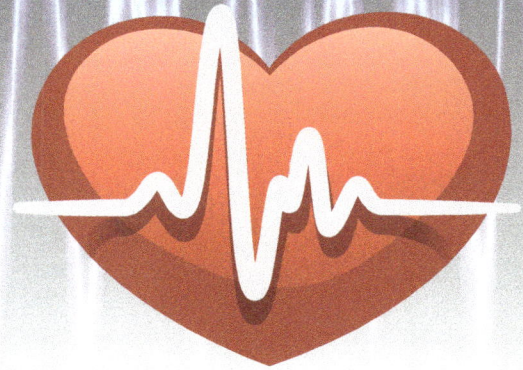

These electrical nerve impulses are called electrical waves.

What is an ECG?

An electrocardiogram, or ECG, is a diagnostic test that records, in a wavy line graph on paper or a computer screen, the activity of the electrical wave that activates our heart.

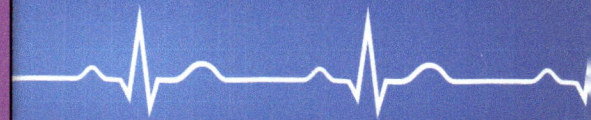

The test is performed using an ECG machine that captures and records the electrical signals produced between the different parts of our heart.

What can the ECG test detect?

The ECG test can detect problems in the generation of electrical waves and in their conduction in our cardiac system.

Conduction Pathway of our Heart

Here is an outline of the conduction pathway of our heart:

Each electrical wave

⬇

generated by the SA node spreads through the cells of both atria and reaches a connection point with the ventricles called the AV node (atrioventricular node).

⬇

As the electrical wave travels through the atria, it causes them to contract. The AV node hinders the electrical wave, enabling the blood passively flowing though the atria to fill the ventricles.

⬇

At this moment, the electrical wave leaves the AV node and travels along a fast pathway, at whose end it splits between both ventricles, causing them to contract while full of blood.

⬇

This entire process repeats itself with each new heartbeat, enabling the atria and the ventricles to coordinate their activity and regulate the rhythm of our heart.

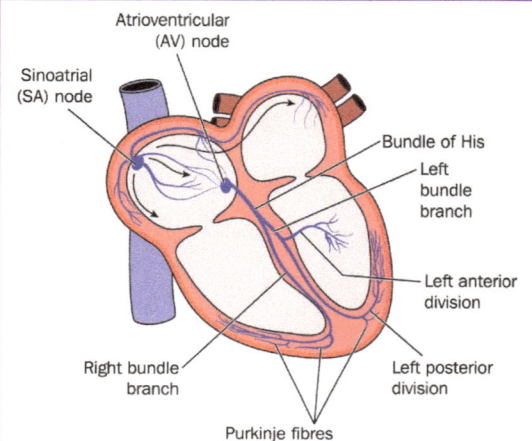

⬇

The SA node functions as the natural pacemaker of our heart, causing it to beat regularly and evenly all our life. In the case of severe problems with a person's natural pacemaker, doctors can decide to replace it with an artificial one.

How is the ECG machine built?

It has 10 interfaces (sensors), called "electrodes", which are divided into two groups:

Four electrodes capture the electrical signals on each of our two legs and two arms.

The remaining six electrodes capture the electrical signals on our chest walls.

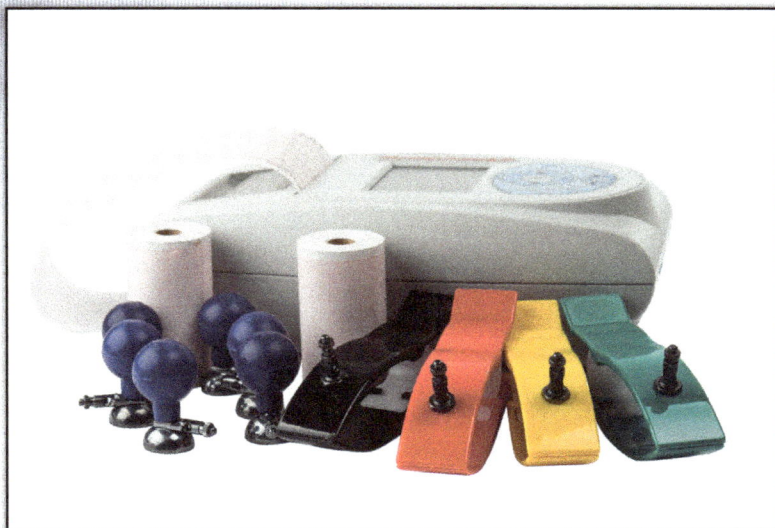

121

Important information

An ECG test takes only a few minutes. It is non-invasive, and doesn't hurt at all.

How does the technician perform an ECG test?

The patient lies down on his back on a bed.

He uncovers his hands, ankles and chest.

The ECG technician attaches four electrodes to his limbs: one to his left wrist, one to his right wrist, one to his left ankle and one to his right ankle.

She places six special sticky patches on the patient's chest, and attaches the six remaining electrodes to them.

She attaches all the 10 electrodes after first dampening them and the patient's skin with water, in order to improve the electrical flow between them.

After attaching all ten electrodes to the patient's limbs and chest, the technician operates the ECG machine. At this stage, the electrical activity of the patient's heart starts being recorded on graph paper.

The paper printout containing the results of the test comes out of an opening at the side of the machine.

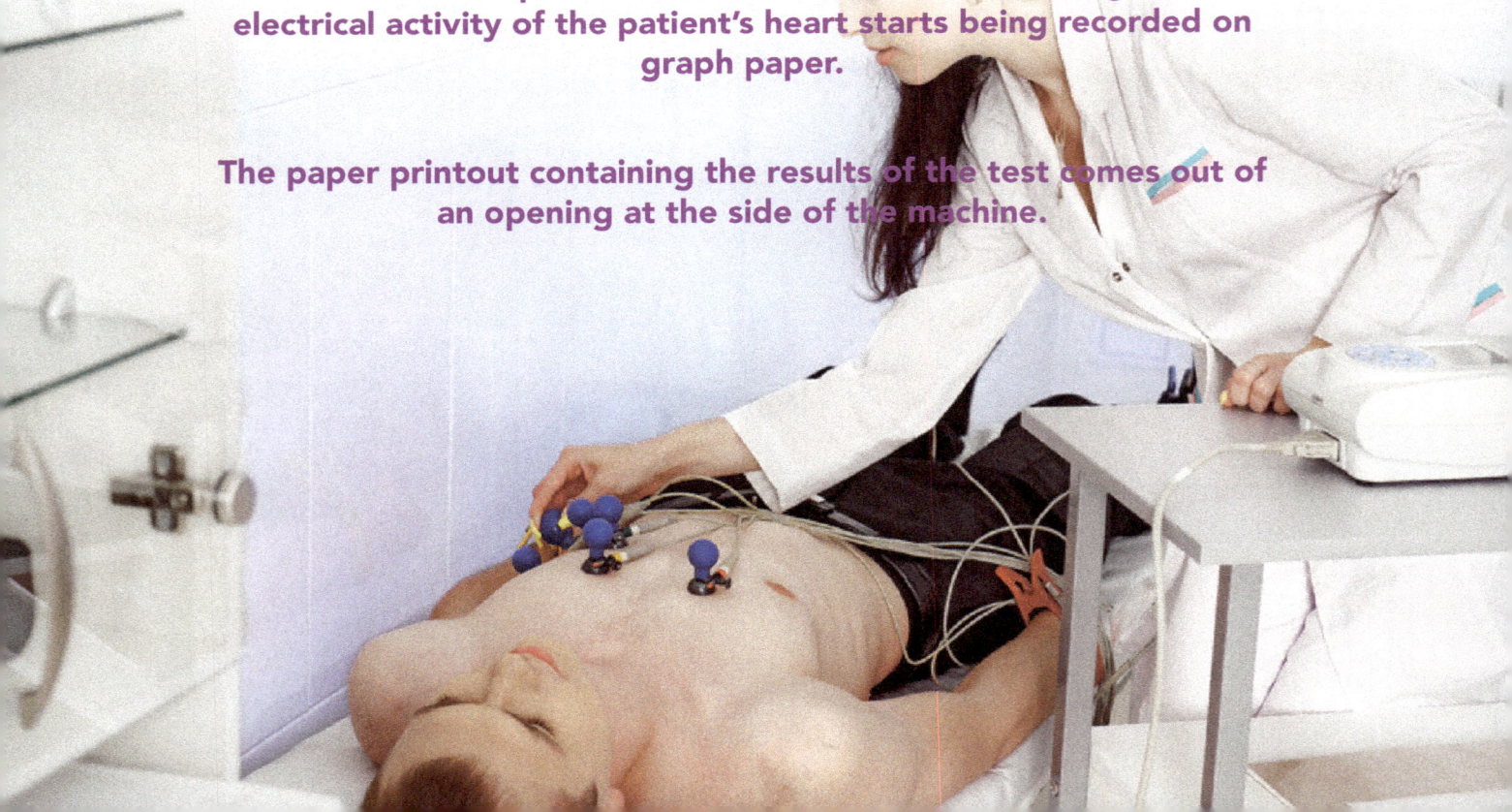

ECG recordings

ECG recordings contain two different types of waves:

> **One wave reflects the contractions of the upper chambers of the patient's heart, the atria.**
>
> **Another wave reflects the contractions of the lower chambers of the patient's heart, the ventricles.**

Important information

The ECG test is an auxiliary test. Its purpose is to identify the source of the problem with the electrical conduction system of the patient's heart.

The findings of the ECG test are matched with the patient's medical imaging and with other auxiliary tests.

A story from the past

The Dutch doctor and physiologist Willem Einthoven invented the ECG machine in 1901. He won the Nobel Prize in Medicine for it in 1924. The basic principles of the ECG in Einthoven's time are still relevant. However, the initial clumsy version was replaced over time by simpler electronic ones, and even by computerised machines.

Did you know?

A Holter Monitor is a recording of the heart's rhythm over a 24-hour period.

Medical advice: Prof. Ovdi Dagan

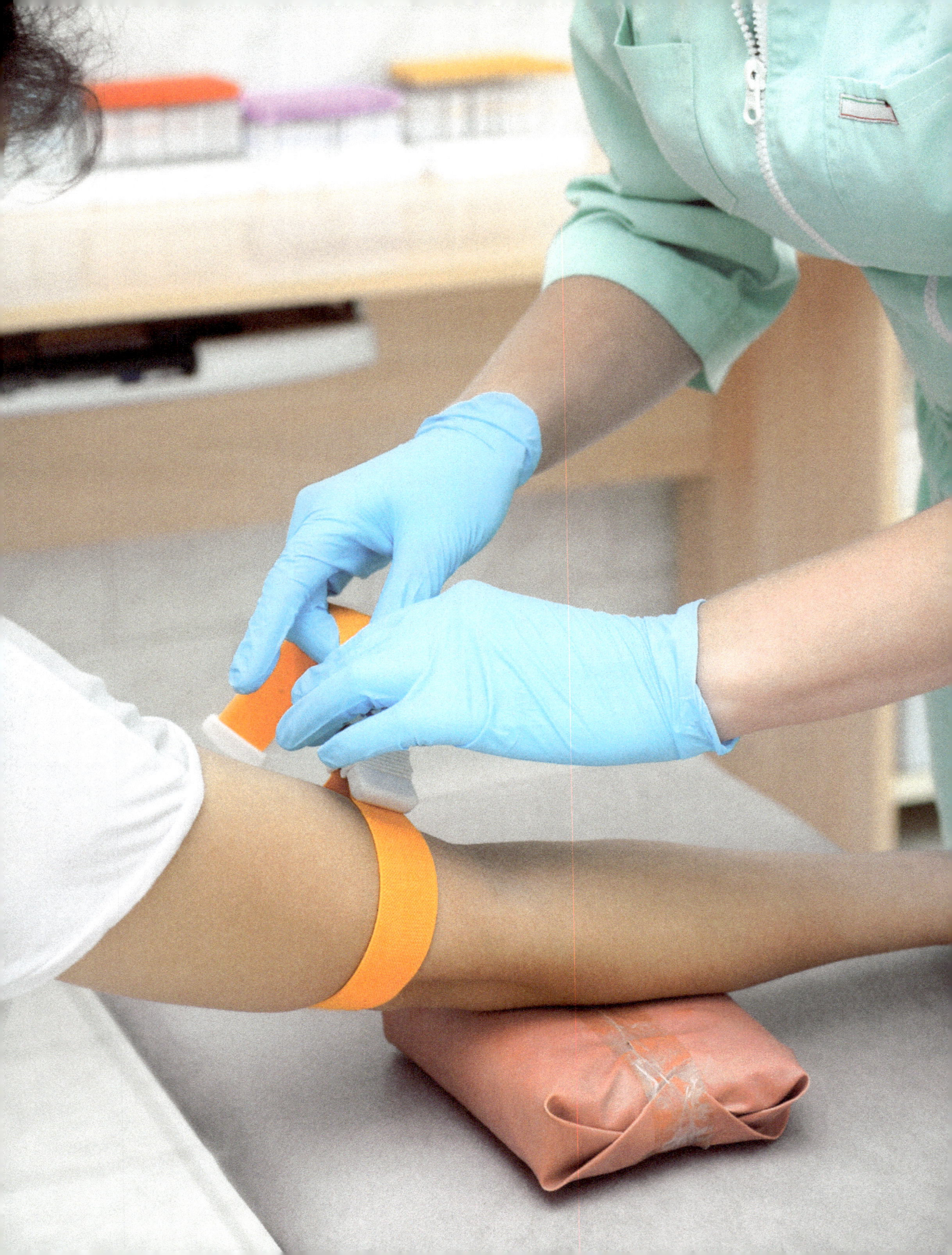

INVESTIGATING YOUR BLOOD

Being sick, doing a blood test, and getting well again

To understand the connection between being sick, having a blood test, and getting well again, it helps to know two things:

> **The components of human blood.**
>
> **What each of the components of your blood tells us about your health.**

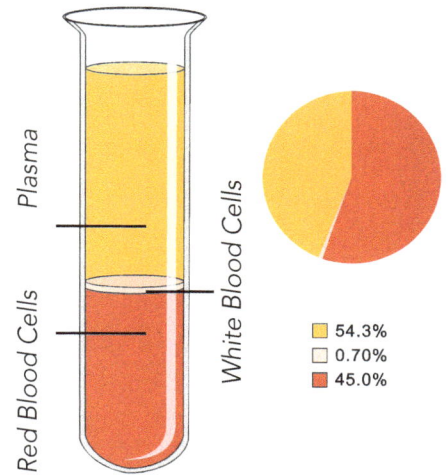

Plasma

Red Blood Cells

White Blood Cells

■ 54.3%
□ 0.70%
■ 45.0%

White Blood Cell

Red Blood Cell

The components of blood

Blood has two main components:

Blood cells are divided into three groups:
- Red blood cells
- White blood cells
- Platelets

Blood cells make up approximately 50% of your blood volume.

Blood plasma is a component of your blood fluid that does not contain cells. It is a clear yellowish fluid, and constitutes about 50% of your blood volume.

Platelet

Did you know?

Blood volume is the amount of blood in your body, and is approximately equivalent to 6-7% of your weight.

Red blood cells

Red blood cells, known by doctors as erythrocytes (a compound word formed by combining the Greek words, erythros and kytos, meaning "red" and "hollow vessel", or "cell", respectively), have several characteristics:

Red blood cells are the most abundant cells in the human body. There are about 5 million red blood cells in each cubic millimeter of blood in your body.

Red blood cells are shaped like concave disks.

Red blood cells contain hemoglobin. This gives them, and your blood, their red color.

Important!

Hemoglobin is a protein molecule found in red blood cells that carries the oxygen from your lungs to the tissues in your body.

White blood cells

White blood cells, known by doctors as leukocytes (a compound word formed by combining the Greek words, leuko and kytos, meaning "white" and "hollow vessel", or "cell", respectively), have several characteristics:

Our blood has only a small amount of white blood cells. There are only about 5,000-10,000 white blood cells in each cubic millimeter of blood in your body.

White blood cells are divided into several types, and represent an important component in your body's defense system.

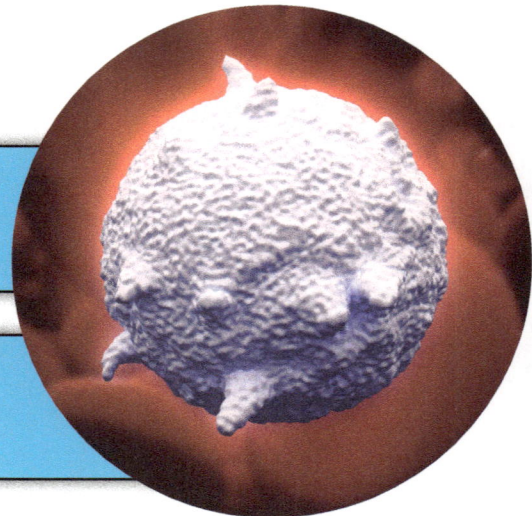

Platelets

Platelets, known by doctors as thrombocytes (a compound word formed by combining the Greek words, thrombo and kytos, meaning "blood clot" and "hollow vessel", or "cell", respectively), have several characteristics:

Each cubic millimeter of blood in your body contains between 150,000 and 400,000 platelets.

Platelets play a key role in blood clotting. If you get a cut, they stop the bleeding.

This is important!

All blood cells are produced in the blood marrow, which is a soft tissue found in the hollow part of most bones in your body.

Why are blood tests performed?

There are several reasons why blood tests are performed:

To help diagnose the functioning of your different body systems.

To understand the patient's medical condition.

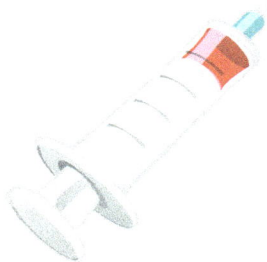

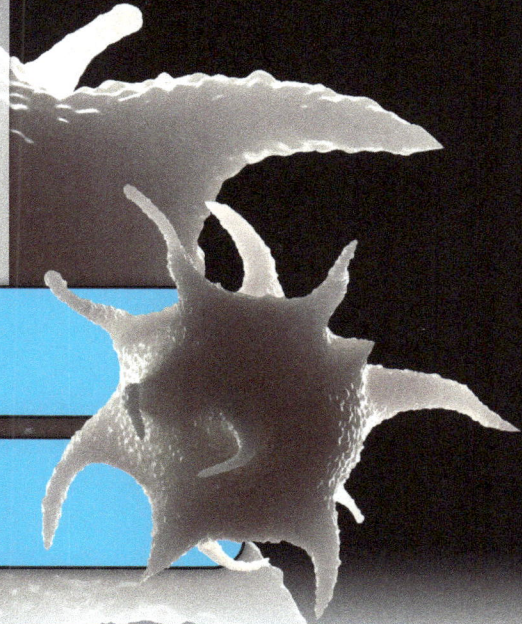

Blood test results are assigned values in numbers, called "normal values" or "values within the range of normal". There are separate norms for children, adults, and the elderly.

If you're sick, the results of your blood test may show deviations from normal values.

Values higher or lower than normal mean that there are changes in the composition of your blood due to illness, malnutrition, the influence of medicines, and so on.

How are blood tests performed?

Blood tests are performed by taking a blood sample from the patient.

How are blood samples taken?

The way a blood sample is taken depends on the type of blood test.

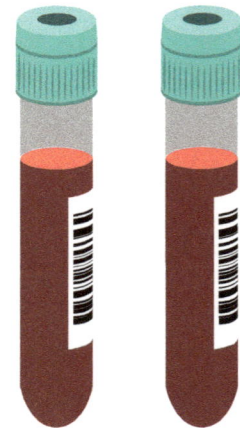

There are two blood sampling methods:

Finger-prick blood tests

In finger-prick tests, the nurse or lab technician pricks the pad of your finger with a sterile plastic needle called a lancet. She then presses the sides of the pad of your finger several times, until blood droplets appear, and draws them into a thin glass tube or a blood collection tube called a vacutainer test tube.

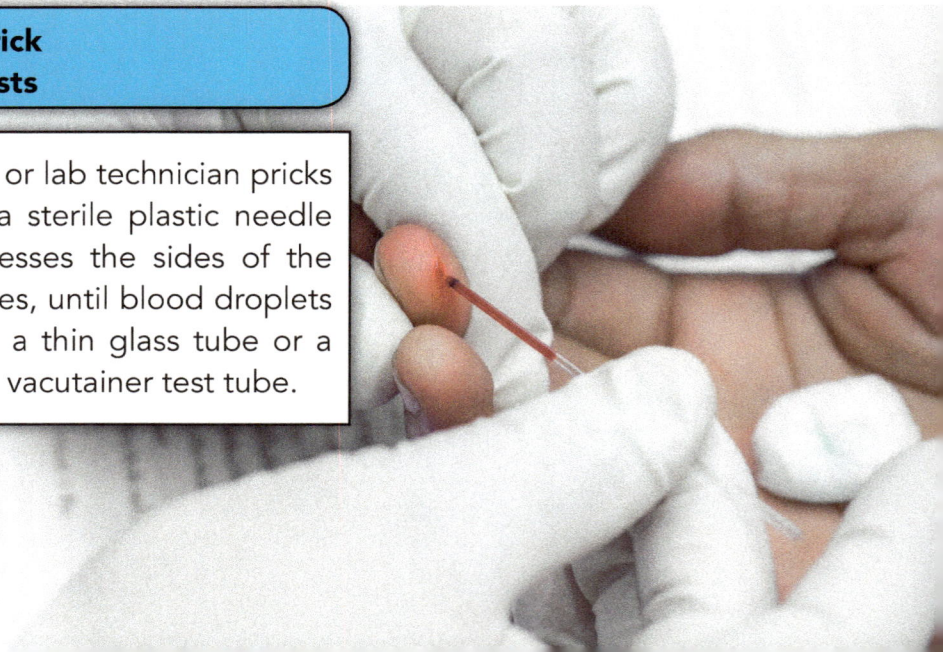

Venipuncture blood tests

In this method, the nurse draws a blood sample directly from the patient's vein.

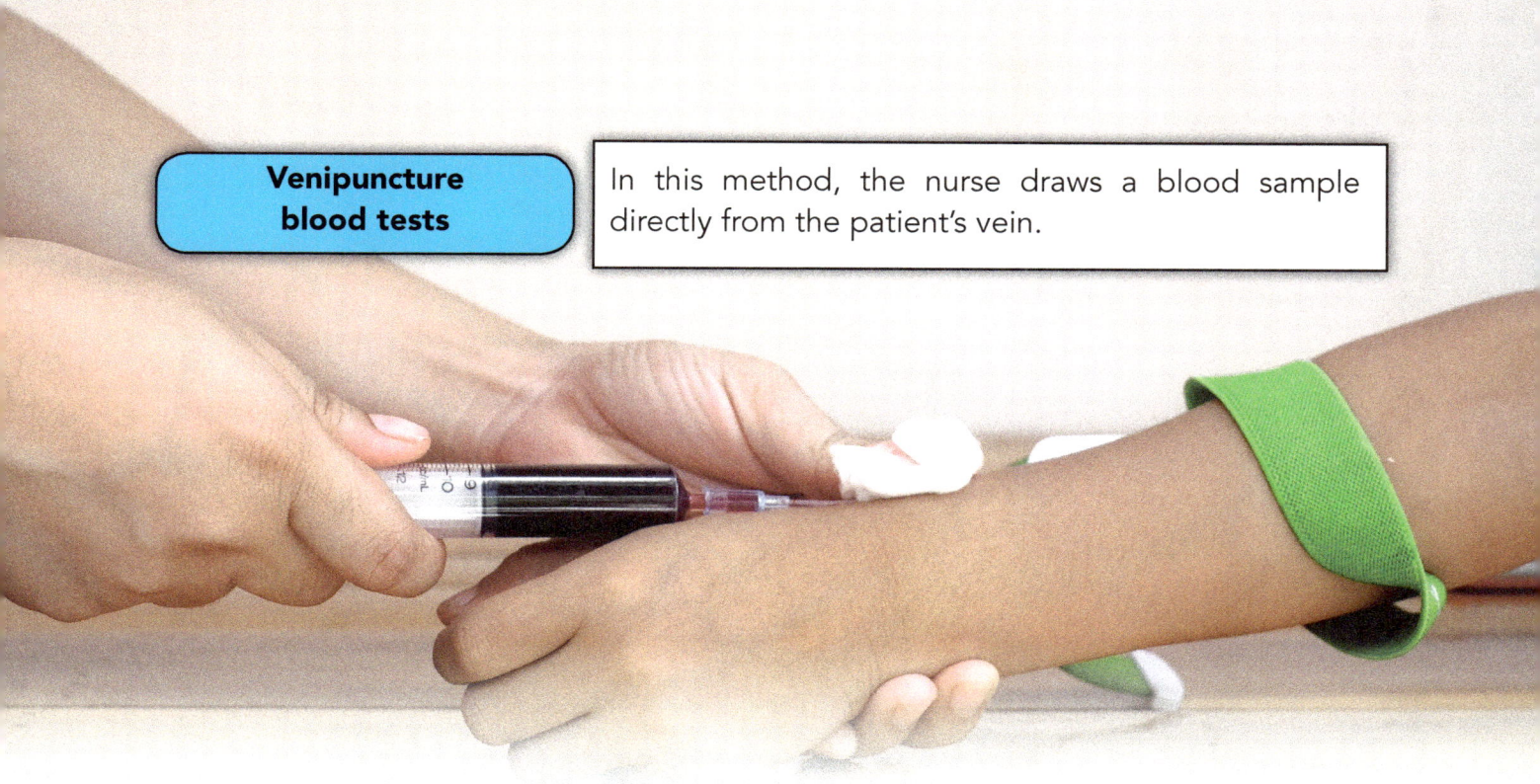

Here is how venipuncture blood tests are performed:

- The nurse or the doctor prepares a different vacutainer test tube for each different blood test, and labels them with the patient number you were given.

- The nurse then washes the area where your blood will be drawn with an antiseptic swab. Then, she ties a rubber cord around your upper arm. After a few seconds, your veins will bulge slightly through your skin and be easily visible.

- The nurse then places a needle into one of your bulging veins, and draws your blood. The other end of the needle is attached to a thin glass tube, through which your blood flows, entering directly into a special, sterile, hermetically sealed vacutainer test tube. The nurse places the vacutainer test tube on a special vacutainer test tube rack.

Where are your blood samples sent?

Your blood samples are sent for analysis to a laboratory with state-of-the-art equipment.

Who examines your blood samples?

The blood samples sent to the laboratory are examined by a lab technician specialized in conducting certain tests.

That is interesting!

It is impossible to examine all the components of all the blood in your body. That is why only a tiny sample is taken of your blood, and components of it that may be connected to your present illness are examined.

This sampling is an initial test that provides information about the state of your health.

132

You don't have to fast before most blood sampling tests.

The only tests that require you to fast beforehand, for 12 hours, are blood sugar level tests and blood fat tests. This is because the nutrients in the food and drinks you consume are absorbed into your blood stream and, if you eat before a test, this could affect the results, making them inaccurate.

The usual blood tests done are:

A blood count

A blood smear

A biochemical test

A blood culture

BASO	RARE	RARE		PROTEIN (BIURET)	5.3-7.8	5.8-7.8	gm%	Bilirubin	[-]
UNCLASS				ALBUMIN	2.3-3.		gm%	Hb/ Blood	[-]
NUCL RBC			/100WBC	GLOBULIN	1.5-		gm%		-]
RETICS	1-2	0-1	%	ELECTROLY					
PLATELETS	200-500	300-800	X10²/ul	CALCIUM			mg%		
PROTEIN (REFRACT)	6-7.5	6-7.5	gm%	PHOSPHORUS			mg%		
BLOOD MORPHOLOGY				SODIUM			mEq/L		
				POTASSIUM					
				CHLORIDE					
				AMMONIA				TALS	
				OTHERS					

BLOOD PARASITE		COMMENT	
Babesia Sp.			
Ehrlichia canis			
Hepatozoon canis			CELLS
Microfilaria			
Ehrlichia platys			
Haemobartonella felis			
Others			

DATE REPORTED.......... REPORTED BY.......... Vet. Technician
.... Pathologist

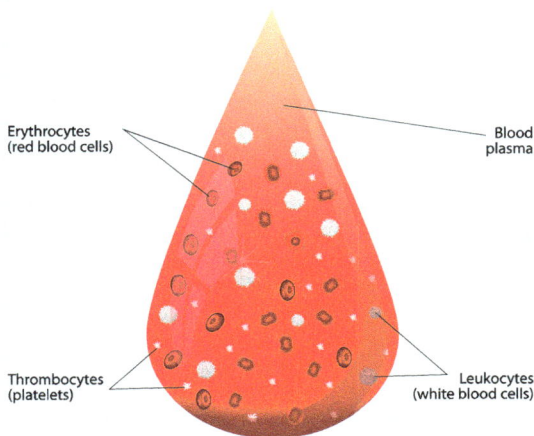

What is a blood count?

A blood count test measures the following:

- The number of white blood cells in your blood.
- The number of red blood cells in your blood.
- The hemoglobin level in your blood.
- The number of platelets in your blood.

Erythrocytes (red blood cells)

Blood plasma

Thrombocytes (platelets)

Leukocytes (white blood cells)

Blood count results usually fall within normal ranges.

However, the blood count values of certain groups of children and adults may be higher or lower than the normal range. In such cases, it is important to find the reason for these higher or lower values.

Blood smears, or differential blood counts

With the help of blood smear tests, it is possible:

- To detect changes in the shapes of the red blood cells, the white blood cells, and the platelets in the patient's blood.

- To identify the different types of white blood cells in the patient's blood.

- To evaluate the patient's medical condition, and to determine whether an illness is infectious, viral or bacterial.

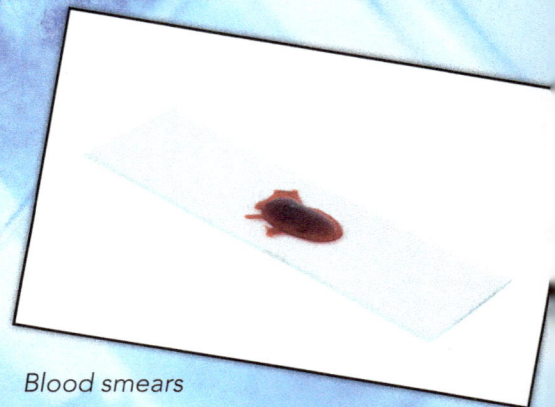

134

Blood smears

How are blood smears prepared?

- The lab technician smears a small drop of the patient's blood on a thin flat piece of glass, called a microscope slide.

- Using an automated instrument, the lab technician then stains the blood smear with a special staining solution. The red blood cells, which lack a nucleus, are stained pink while the nuclei of the white blood cells are stained bluish.

Who examines the blood smear?

A hematologist, who is a doctor specialized in the field of blood and of blood-forming tissues, examines the stained blood smear under a microscope. He can distinguish between the red blood cells, the white blood cells, and the platelets, and is also able to determine their size, shape, and maturity, and to assess their condition. Based on this information, he diagnoses the patient's medical condition.

Important!

Blood smears are part of the set of blood tests that enable your doctor to arrive at a precise diagnosis of your medical condition, and to make professional decisions on how to proceed with the further clarification of your health.

Interesting

Although the new-generation automated cell counters are highly sophisticated, they cannot replace the hematologist, who is specialized in interpreting the appearance of the blood smear.

Biochemical tests

Biochemical tests are blood tests that tell us several things about:

Your blood sugar level

Your blood mineral level

Your blood protein level

Your blood fat level

Your blood vitamin level

The number of biochemical tests available is rising from year to year.

- They help your doctor determine why you aren't feeling well.
- They enable your doctor to make a more accurate diagnosis of the state of your health.

Your doctor's diagnosis is needed in order to determine the appropriate course of treatment that will help you get better.

Blood culture tests

Blood culture tests check whether bacteria have penetrated into your blood. If any are indeed found, that means that you have an infection that requires immediate attention.

In this test, a blood sample is placed on a special growth medium, to enable any bacteria or fungi present in the sample to grow. The test also investigates the sensitivity of the bacteria to specific antibiotics, so that your doctor can recommend an effective course of treatment for your particular infection.

These experiments are worth trying out!

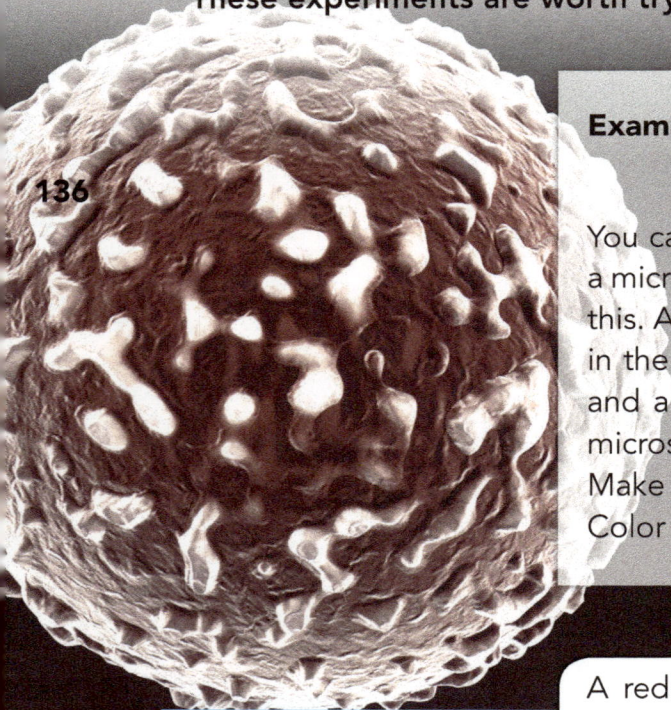

Examine a blood sample under a microscope:

You can examine the various components of blood under a microscope. You will need your biology teacher's help for this. Ask her for a prepared blood smear slide, and place it in the appropriate location in the microscope. Get paper and a pencil ready. Examine the blood smear under the microscope, and identify the different types of blood cells. Make a drawing of how they look under the microscope. Color them. Summarize your findings.

Red and white

A red blood cell and a white blood cell meet. They have a conversation. Try to portray this conversation in a drawing, in music, in writing and in any other way you like.

Medical advice: Prof. Yaakov Amir

SYRINGES, NEEDLES AND INJECTIONS

What Is a Syringe?

A syringe is a cylindrical instrument with a slender, hollow needle at its end.

It is used for several purposes:

To inject substances into our body.

To extract a blood sample from one of our veins.

How Are Syringes Built?

Syringes have two parts: The Plunger and The Barrel.

- The cylindrical tube, called a **barrel** has graduation lines on it, indicating the volume of fluid in the syringe. The number of graduation lines depends on the size of the syringe. A slender, hollow needle is attached to a protrusion at its end.

- Inside the barrel is a **plunger**, which can be moved up and down.

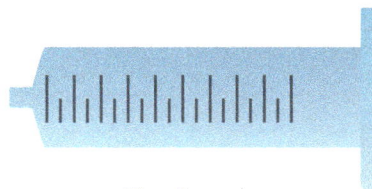

The Barrel

The Plunger

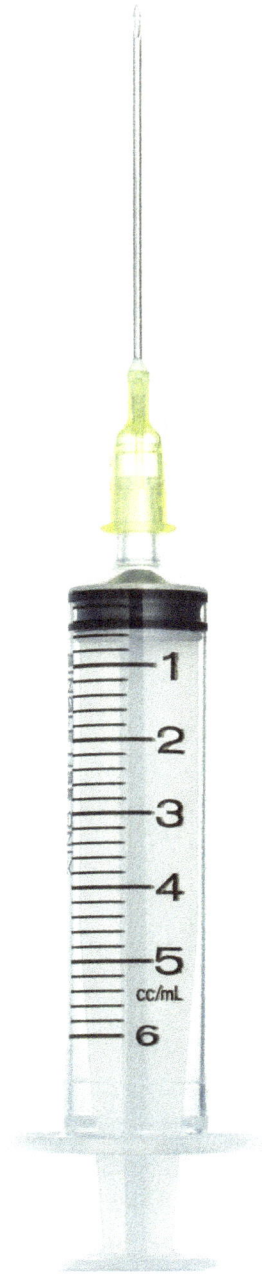

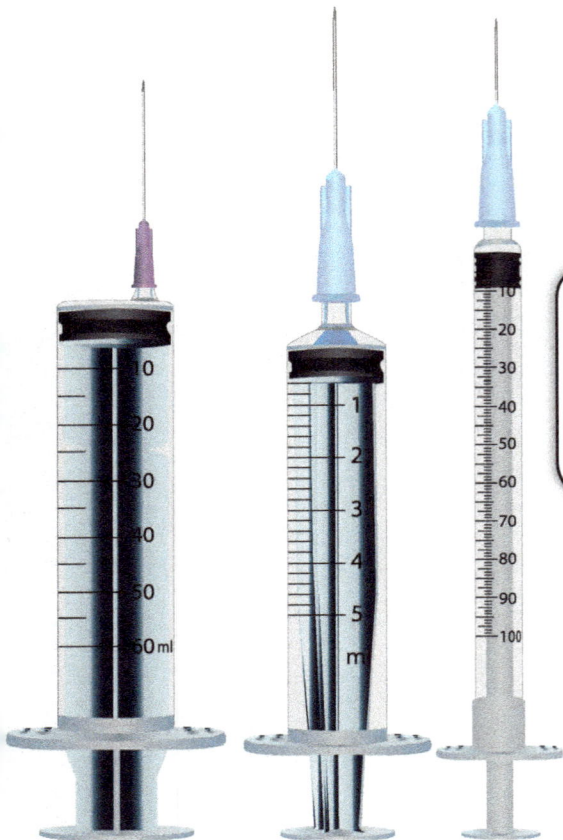

Different Types of Syringes

There are different types of syringes:

> **Long, very slender syringes, used for extracting small, exact quantities of blood.**
>
> **Wide, short syringes, used both for giving injections and for extracting blood.**

The Structure of the Needle

Needles have three parts:

1. The **hub**, which is the plastic part attached to the protrusion at the end of the syringe barrel.

2. The **shaft**, which is the long part of the needle and is embedded in the hub.

3. The **bevel**, which is the slanted part of the tip of the shaft.

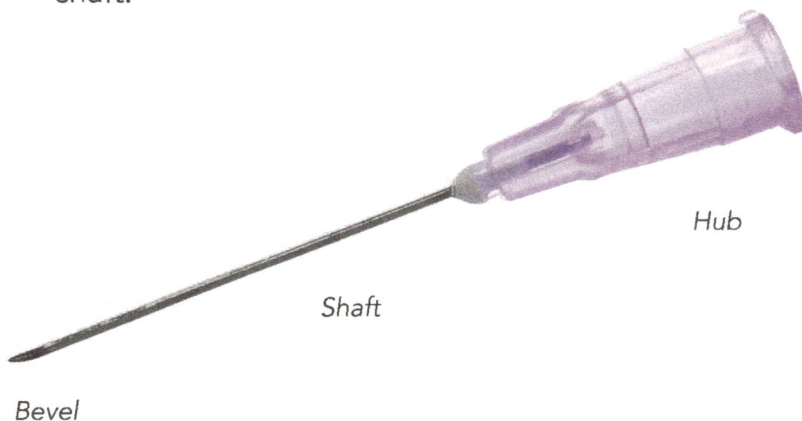

Hub

Shaft

Bevel

Types of Needles

Needles come in different sizes. The length of the needle depends on the purpose of the syringe.

Needles are differentiated by the color of the plastic part, the hub, which is attached to the protrusion at the end of the syringe barrel.

How the Syringe Is Filled

Health care professionals fill the syringe with the substance to be injected into the patient.

> **They attach a suitable needle to the protrusion at the end of the syringe barrel.**
>
> **When they pull back the plunger, the substance is drawn into the syringe through the needle.**

Important Information

When do we take medicine in the form of tablets or syrup, and when is it injected into us?

Some substances cannot be administered orally. There are several reasons for this:

Our digestive juices would destroy them	**They would irritate our bowels and give us a stomachache**	**They would not have an instant, precise impact.**

In such cases, the medicine is administered by injection, and not in liquid or tablet form.

Into What Part of Our Body Is Medicine Injected?

Medicine can be injected into different parts of our body:

- Into a muscle in our upper arm or into our thigh
- Under our skin
- Into our buttock
- Into an infusion pump used for slowly dripping fluids such as solutions, medicine and blood into one of our veins.

Who Is Licensed to Give Injections?

Not all injections are the same, and we inject different substances into different locations in the bodies of human beings and animals.

That is why various health care professionals have different licenses for giving the different injections.

Nurses and paramedics administer injections into our muscles.

Only specialist doctors are authorized to administer rarer, more complicated injections.

It is easy to inject medicine into our body anywhere under our skin. People with diabetes are allowed to inject themselves with medicine without prior medical knowledge.

What Can Patients Do To Make the Injection Hurt Less?

When you are being given an injection, do your best to relax the muscles in your arm or thigh.

Important!

When a needle is inserted into a relaxed muscle, it hurts less.

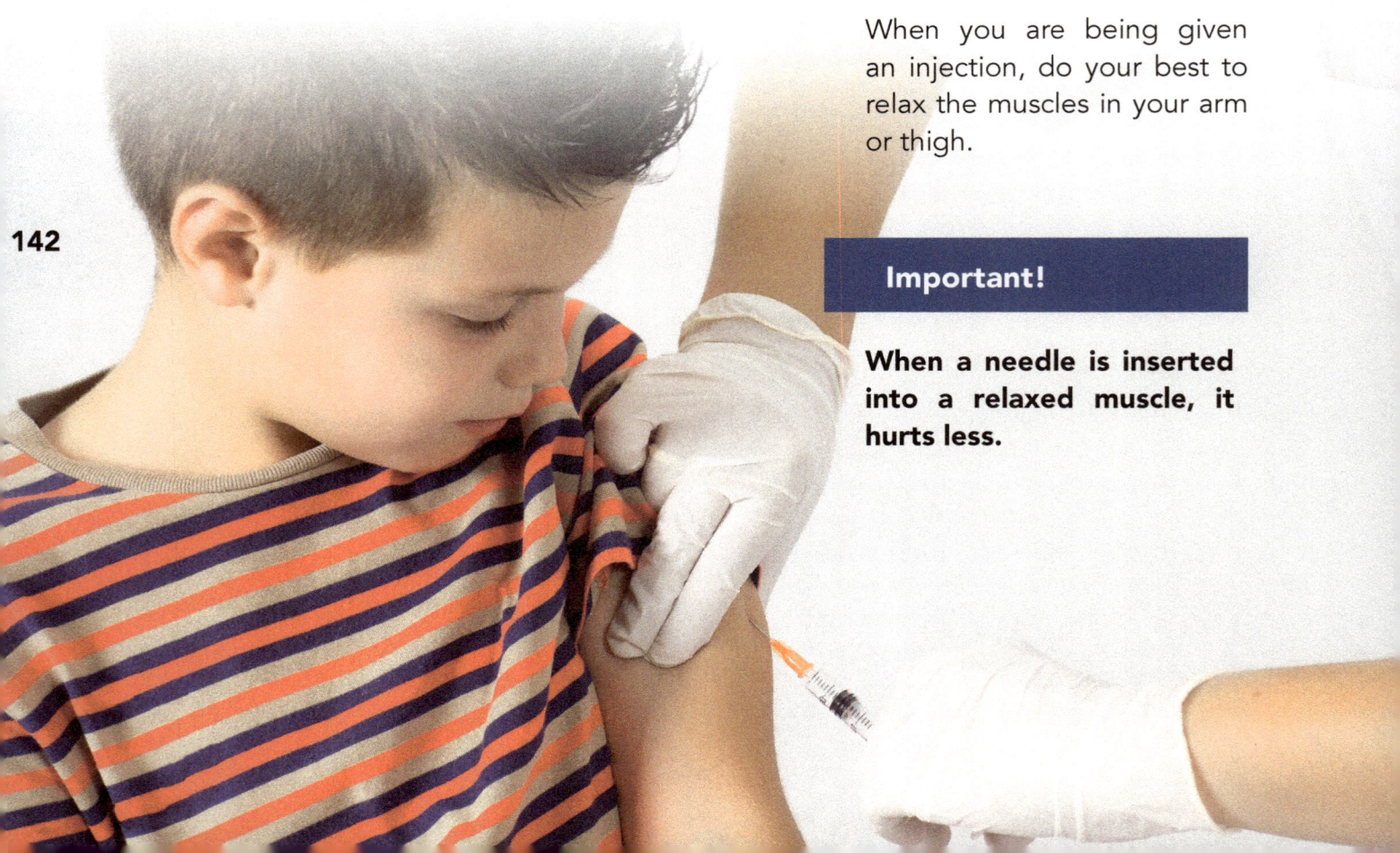

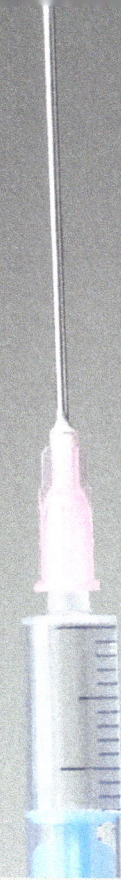

Discoveries from the Past

The French mathematician and philosopher, Blaise Pascal, whose scientific activity encompassed many different fields, invented the syringe. He was born on June 10, 1623 and died on August 10, 1662.

Development of the Use of Syringes

The year 1760 marked the introduction of intravenous injections and infusion pumps into the medical profession.

In 1853, Charles Gabriel Pravaz and Alexander Wood developed a hypodermic syringe with a fine needle that penetrates the skin with ease.

In 1956, New Zealand pharmacist and inventor Colin Murdoch registered a patent on syringes made of plastic.

In 1974, a patent was registered on disposable plastic syringes in the USA.

Professional Advice: Prof. Yaakov Amir

YOUR EARS AND THROAT

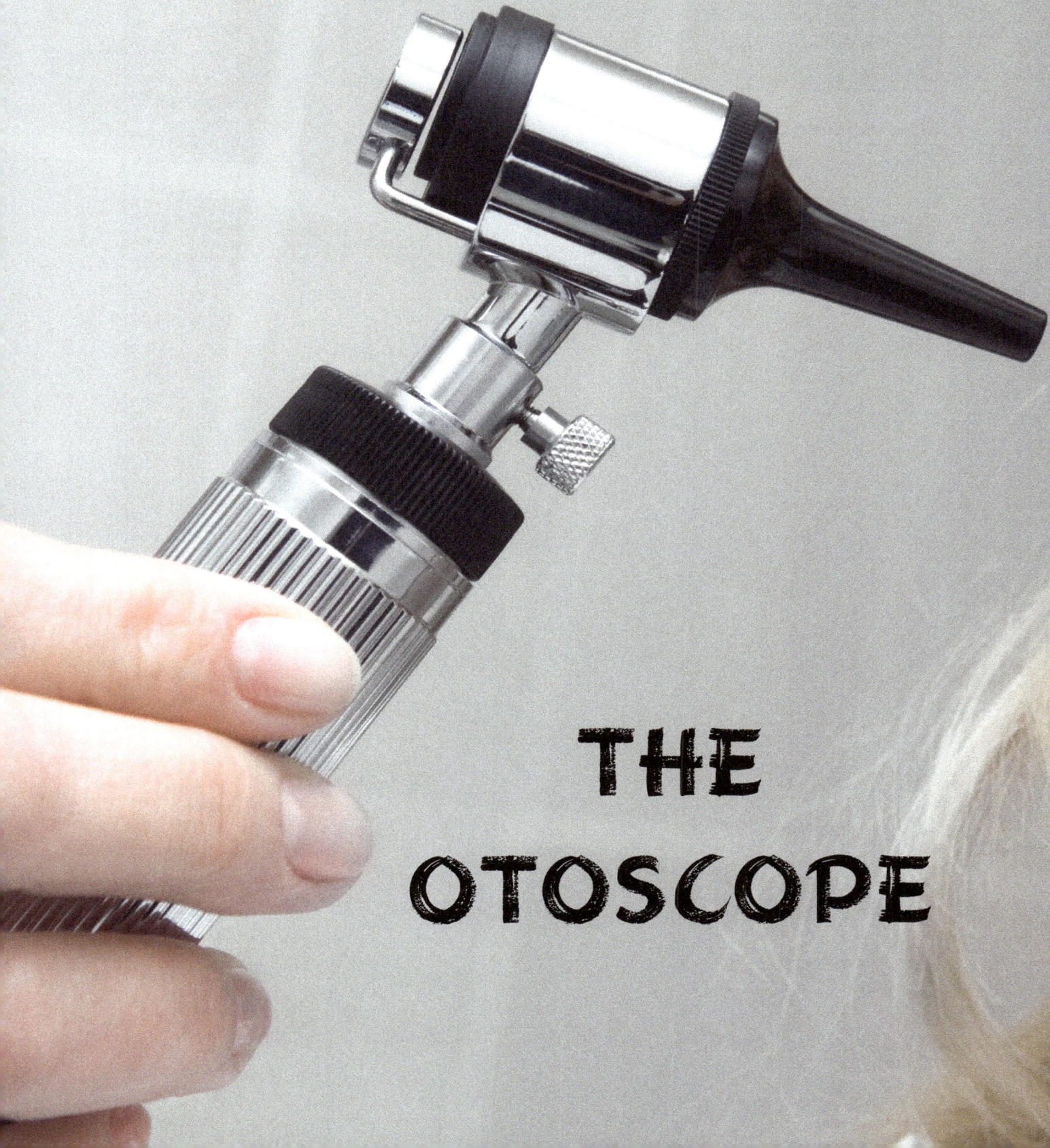

THE OTOSCOPE

Your Ear and the Otoscope

Your ear is the organ responsible for hearing and for balance.

The structure of your ear

Your ear has three parts:

The outer ear	The middle ear	The inner ear

Anatomy of the Ear

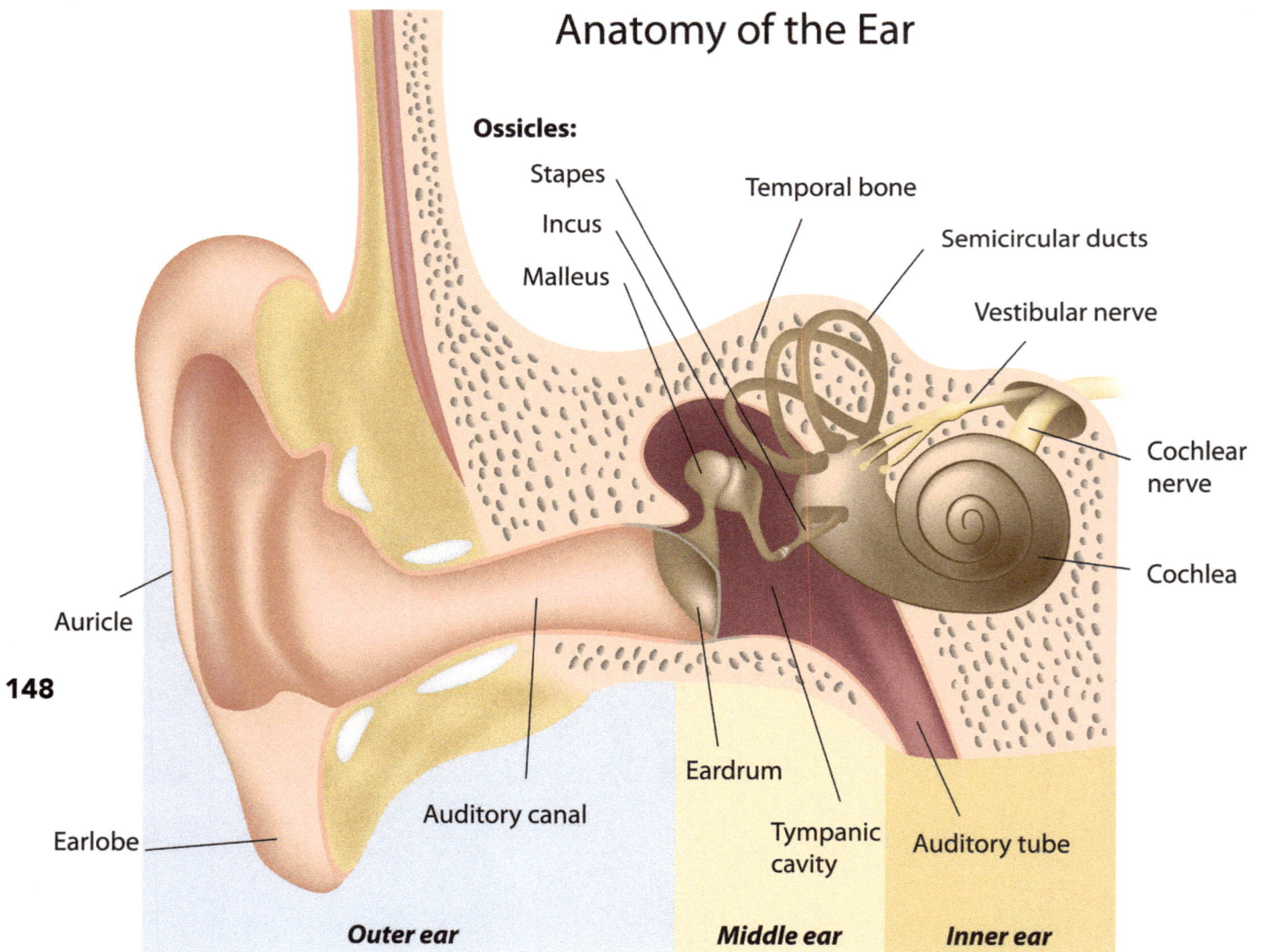

Ossicles:
Stapes
Incus
Malleus
Temporal bone
Semicircular ducts
Vestibular nerve
Cochlear nerve
Cochlea
Auricle
Eardrum
Earlobe
Auditory canal
Tympanic cavity
Auditory tube
Outer ear
Middle ear
Inner ear

The outer ear

The outer ear consists of:

1. The auricle (also called pinna)

The auricle is the only visible part of a person's ear, and is located on the both sides of the head.

2. The auditory canal, or ear canal (also called the external auditory meatus)

The skin of the auditory canal is lined with hair follicles. These hair follicles prevent dust from entering your ear and damaging it.

At the end of the auditory canal is the eardrum. The eardrum is a semitransparent thin membrane that separates the outer ear from the middle ear. When sound waves enter your ear from outside, they cause your eardrum to vibrate.

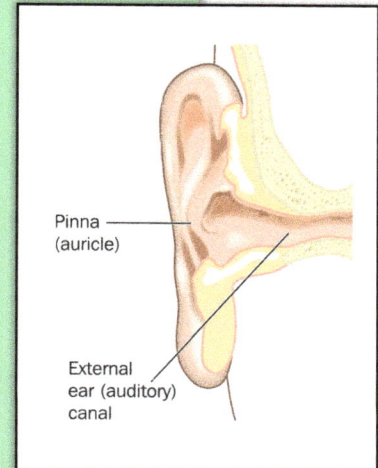

Pinna (auricle)

External ear (auditory) canal

The middle ear

The middle ear consists of:

1. An air cavity

The air cavity is situated behind the eardrum.

Inside the air cavity are three tiny bones, called auditory ossicles

2. The auditory tube, or Eustachian tube

The auditory tube connects the middle-ear cavity to the pharynx.

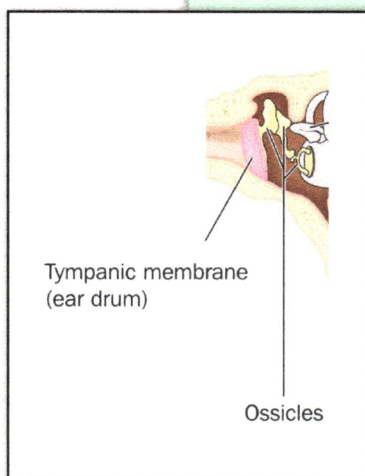

Tympanic membrane (ear drum)

Ossicles

The inner ear

The inner ear consists of:

1. An organ called a cochlea

There are sensors in the cochlea. These sensors transform sound waves into nerve impulses that are transmitted to our brain's hearing center.

2. The semicircular organ responsible for our body's balance.

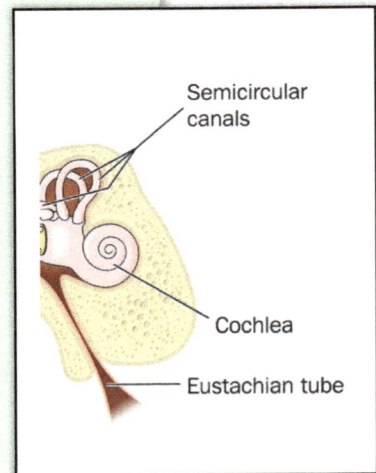

Semicircular canals

Cochlea

Eustachian tube

The structure of the otoscope

The otoscope is the mirror of the ear. It's the instrument your doctor uses to examine your ears, and to determine why you are suffering from otitis (an infection in your ear).

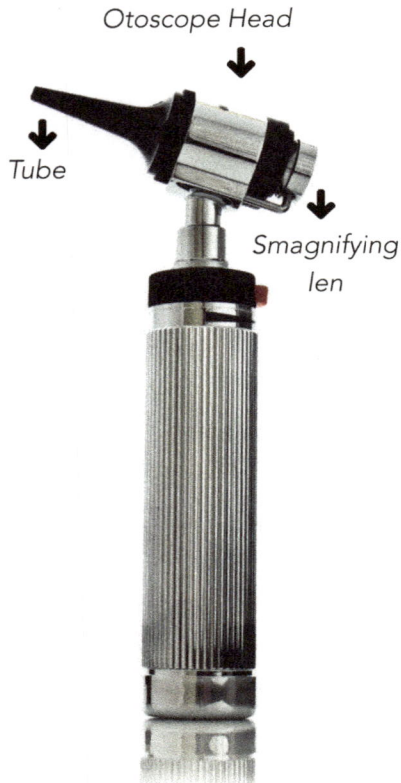

These are the parts of the otoscope:

Otoscope Head

Tube

Smagnifying len

A hollow metal cylinder, on top of which the otoscope head is fitted.

A tube called an ear speculum, which comes in a variety of sizes adapted to the patient's age, is secured to the front side of the otoscope head.

Inside the otoscope head, at the back, is a light source, which lights up the tube cavity. At the back of the tube is a magnifying lens. The light source and the magnifying lens help your doctor to see your eardrum better and with greater precision.

150

An innovative version of the otoscope has been developed, with a camera. With its help, doctors can see the structure of the patient's ear clearly and with great precision. It can also be attached to a television screen, and the picture can be stored and processed for follow-up and analysis of the patient's medical condition.

The purpose of the examination

The purpose of the ear examination is to identify signs of an infection, based on the appearance of the patient's eardrum.

How is the examination carried out?

Your doctor gently inserts the ear speculum into your outer ear canal.

Your doctor directs the beam of light into your eardrum, and examines it.

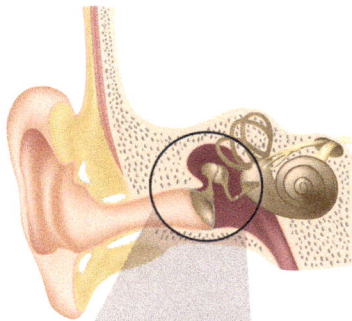

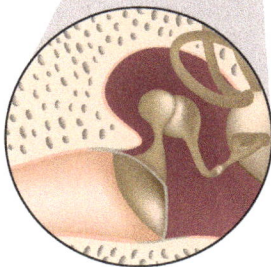

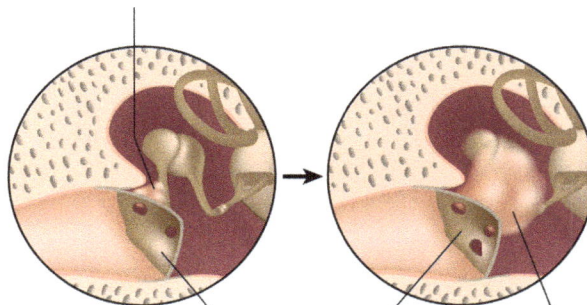

Normal *Retracted and perforated eardrum* *Cholesteatoma*

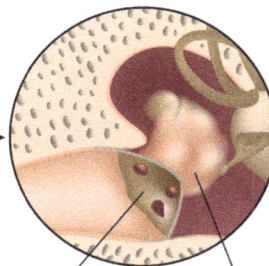

How does your doctor diagnose an infection in your ear?

When your doctor looks through his otoscope inside your ear when you have an earache, he may detect changes in your eardrum.

> **The normal light grey or shiny pearly-white color of your eardrum may have turned red.**

> **The smooth taut membrane may be pushed by the buildup of pus and mucus behind it, and may become retracted or bulging.**

If your doctor detects these symptoms, this indicates that you have an ear infection.

How Do Ear Infections Develop?

Ear infections usually develop after you get a cold, like this:

↓

A bacterium or virus gets into your throat,

↓

causing an infection in your upper respiratory tract.

↓

As a result of this infection,

↓

the mucus of the upper respiratory tract and the mucosal lining of the auditory tube become edematous, accompanied by excessive mucus secretion.

↓

The abnormal collection of fluid blocks the auditory tube.

↓

The blocked auditory tube prevents the middle-ear cavity from draining into the pharynx.

↓

Fluid accumulates in the middle-ear cavity, providing a favorable environment for bacteria and viruses to multiply. That is how an infection develops in your middle ear.

152

Just as changes occur in the external layers of our skin after we get a bruise, similarly changes occur in our eardrum if we get a bacterial or viral infection.

Treating ear infections

Your doctor determines the appropriate treatment for your specific type of infection.

What causes repeated repeat ear infections?

The most important causes of ear infections in children are:

Swimmer's Ear

Eardrum

Infection in ear canal

Clear discharge

Outer ear　　**Middle ear**　**Inner ear**

- The auditory canal is especially narrow in children.
- When you have a cold, the abnormal collection of fluids and excessive mucus secretion easily causes it to be blocked.
- The fluids and mucus in your middle ear cavity cannot drain.
- A favorable environment is created in your ear cavity for bacteria and germs to multiply.
- From time to time, a different kind of bacterium causes a different kind of infection.

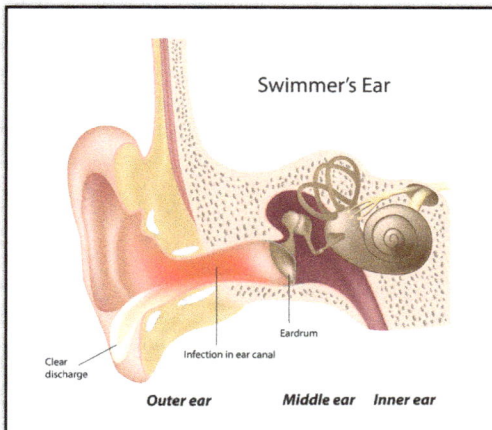

This is worth remembering

The most common type of ear infection occurs in the middle ear.

Outer ear infections are far less common. They are caused by water getting into your ear at the swimming pool or in the shower, and cleaning the auditory canal with swab.

This is worth knowing and trying!

The sculptures and pictures of ancient and modern-day artists are publicly displayed in museums, for all to see.

Works of art draw our attention to their beauty, as revealed by the talented artists who created them. Here is how the ear is presented in different forms and ways in different works of art:

You can try to do it yourself

Medical advice: Prof. Yitzhak Versano

THE PHARYNX AND THE TONGUE DEPRESSOR

Tongue Depressors, Tonsils and Tonsillitis?

Here is some important information that will help you understand the connection between tongue depressors, tonsils and tonsillitis:

What are Tonsils?

- Tonsils are lymph nodes and are an inseparable part of our lymphatic and immune systems.
- Our tonsils are located in our pharynx, at the back of our mouth cavity.
- Tonsils are almond-shaped and pink in color.
- Children's tonsils are 1-2 cm in size.
- We have two tonsils, one at each side of our pharynx.
- Tonsils differ in size from person to person.

| Bacterial infection | viral infection |

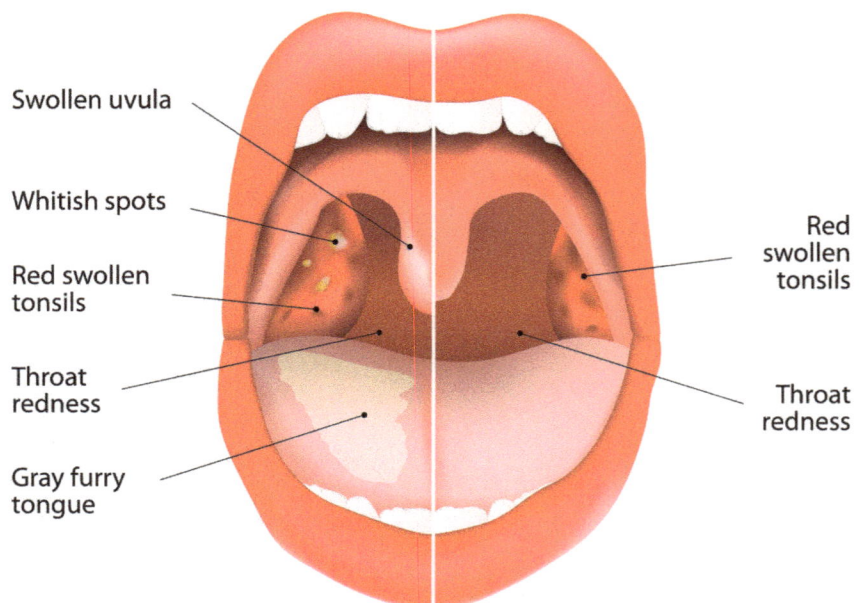

Swollen uvula

Whitish spots

Red swollen tonsils

Throat redness

Gray furry tongue

Red swollen tonsils

Throat redness

What Happens When Bacteria and Viruses Get into our Throat?

When bacteria and viruses get into our throat, they attach themselves to the mucous lining of our pharyngeal cavity and to our tonsils. They then multiply.

At this stage, our tonsils activate an immune response by dispatching white blood cells to destroy the invaders. The "enemies" clash and the white blood cells release substances that:

- Cause our pharyngeal cavity and its mucous lining to swell.

- Enlarge our tonsils and change their color from pink to red.

This process is called tonsillitis.

Important Facts

There are two kinds of tonsillitis, depending on the cause of your infection.

Strep throat bacterial tonsillitis	→	**This kind is caused by streptococcus bacteria.**
Viral tonsillitis	→	**This kind is caused by a virus.**

Virus

How Are Strep Throat and Viral Tonsillitis Diagnosed?

Your doctor must see as much of your pharyngeal cavity as possible in order to be able to diagnose what kind of tonsillitis you have, based on its characteristic symptoms.

That is where the tongue depressor enters the picture, along with appropriate lighting.

What Is a Tongue Depressor?

A tongue depressor is a flat wooden stick that your doctor or nurse uses to examine your throat. She presses your tongue down with it, and looks deep inside our pharynx with the help of a flashlight or other suitable lighting.

That is how she sees whether your tonsils are swollen, what color they are, and whether they are flecked with white exudates. She may recommend an appropriate course of treatment in accordance with her findings.

Germs

Important!

Usually, a physical examination and existing symptoms provide your doctor with important information to diagnose whether you have tonsillitis. To conclusively determine the cause of your infection, she may take a throat swab, that is, a sample of the secretions containing the cause of your infection.

How Are Throat Swabs Taken?

Your doctor or nurse uses a tongue depressor with cotton wool to take a throat swab. She asks you to open your mouth wide, presses your tongue down with it, and rubs the cotton tip gently along your tonsils and the flecks at the back of your pharynx, where the bacteria are, to get a sample. She then takes the tongue depressor back out of your mouth, and places the sample in a sterile test tube, which she sends to the laboratory.

How are Throat Swab Samples Tested in the Laboratory?

A laboratory technician tests your throat swab sample in the laboratory.

She removes it from the sterile test tube.

She then spreads it on a bacterial growth medium.

If the sample contains bacteria, they will multiply on the medium. After a day, the laboratory technician will be able to identify the kind of bacteria causing your infection and their susceptibility to a particular type of antibiotic. Your doctor will prescribe a course of treatment on the basis of your throat swab sample.

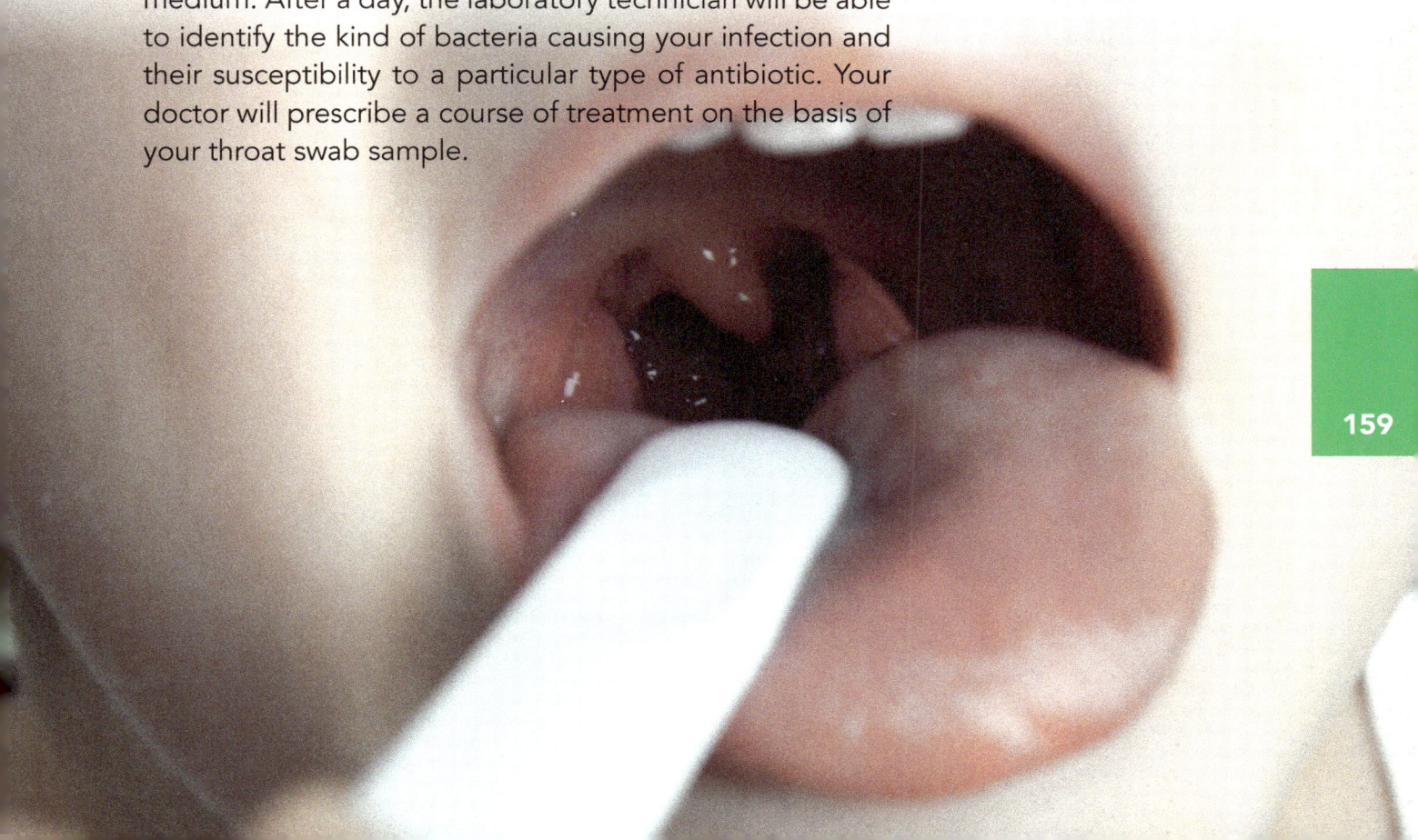

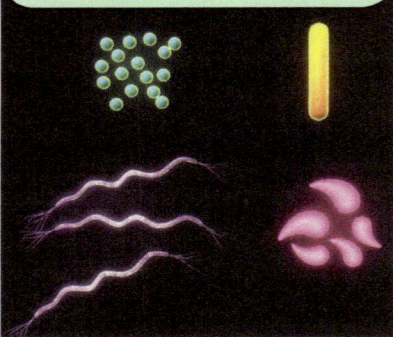

It all Goes back to the Cause

Many different types of viruses may attack your tonsils. Each case of viral tonsillitis is caused by the invasion of a different type of virus.

That is why you can get viral tonsillitis again and again.

I Don't Get it

Why can children get strep throat more than once?

Strep throat is caused by streptococcus bacteria. There are several strains of this bacterium.

Each time you get strep throat, it is because a different strain of streptococcus has invaded your throat.

Fun Things To Do

Making Sounds

Do this activity in pairs.

Each child makes a sound while her throat is being examined. Have a conversation with these sounds. Try to find out what your friend is saying.

Brighten up a Pair of Tongue Depressors

160

Tongue depressors are usually bare. Color each of them, or decorate them in whatever way you want to. Give each of them a name.

Professional Advice: Prof. Izak Versano.

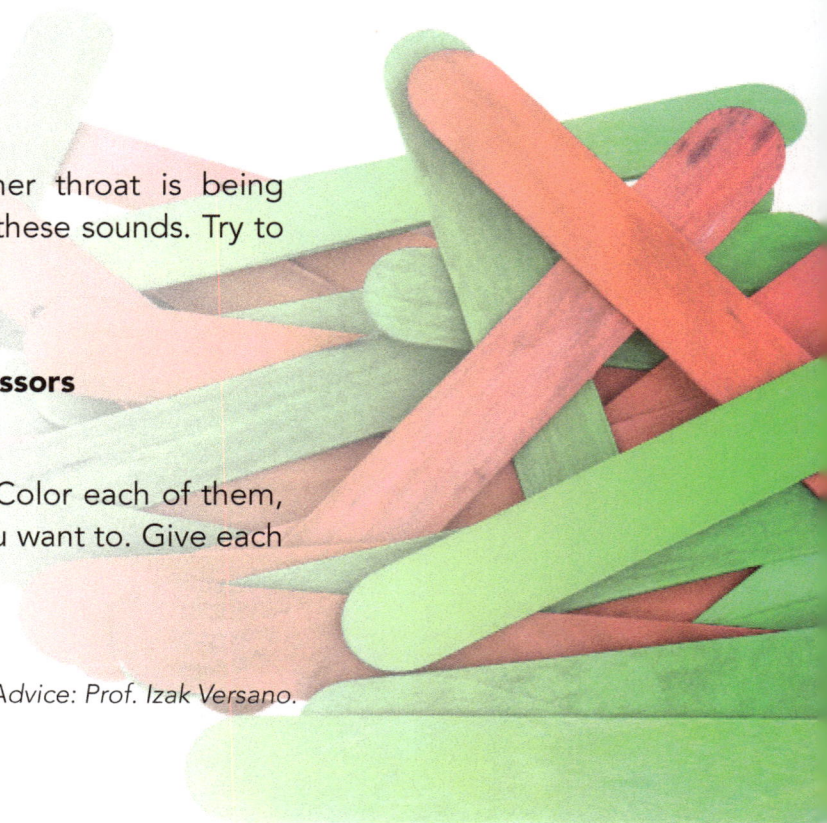

THE IMAGING CENTER

Imaging
A Little History

For many years, scientists searched for ways to be able to observe the internal organs of their patients. They wanted to be able to obtain information about them, their shape, their size, their functioning and the pathological processes occurring in them without inflicting bodily harm on their patients.

In 1895, Wilhelm Roentgen discovered rays that he called X-rays (subsequently formally named Roentgen rays, after him), causing an upheaval in the methods of medical diagnosis.

X-rays made it possible "to see what could not be seen" and view the patient's internal organs. The method was simple and nondestructive. The X-rays passed through the patient's body, recording images on photographic film.

In the last 40 years, a significant breakthrough has occurred in the Roentgen method, in addition to its perfection and expansion.

Thanks to the development of the computer, many additional methods now also make it possible to "view" the body's internal organs in simple, harmless ways.

All these imaging methods are used for the medical diagnosis of the patient's tissues and organs. Each method has its advantages and disadvantages.

It is the doctor's role to choose the appropriate imaging method for the patient's specific medical problem.

All such tests are performed at an imaging center.

The Imaging Center

Imaging centers sometimes use incomprehensible medical terms, such as:

1. **Imaging center:** This is the place where medical photographs are taken with the aid of suitable instruments for the type of test required.

2. **Imaging:** This term refers to the methods used for performing diagnostic tests and looking inside the patient's body.

3. **X-ray:** An X-ray is a medical photograph taken using radiation.

4. **Fluoroscopy:** Fluoroscopy is a type of medical imaging that displays the organ being photographed, in motion in real time over a continuous period.

5. **Ultrasound scan:** A method of medical imaging performed by transmitting high-frequency sound waves to the body part or organ being examined.

6. **CT (computed tomography):** Computed tomography is an imaging technology that uses computers to scan an organ layer by layer, from different angles, and create pictures of cross-sections of it.

7. **MRI (magnetic resonance imaging):** MRI is an advanced state-of-the-art computerized technology that uses a combination of a powerful magnetic field and radio waves to form images of the tissues in your body.

8. **Contrast agent:** A contrast agent is a liquid medicine that the patient swallows or that is administered to her by injection before or during the test.

9. **X-ray technician:** An X-ray technician is a professional who is specialized in performing imaging tests, X-rays, ultrasound scans, CTs, and MRIs.

10. **Radiologist:** A radiologist is a doctor who is specialized in imaging. He determines the patient's medical diagnosis on the basis of the X-ray tests that she underwent at the imaging center.

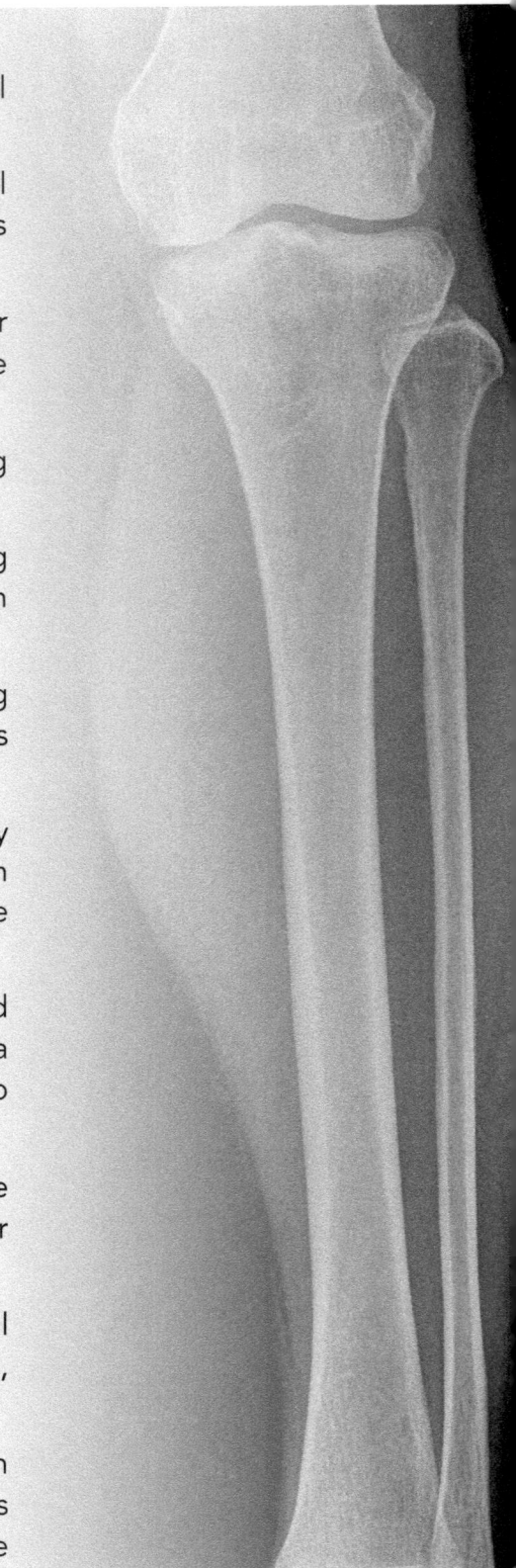

Important!

Every imaging center has a computer workstation, which fulfills several roles:

Registration of the patient's personal details.

Registration of the type of test.

Transfer of the electrical signals to the computer's data processing and presentation unit, based on the type of test.

Conversion of the electrical signals into an image that is registered on an X-ray picture screen attached to the equipment.

X-rays

What are X-rays?

An X-ray is a special form of radiant energy that is invisible to the human eye and that has very short wavelengths.

What are the special characteristics of X-rays?

The special characteristics of X-rays:

- X-rays can penetrate deep into human tissue, in contrast with standard light rays, that do not have such a power of penetration.

- X-rays make it possible to photograph different parts of your body.

- X-rays can detect fractures in your bones.

- X-rays can detect foreign objects in your body.

- X-rays examine various internal organs with the help of a contrast medium.

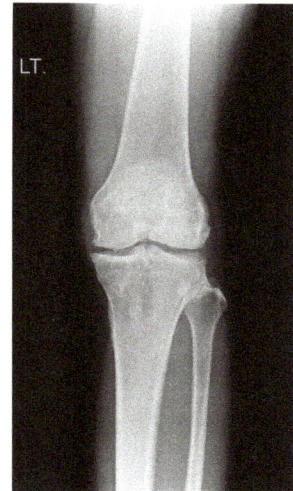

Healthy Bone

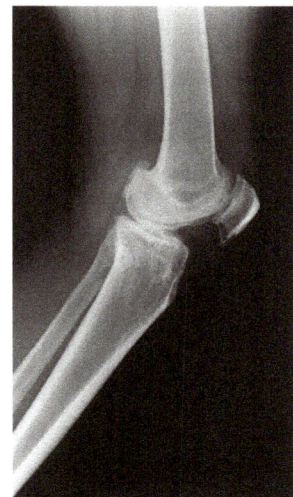

Fractured Bone

What are contrast agents?

Contrast agents are liquid medicines that are used as an aid in examining the internal organs of your body.

Due to their chemical composition, contrast agents have a high X-ray absorption coefficient.

They enhance the contrast between the organ being photographed and its internal environment, thereby improving its visibility.

Imaging using X-rays

Radiologists use three different types of X-ray imaging technologies:

Photography   **Fluoroscopy**   **CT (computed tomography)**

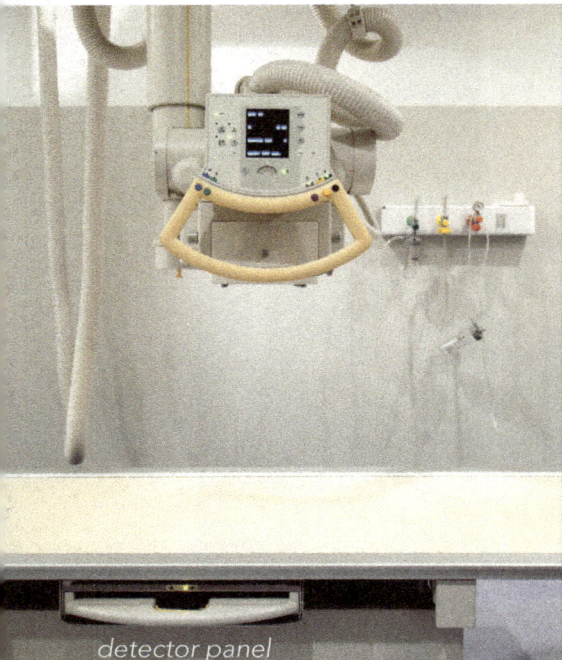

detector panel

The structure of x-ray machines

Here are the main parts of the x-ray machine:

- A cylinder-shaped tube, called an X-ray tube, where the X-ray is produced.

- A detector panel. This is a small flat box. One side absorbs the radiation, while the other converts it into electrical signals that are transmitted to a computer.

- Additional components on which the X-ray tube is mounted, or that allow it to be moved, or make it mobile, depending on the needs of the test.

166

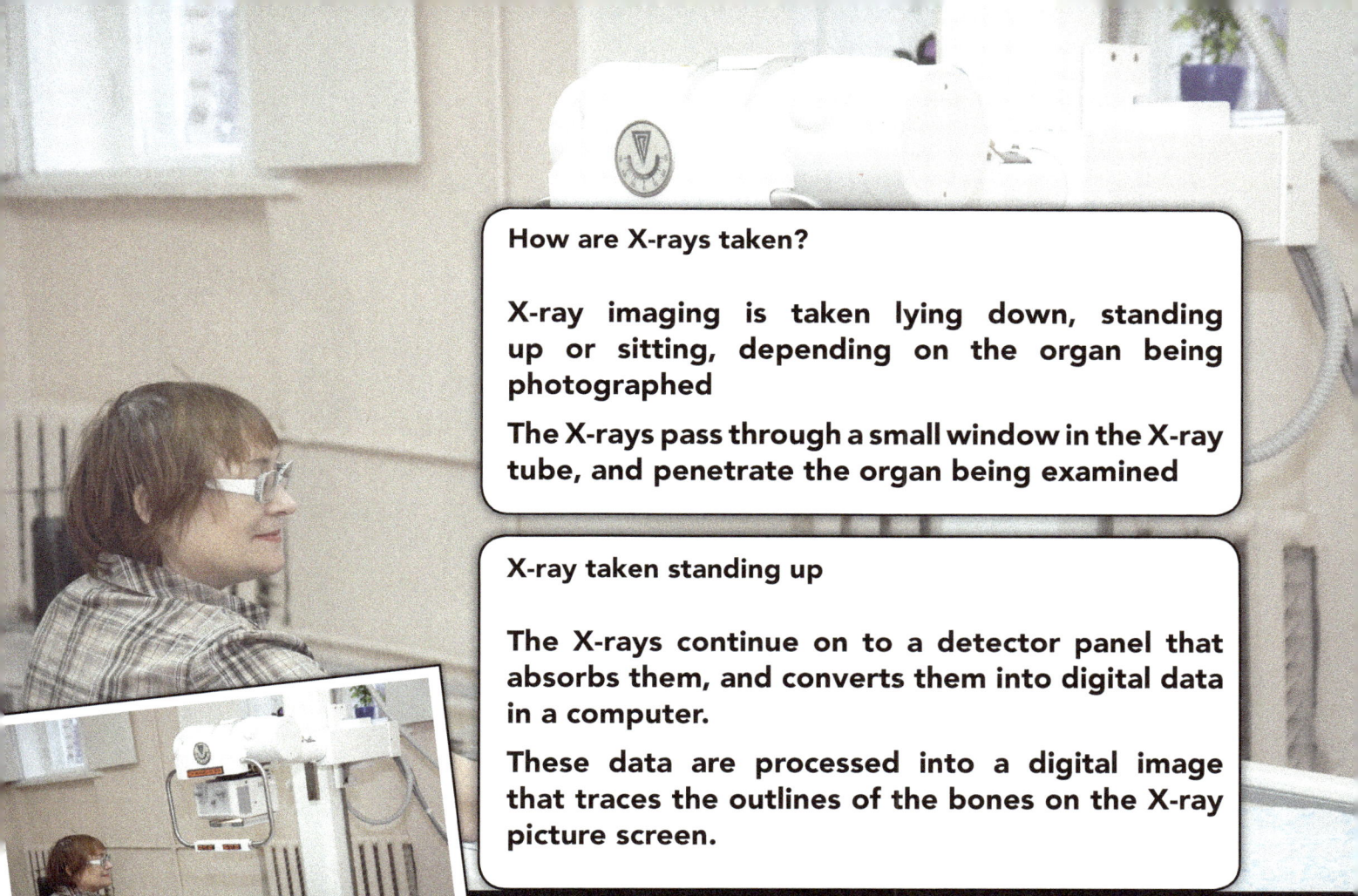

How are X-rays taken?

X-ray imaging is taken lying down, standing up or sitting, depending on the organ being photographed

The X-rays pass through a small window in the X-ray tube, and penetrate the organ being examined

X-ray taken standing up

The X-rays continue on to a detector panel that absorbs them, and converts them into digital data in a computer.

These data are processed into a digital image that traces the outlines of the bones on the X-ray picture screen.

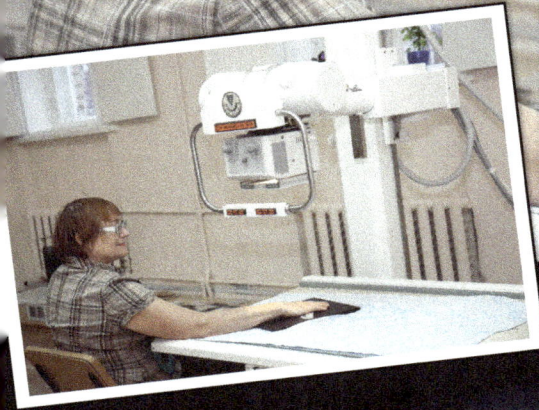

What does the radiologist see in an X-ray?

The radiologist sees your bones and your tissues in the x-ray.

- Your bones appear as pale areas.
- Your body tissues appear as darker areas.

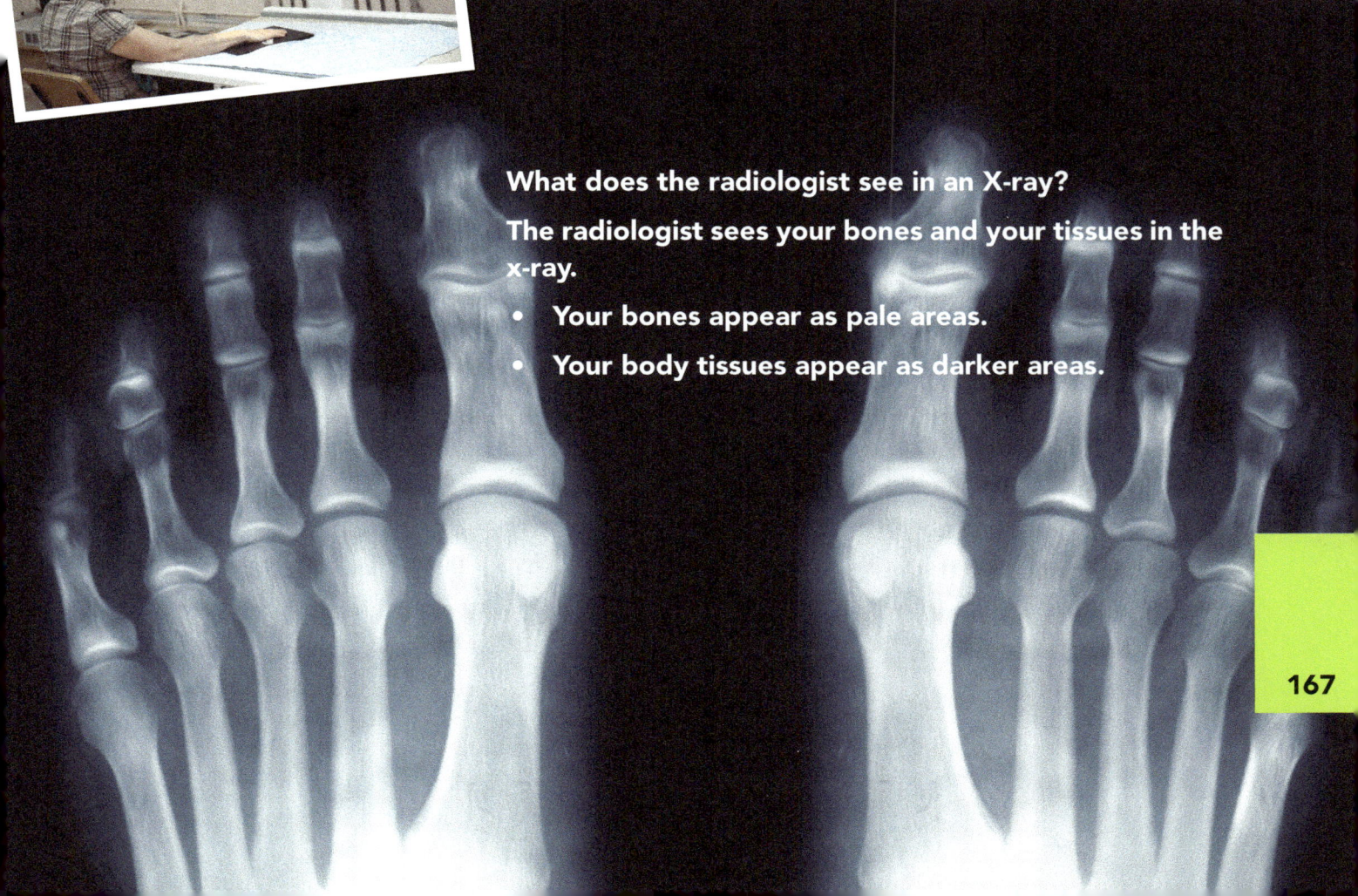

Different tissues in your body absorb x-rays to varying degrees when photographed. Thus, for example, your bone tissue absorbs a larger quantity of X-rays than does your muscle tissue. In medical terminology, your bone tissue is more radiolucent than your muscle tissue. This leads to differences in shading on the X-ray picture screen.

Here are the different shades that may appear on an X-ray picture screen, and what they stand for:

- Black: Air

- Dark grey: Fat

- Light grey: Soft tissue

- White: Bones

Who interprets the X-ray?

The radiologist examines the X-ray, and develops his diagnosis about the medical condition of the photographed organ.

Precautions to prevent the harmful side effects of X-rays

Several steps are taken to protect you against the harmful side effects of x-rays:

The X-ray field diameter is limited by means of a shutter located next to the small window in the X-ray tube.

All the equipment is regularly checked for radiation leaks.

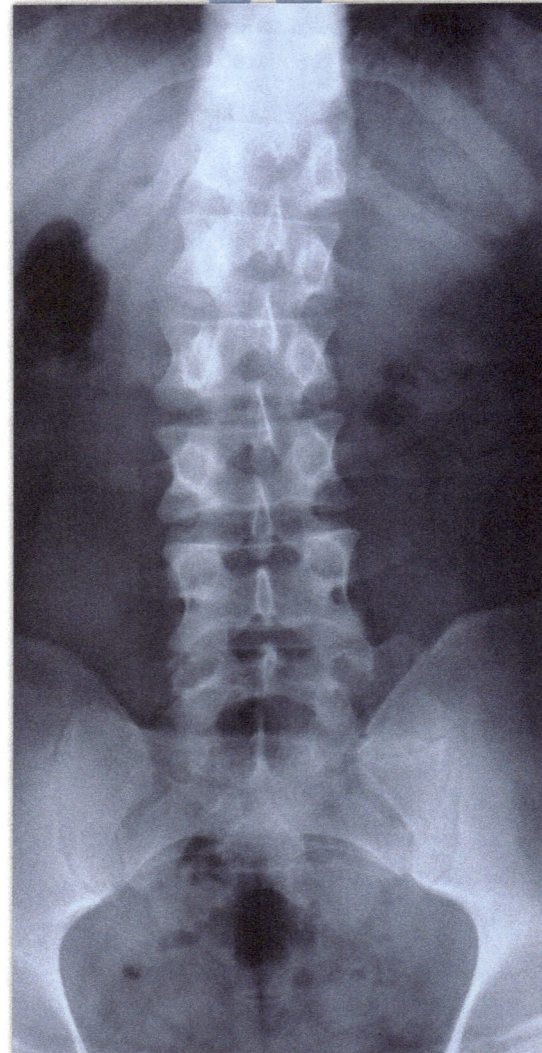

The X-ray technician takes the X-ray at a computer station in the corner of the room, where she is protected against radiation.

The X-ray technician protects the patient, as need be, against avoidable, possible harmful side effects of X-rays, by covering sensitive organs with a lead apron.

Children are accompanied by their parents, whose presence is essential in the X-ray room, and both receive a lead apron that protects them against radiation.

The camera is attached to a pole, or to the ceiling. The camera is stable, and there is no risk of it falling.

These measures are taken to protect the patient and the staff at the imaging center.

Medical apron

Important information

While the X-ray is being taken, it is important for the patient to cooperate with the X-ray technician, and to follow her instructions. This way, the picture will not come out blurred.

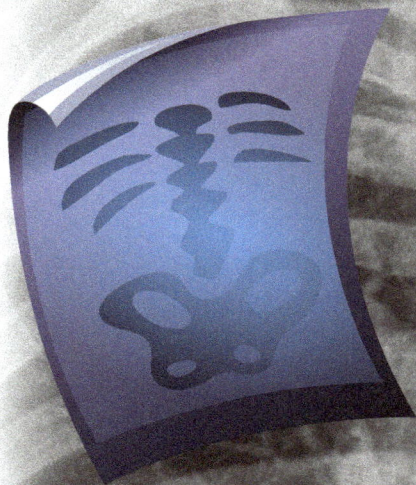

Dental X-rays

When does your dentist take X-rays of your teeth?

Your dentist may decide to take X-rays of some or all your teeth. This is to be sure there are no problems that he could not see when he looked inside your mouth during his initial exam of your teeth and gums.

What types of dental X-rays does your dentist use?

Your dentist uses two main types of dental X-rays:

An X-ray of a single tooth or of two teeth.

A panoramic X-ray of your whole mouth.

How does your dentist take the x-ray?

- Your dentist (or his assistant) inserts a tiny plastic packet, containing film sensitive to x-rays, into your mouth.

- He then leaves the room to take the X-ray by remote control.

- He attaches the tiny plastic packet with the X-ray film to the tooth to be X-rayed, and asks you to press tightly down on it with your finger.

- He asks you not to move, and operates the dental X-ray machine with the remote control.

- He immediately removes the tiny plastic packet with the X-ray film from your mouth.

- The X-ray is then analyzed and your dentist makes his diagnosis and determines the treatment required.

How are panoramic dental X-rays taken?

A panoramic dental X-ray is an image of all your teeth and of your two jaws.

It is taken at a panoramic dental X-ray center.

You sit on a chair, and the X-ray tube rotates in a semicircle around your mouth, starting at one side of your jaw and ending at the other.

Who analyses the panoramic dental X-ray?

Your dentist analyses the panoramic dental X-ray, and determines the appropriate treatment based on his findings.

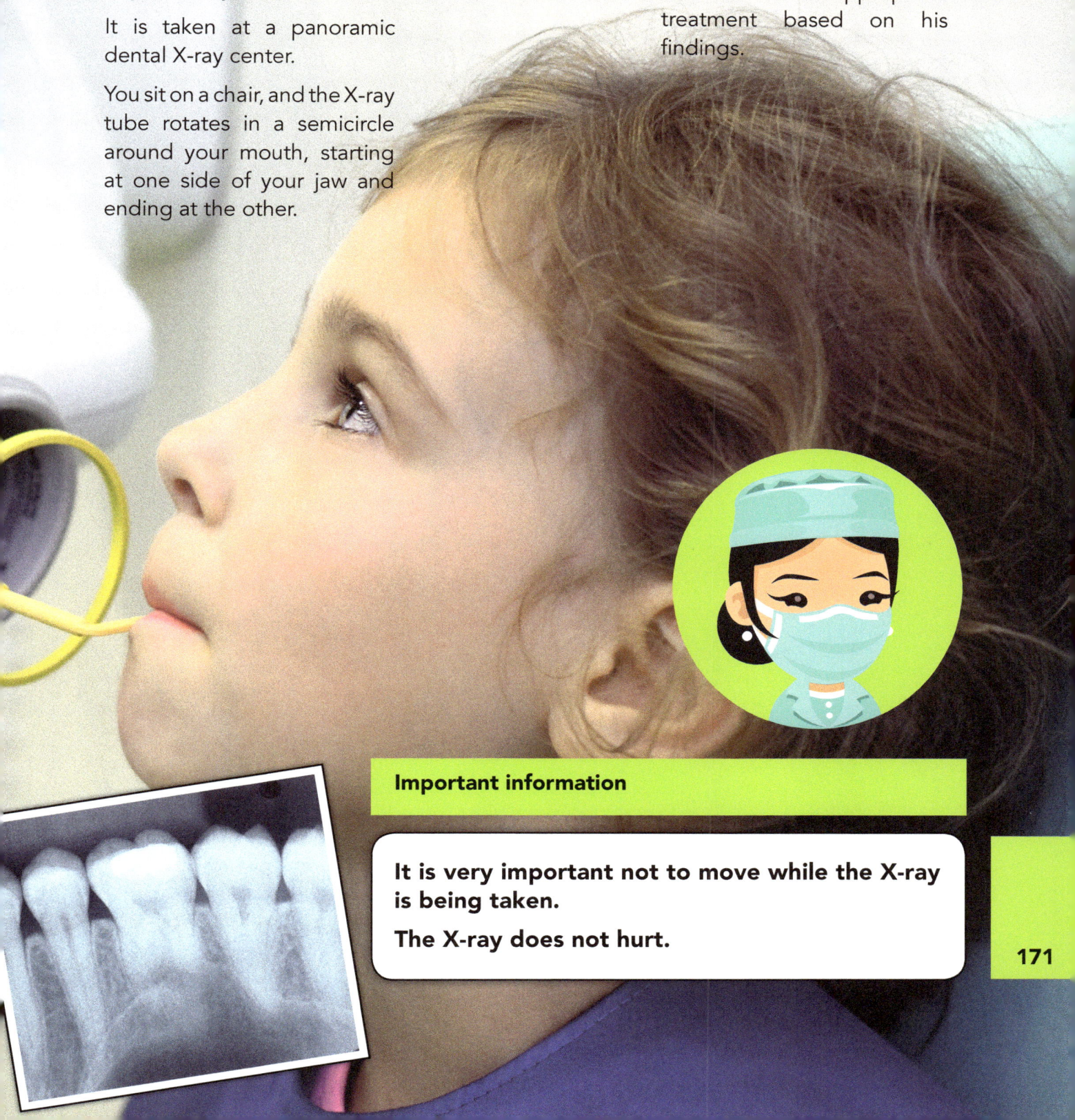

Important information

It is very important not to move while the X-ray is being taken.

The X-ray does not hurt.

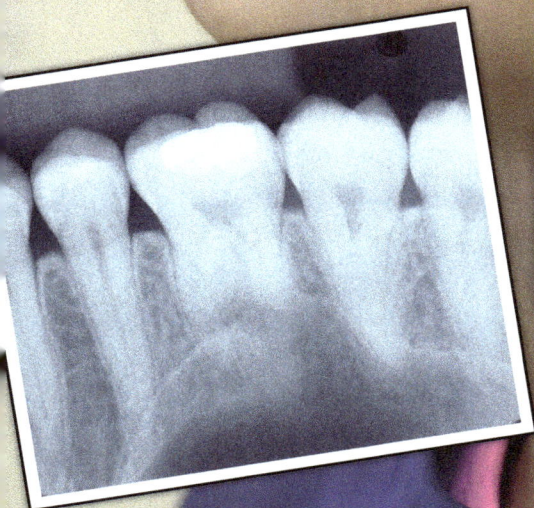

171

Jumbled letters

The letters in the words below got all jumbled up. Sort them out and find the right order. What words did you find?

Gingami _____

Tisoloidar_____

Tasrtnoc tnega _____

X- Yar gnigami _____

Dunosartlu Nacs _____

Rtoceted Lenap _____

Yopcsoroulf _____

TC _____

IRM _____

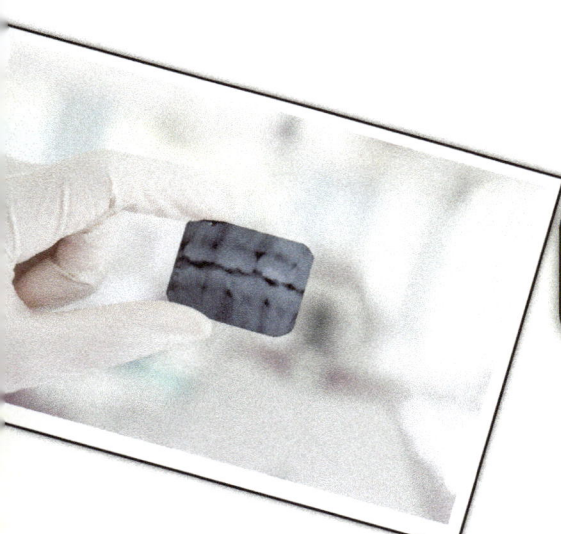

Fluoroscopic imaging

What is fluoroscopy?

> **Fluoroscopy is an imaging technique that uses X-rays to obtain continuous real-time images of mobile organs in your body over time.**

Examples of mobile organs in your body:

- The breathing process taking place continuously in your lungs

- Your blood flowing in your blood vessels

- Your heart beating

172

When does your doctor decide to do a fluoroscopy?

Your doctor may decide to do a fluoroscopy in order to check an organ in motion in your body.

How are fluoroscopic images taken?

Just like X-rays, fluoroscopic images are taken while the patient is either lying down or standing up, depending on the organ being pictured. Fluoroscopes are operated in the same way as X-ray machines.

Interesting!

What is the difference between X-ray imaging and fluoroscopic imaging?

In x-ray imaging, a single picture is generated.

On the other hand, in fluoroscopic imaging, cycles of about 20 frames of per second of the organ are filmed in quick succession over period of time.

The latest image taken is portrayed on the picture screen, while the previous image is stored in the computer memory. Due to this filming method, there is continuity between the images, enabling the organ to be portrayed in motion.

Important information

Fluoroscopic images serve as "eyes" for the operating surgeon and the catheter specialist, enabling them to see the organ being treated in motion as they work.

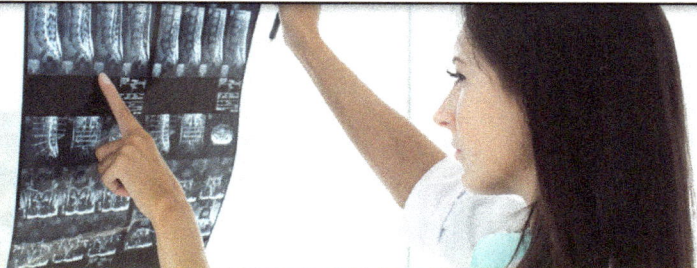

Did you know?

Roentgen rays are named after the German physicist who discovered them, Wilhelm Roentgen (1845-1923). He himself called his discovery X-rays, the name by which they are commonly known in English.

A story from the past

On November 8, 1895, Roentgen was doing an experiment in his darkened laboratory when he accidentally discovered a new and different type of ray. He did not know what these mysterious rays were, so he called them X-rays, after the mathematical symbol "x" for an unknown. They were subsequently named after him. In 1901, he received the first Nobel Prize in Physics for his discovery.

CT (computed tomography)

What is CT?

> CT is a methodology that uses computer processed X-rays to produce virtual "slices" or layers of specific areas of a specific organ.

What is so special about the CT imaging technique?

The CT imaging technique is special because:

- It is a sophisticated technique, and displays the organs in your body more effectively than other X-ray pictures.

Additional uses of X-rays in industry and in everyday life

X-rays are also used:

- To detect cracks in buildings and in airplanes.

- To analyze crystal structures.

- To scan the luggage of air passengers for explosives before they board their plane.

- To examine shells, to see if they contain pearls.

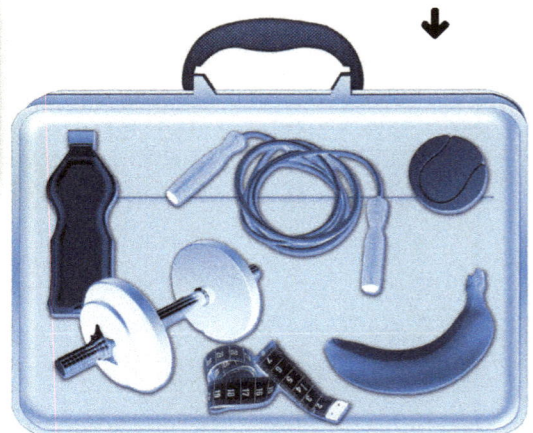

- The organ under examination can be visualized from different angles.

- Three-dimensional imaging of the inside of your body can be generated from the virtual '"slices" produced of specific areas.

- The procedure can be extremely helpful in the diagnosis of illnesses that cannot be detected by an ordinary X-ray examination.

CT SCAN

How are CT scanners built?

This is how CT scanners are built:

A large instrument, called a CT gantry, contains the X-ray tube and the X-ray detectors

The patient lies down on a sliding bed, located in the circular opening of the CT gantry.

The bed, with the patient lying down on it, slides forwards and backwards several times. The X-rays are taken each time the bed slides back into the circular opening, and the signals are transferred to the computer for image reconstruction

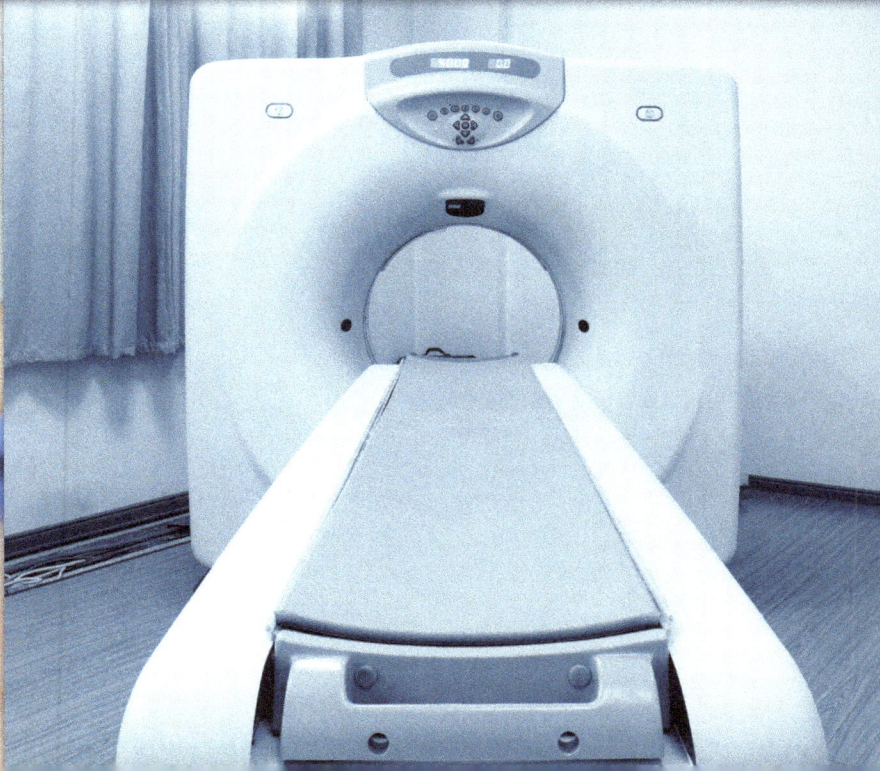

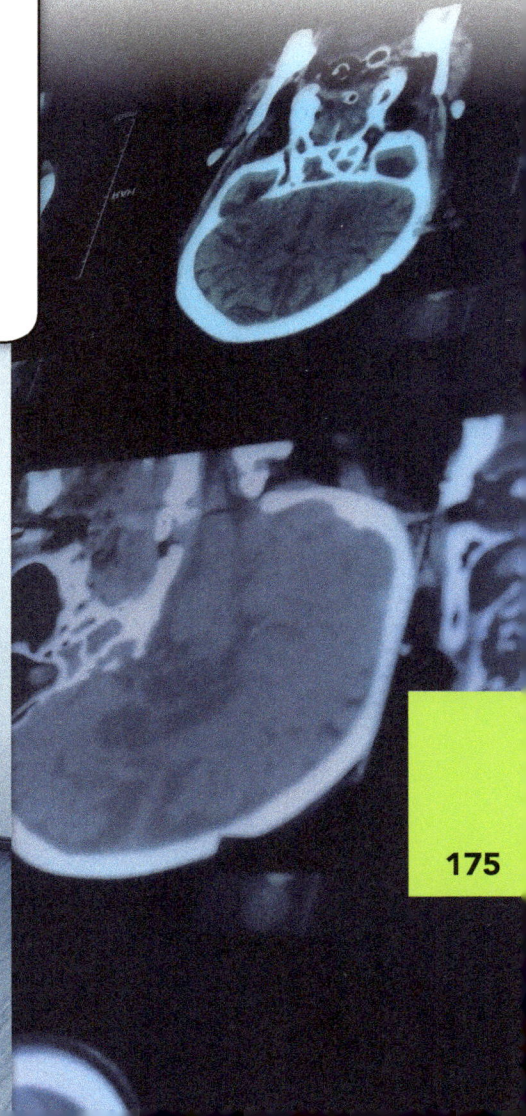

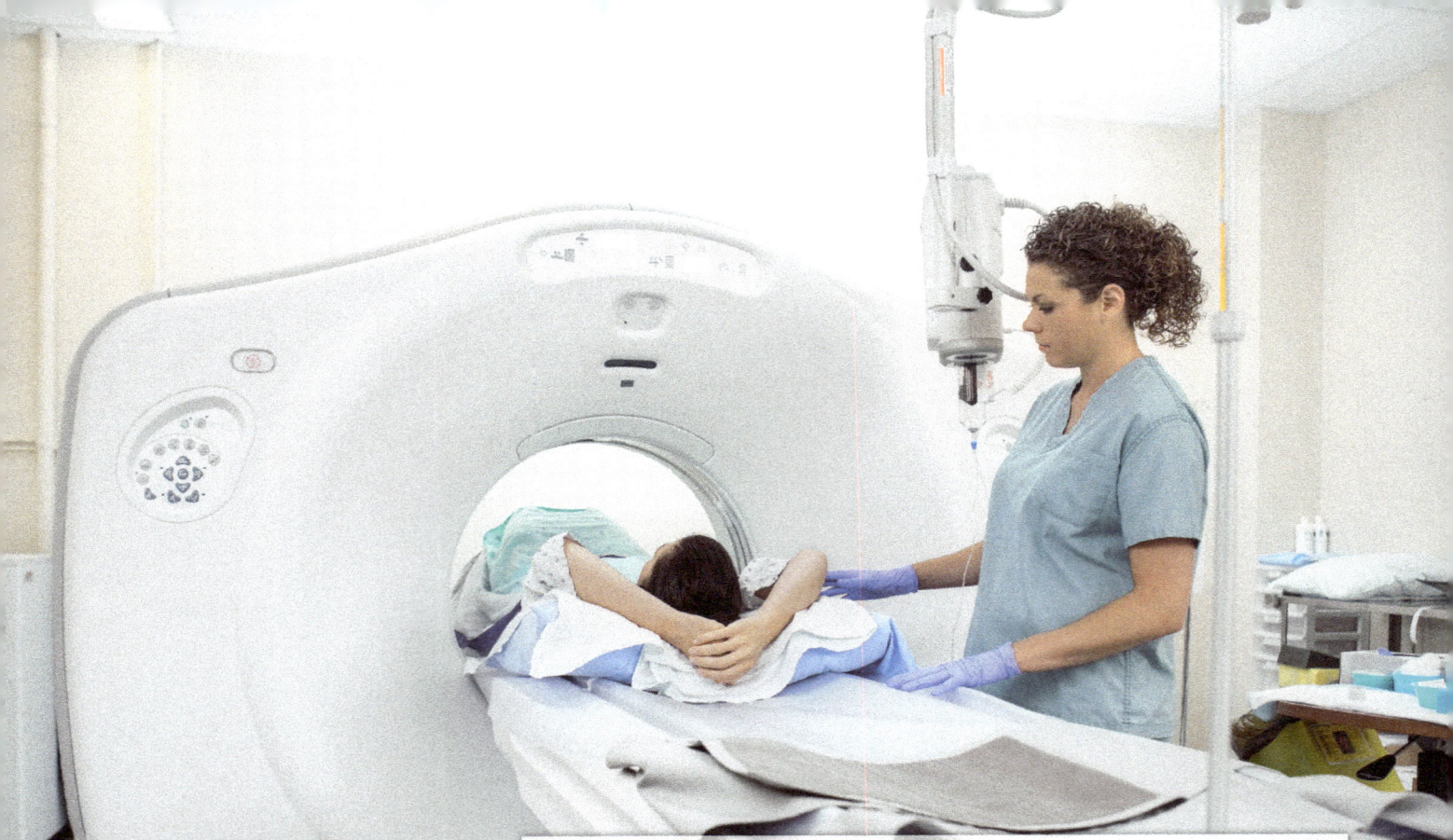

How do CT scanners work?

During the examination, the X-ray tube and detectors make a 360-degree rotation about the organ being scanned.

The X-ray tube emits X-ray beams.

The X-ray beams pass through the patient's organ at multiple angles, and are recorded by the detectors.

The computer processes the data, and generates a three-dimensional image of the organ

This image appears on the computer screen, and can be printed out. It can also be saved for future analysis.

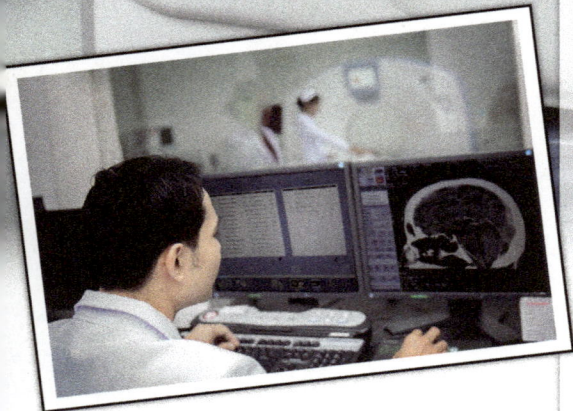

Did you know?

The traditional, front-illuminated digital camera also has detectors. These detectors are sensitive to electromagnetic radiation, which is the light that is visible to the human eye.

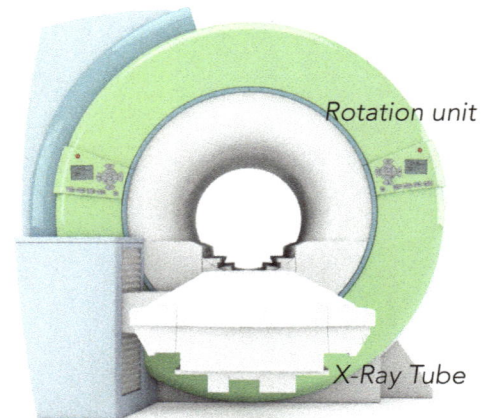

Rotation unit

X-Ray Tube

CT Gantry

176

- The light passes through the camera lens.

- The light is received by the photodetectors at the back of the camera.

- The light on the photodetectors is converted into electrical signals, which are transmitted to the camera's internal computer.

- The computer transforms the electrical signals into a photograph.

- The photograph appears on the screen, and is also saved in the camera's internal memory.

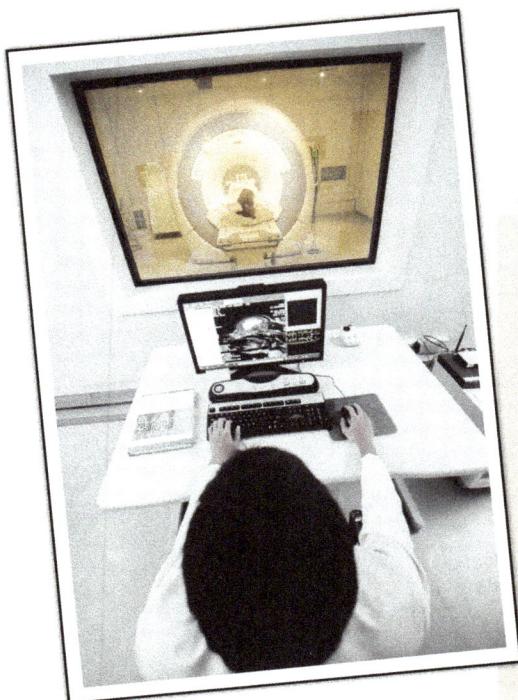

A story from the past

The CT scanner was invented in 1972 by the British engineer Godfrey Hounsfield. He was awarded the Nobel Prize for his discovery in 1979, together with scientist Allan Cormack, who investigated related subjects. It took the first CT scanners several hours to acquire the raw data and process them into images. Nowadays, it takes only a few seconds to scan specific mobile body parts, such as the breathing lungs and the beating hearts of human beings and of animals.

Ultrasound imaging

Ultrasound refers to sound waves with a frequency too high for human beings to hear.

Ultrasound imaging is a diagnostic tool that visualizes an internal body organ by transmitting high frequency sound waves. The echoes of these sound waves reflect from the tissue, and are recorded and displayed as an image on a screen.

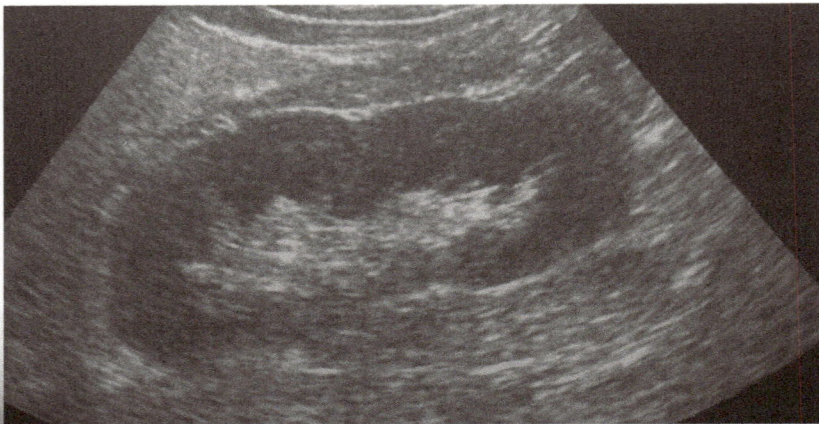

When sound waves are transmitted into the tissues, their echoes are reflected at a different intensity.

The reflected sound waves are displayed as an image on the ultrasound scanner screen.

When is ultrasound imaging performed?

Ultrasound imaging is performed for the following purposes:

To diagnose disorders in one of the body's internal organs.

To visualize soft tissue and fluid-filled spaces, such as the bladder, muscles and blood vessels.

To view a fetus in the womb of its mother.

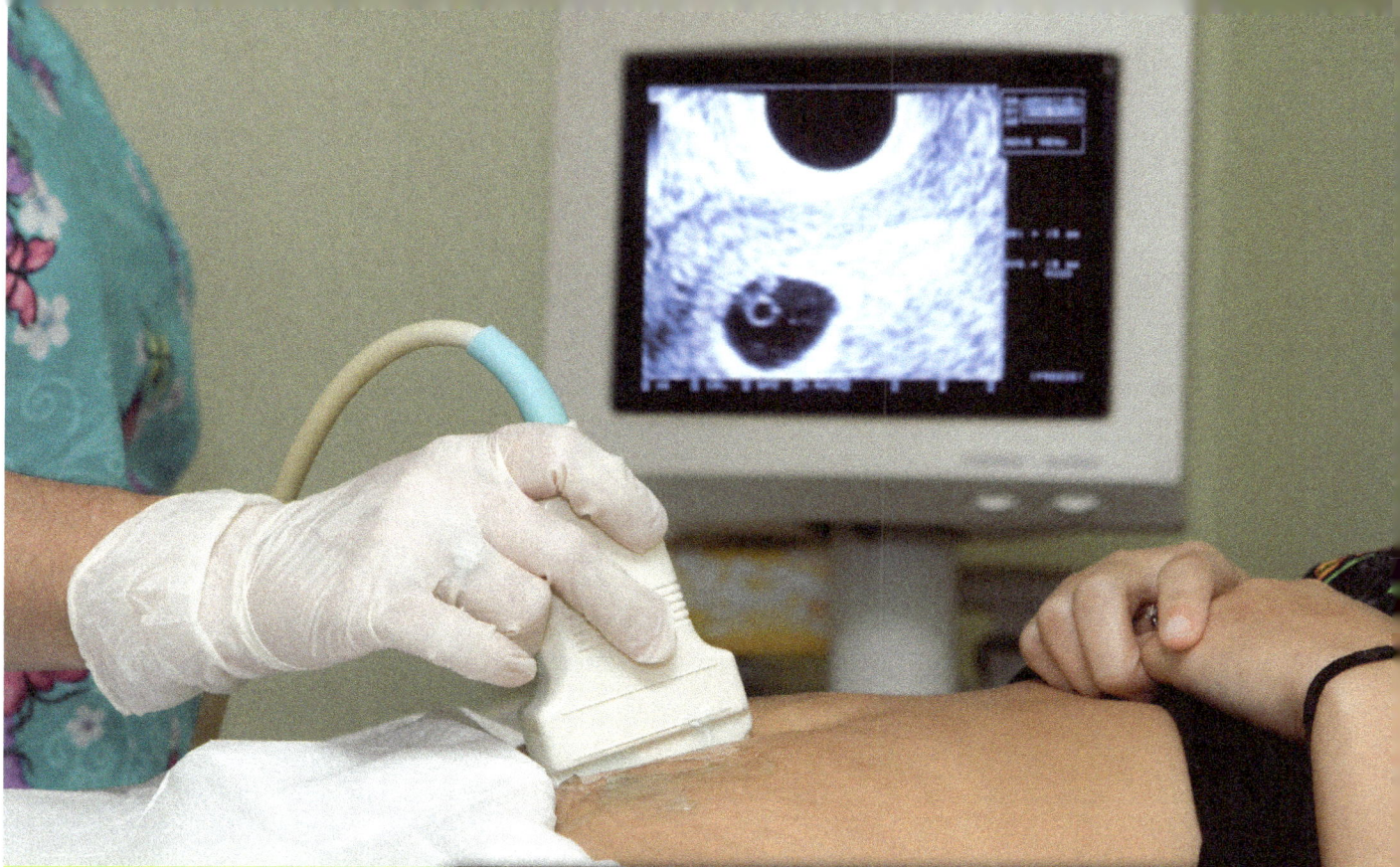

Ultrasound imaging does not do a good job at displaying your lungs or your bones.

How ultrasound images are taken

Ultrasound images are taken like this:

1. The patient lies down on a special bed next to the ultrasound equipment.

2. The skin over the organ to be examined is exposed.

3. The sonographer (ultrasound specialist) or doctor sits next to the bed and to the equipment.

4. The sonographer or doctor applies a special gel to the patient's skin, over the area to be examined.

How ultrasound scanners work

Probe

The sonographer or doctor places an instrument, called a probe, over the area on your skin to which the special gel was applied.

The probe scans the area to be examined, transmitting high-frequency sound waves through the gel into your body, collecting the reflected echoes that bound back, and converting them into electrical signals.

The electrical signals are conveyed to the processing and display unit.

The processing and display unit converts the electrical signals into an image that is displayed on a screen attached to the ultrasound scanner

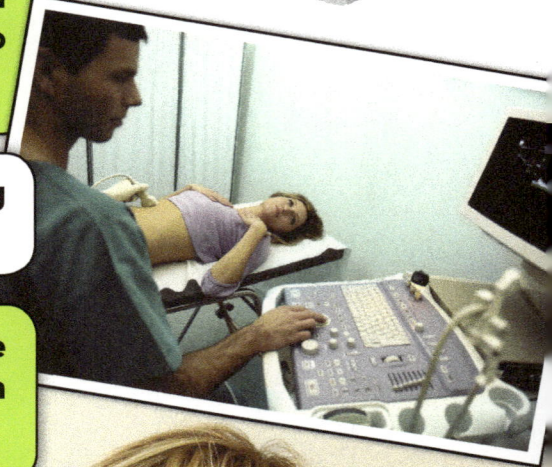

Ultrasound scanners consist of a control table and a computer

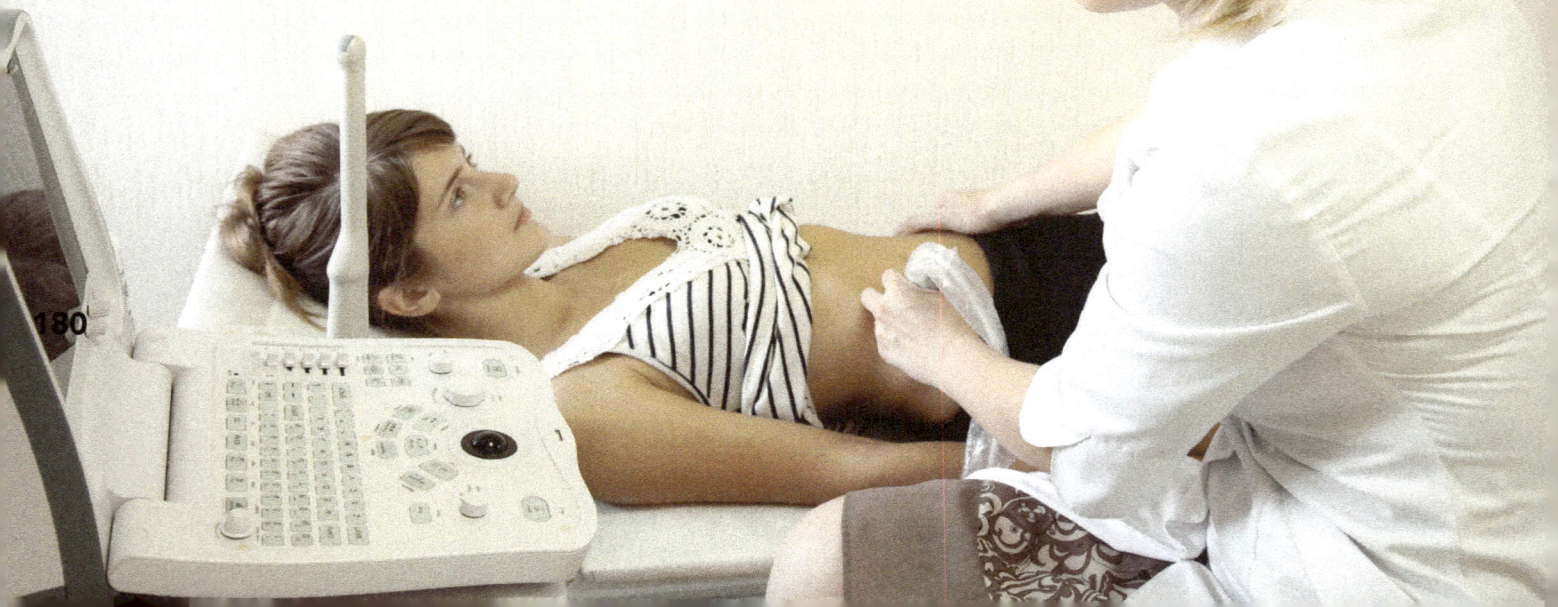

The gel's special components prevent the air from interfering with the transmission of the high-frequency sound waves from the probe through it into your body, or with the echoes bounding back. So, thanks to the gel, high-quality images are obtained.

Who performs ultrasound scans?

A sonographer or doctor perform ultrasound scans.

Who interprets the results of ultrasound scans?

A doctor interprets the results of ultrasound scans.

Stories from the past

The first ultrasound scans performed, in the early 1900s, were for military purposes. In 1912, the disaster of the sinking of the Titanic, which collided with a massive iceberg, was one of the factors accenting the need to search for methods of detecting underwater obstacles. In 1917, during World War 1, the French physicist Paul Langevin invented the first sonar device for detecting submarines.

After World War 2, with continued technological progress, ultrasound waves began to be used in the field of medicine, too. In 1957, a Scottish doctor called Ian Donald started using ultrasound as a medical diagnostic tool. Following the development of electronics, the early 1970s saw enormous developments in the field of ultrasound imaging.

Ultrasound scans do not hurt. Moreover, they only take about 10–15 minutes.

The gel comes off easily, and does not leave any stains.

The sound energy is not harmful.

Did you know that?

Bats have natural sonar systems. Their sense of distance and direction is based on the production of sounds at a frequency too high for human beings to hear. The sound wave vibration system of bats is similar, in how it works, to ultrasound systems used at imaging centers.

MRI (magnetic resonance imaging)

What is MRI?

MRI is a diagnostic technique that uses powerful magnetic fields, radio waves and a computer to form images of internal body tissue.

What is unique about MRI?

MRI is unique because it is more sophisticated and advanced than other imaging techniques. It is capable of detecting illnesses and of providing diagnostic solutions to obstacles where other imaging techniques fail or find them hard to identify.

Magnetic Resonance Imaging Machine

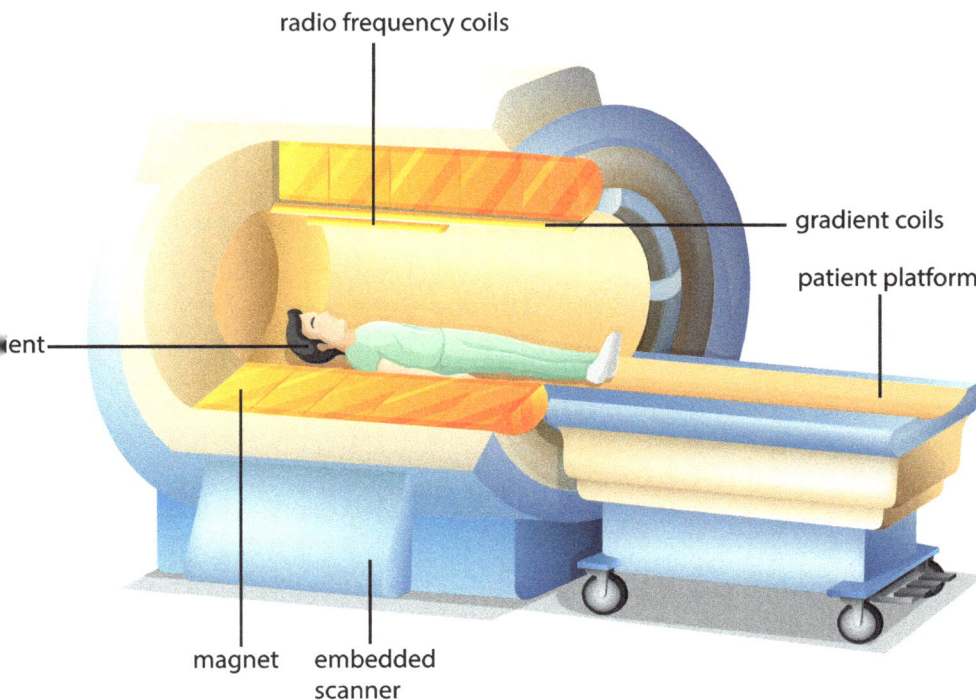

radio frequency coils

gradient coils

patient platform

ient

magnet   embedded scanner

Components of the MRI:

An enormous gantry (larger than a CT gantry).

A magnet, that is, an object that produces a magnetic field. A magnetic field is the three-dimensional area surrounding a magnet, where its force is active.

A radio frequency transmitter. The radio frequency transmitter creates radio wave energy that is transferred to the tissue to be examined in the patient's body.

Specialized receiver coils. These are placed over the area to be examined, and transmit the signals emitted by the patient's body to the computing system.

A special narrow bed, the same length as the patient, on which she lies. The bed moves slowly back and forth, and back again into the hollow tube inside the gantry, where the images are created.

Did you know?

Radio wave energy is similar to light energy. The difference lies in their different wavelengths.

How do MRI machines work?

In order to better understand how MRI machines work, consider the fact that the human body contains a large amount of water and that a single molecule of water is made up of two atoms of hydrogen and one atom of oxygen.

Hydrogen Atom

MRI machines work like this:

During the scan, a magnetic force causes the nuclei of the hydrogen atoms in your body's fluids and in nearly all its tissues to line up in one direction.

The radio wave energy transmitted to the organ being examined causes the hydrogen nuclei to change direction, relative to the amount of water in your body tissues.

When the radio waves are turned off, the hydrogen nuclei resume their original position, and realign with the magnetic field.

The computer measures the changes in position of the hydrogen nuclei, and converts the signals emitted by the organ into an image that visualizes the density of each tissue.

184

The time it takes the hydrogen nuclei to resume their original position is called relaxation time, and varies from tissue to tissue. It is because of these differences in tissue relaxation times that a precise diagnosis can be made.

MRI scans are not harmful. Neither do they hurt. The examination takes about 20-60 minutes.

This is worth remembering!

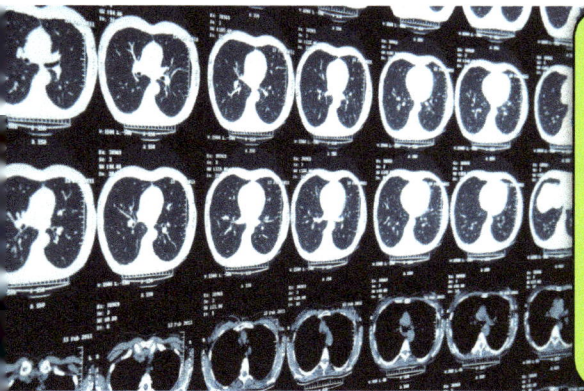

During the MRI scan, you will hear tapping and knocking noises as the scanner works and the magnet moves.

The technologist who performs the MRI scan is able to see, hear and speak with the patient at all times. The patient can talk to him through the intercom system.

What are the advantages of an MRI scan?

MRI scans have several advantages:

- MRI scans visualize internal organs and detect pathological changes in the human body that other diagnostic tools are unable to identify.

- MRI scans do not use X-rays.

- MRI scans can show differences between healthy and unhealthy tissues.

Medical advice: Mr. David Tveta, Director school of Radiographers, Clalit Health Services, Kaplan Medical Center, Rehovot

That's interesting!

The development of MRI paved the way for a revolution in the world of medicine. Science and technology continue to strive to meet the constant need to improve examination techniques, so that even more precise diagnoses of illnesses can be made and patients can be helped even more.

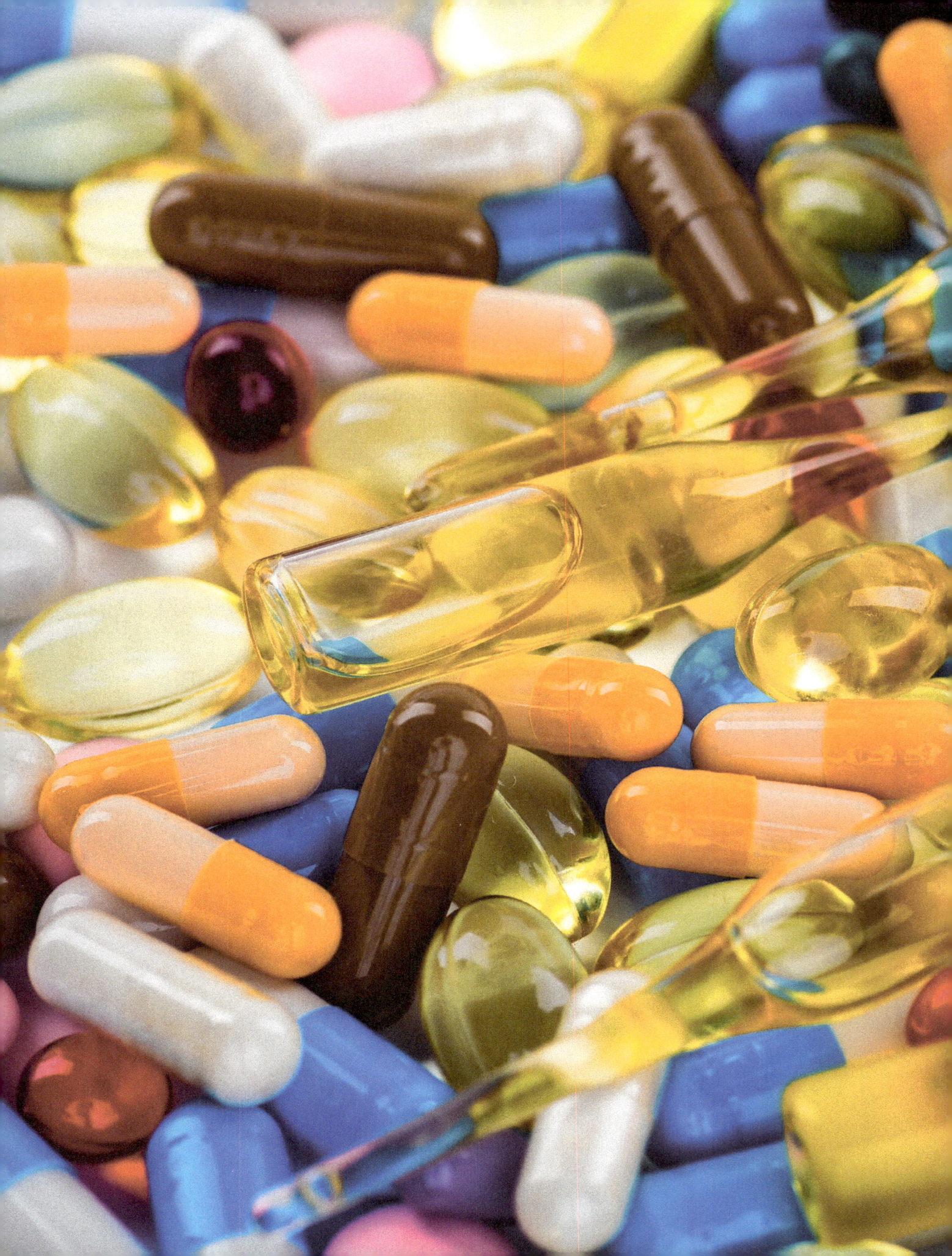

MEDICINES

What is medicine?

A medicine is a compound containing an active chemical ingredient that influences the living cells in our body and alters their activity.

What are the characteristics of the active chemical ingredient?

Here are the characteristics of the active chemical ingredient contained in medicines:

- This active chemical ingredient is synthetic or natural, and can mimic the activity of the substances created in our body.

- When the active chemical ingredient is prepared in the right dosage strength, it can alter the functioning of the living cells in our body and influence them.

- The molecules of the medicines interact with molecules found on and inside cells in our body. The receptors on these cells can sense the changes in the enviroment, and trigger a range of reactions in them.

- The active chemical ingredient does not remain permanently in our body. Rather, it is disintegrated with the help of catalysts called enzymes, becomes inactive and is eliminated from our

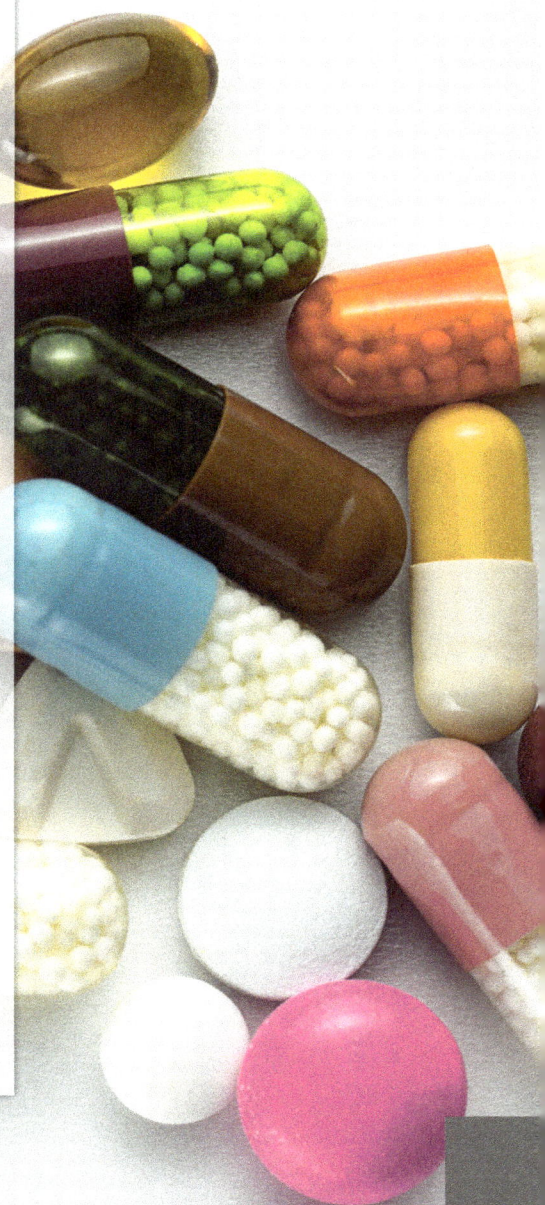

body by feces or urine.

Stories from the past

Since time immemorial, people have prepared remedies as medicines

In bygone times, doctors were the wise people of the nation (priests, philosophers and teachers) who recognized the remedial powers of certain plants. The experiences of these first doctors paved the way for the development of appropriate effective treatments for many diseases.

The ancient Greeks, who gained glory as valiant warriors and healers of wounds sustained on the battle field, were especially renowned for their recognition of the powers of medicinal herbs.

In the Middle Ages, however, the achievements of the Greeks were forgotten. It was only a century later that interest was renewed in the healing powers of herbs.

In recent generations, specially trained pharmacists started engaging in the preparation of medicines. These pharmacists had books containing numerous formulae, on the basis of which they prepared powders and ointments in their pharmacies.

Medicines are prepared in several ways:

- **Medicines prepared from plants**

  Antibiotics are prepared from secretions of mold fungi that are effective against pathogenic bacteria, destroying them.

Blue and green mold

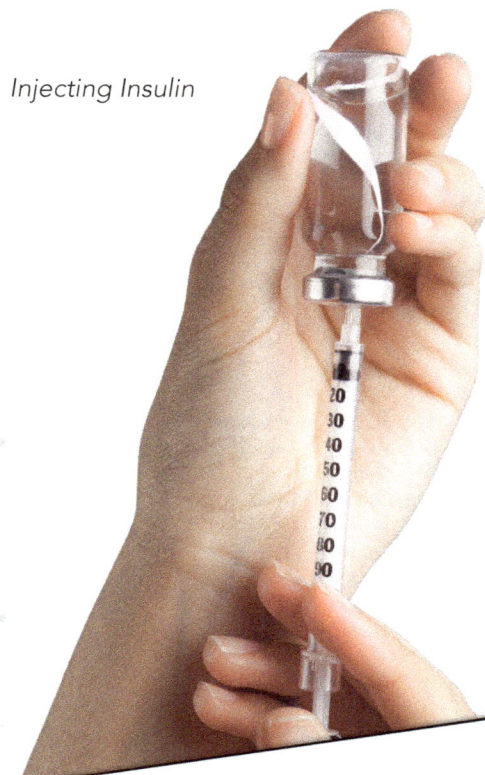

- **Medicines prepared from animals**

  Insulin

  By various means, a protein hormone called insulin was extracted from the pancreas of oxen. Insulin obtained in this way helped regulate the amount of sugar in the blood, and was effective in the treatment of diabetes.

  Vaccines

  Vaccines contain a serum and are administered to prevent such serious diseases as polio.

- **Medicines prepared from a wide variety of minerals and their compounds**

  Compounds are prepared from a wide variety of minerals, such as calcium and vitamin D in order to strengthen people's bones and teeth.

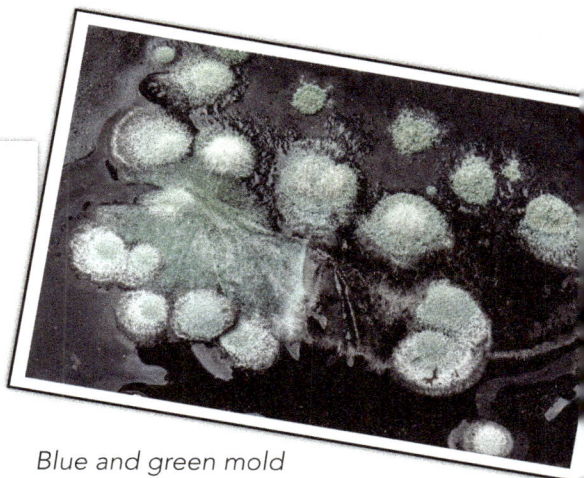

Injecting Insulin

Hep

HepB, Hib-HepB,

HepB, DTaP-HepB-IPV)

Diptheria, Tetanus, Pertussis

(DTaP, DTP, DT, Td, Tdap, DTaP-HepB-IPV, DTaP-IPV/Hib, DTaP-IPV,

Some species of mold are fungi. Like other fungi, mold has a mycelium, which is its vegetative threadlike part.

The mycelium and its network of threads, known as hyphae, branch out and spread over the surface of food.

Short upright threads whose tips are full of spores grow out of the mycelium.

Some species of mold fungi are very dangerous, and destroy cows, food and other organic substances.

However, green mold, whose spores are bluish-green and which is also known as blue mold, is invaluable to medicine. For it is from it that penicillin, which destroys bacteria, is extracted and prepared.

This is important!

After uncovering the precise chemical substances present in medicines concocted from various plants, animals and minerals, it has been possible to prepare them synthetically.

The story of PENICILLIN

Alexander Fleming, the doctor and scientist who discovered penicillin, was born in Scotland on August 6, 1881, and died on March 11, 1955 at the age of 73. He began studying medicine when he was 20. In the course of his studies, he met the bacteriologist Sir Almroth Wright, who introduced him to the world of bacteria and whose laboratory he joined as a researcher. Alexander Fleming spent years searching for a substance that could kill bacteria without attacking and harming the sick person. Like other scientists, he grew bacteria cultures in Petri dishes. Then, in 1928, he noticed that mold had developed in one of the Petri dishes, which was full of the food used for laboratory bacterial-cultures and contained a colony of bacteria, and that the mold was surrounded by a bacteria-free ring. He started researching the properties of mold as a bacteria-killer, and discovered that it contained an active substance that he called penicillin.

Fleming soon became aware of the fact that highly diluted, small concentrations of penicillin were capable of effectively killing bacteria. He subsequently also realized that penicillin was not toxic, and did not harm the sick person's body, either.

It was only in 1941, twelve years after Fleming first published his findings, that the manufacture of penicillin began. The scientific community bestowed its highest medals of honor on Fleming for his first achievement in recognizing the benefits of penicillin. A title of nobility was conferred on him in 1944, and he was awarded the Nobel Prize in 1945.

How medicines are manufactured today

Today, medicines are manufactured in special factories. The ingredients of the medicines are carefully monitored, and they are manufactured with great precision, under the supervision of specialized doctors and pharmacists.

There is a great variety of medicines, and they are used for many different purposes:

- Alleviation of symptoms, rather than of the illness itself, as when you get the flu.

- Destruction of the bacteria causing the illness and, in so doing, healing of the illness.

- Relief of pain, lowering of temperature, healing of wounds and formation of scars.

- Prevention of disease, as in the administration of a vaccine.

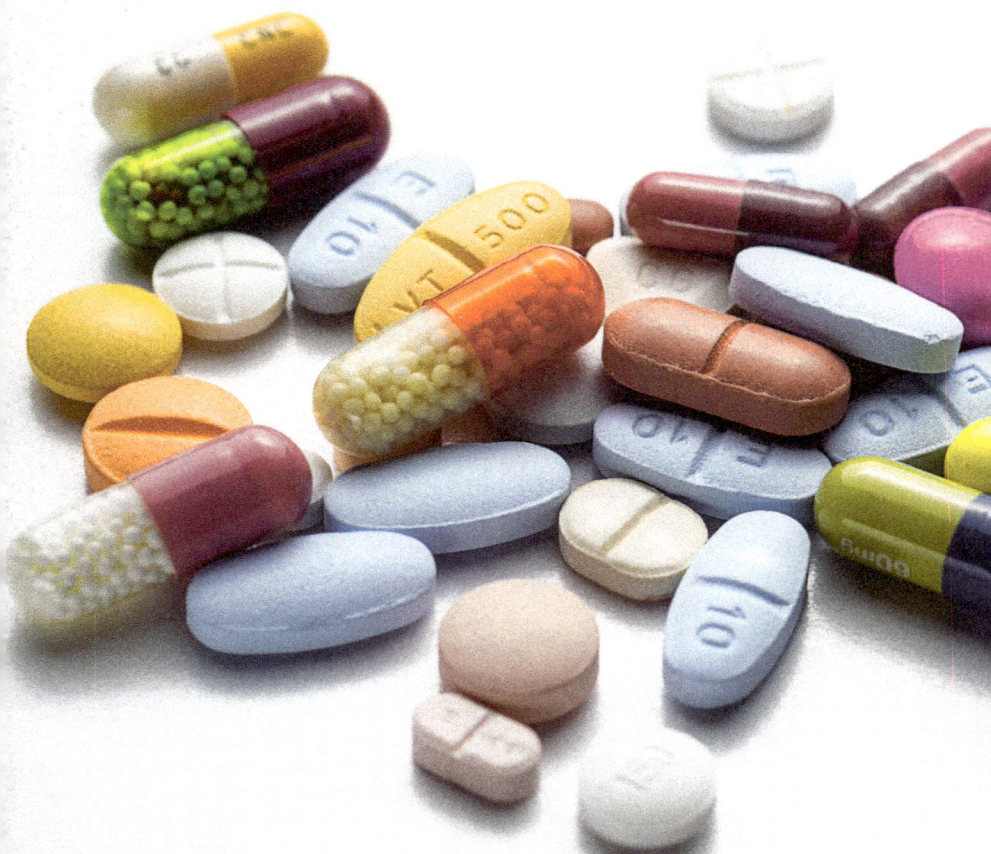

Here is some interesting information

The process of developing a new medicine and having it approved is lengthy and costly.

Nowadays, it takes at least five years to develop a new medicine and costs several million, or even several billion, dollars.

A new medicine must be approved by the health authorities of the country where it is manufactured before it can be marketed.

Ready-made medicines come in diverse dosage forms, such as powders, pills, tablets, capsules, serums, granules, solutions, syringes, ointments, suppositories, drops, syrups, and solutions for intraveneous infusion and injections.

Medicines are marketed to hospitals and pharmacies by pharmaceutical companies.

How medicines are used

Medicines can be divided into two groups, according to their method of use:

Medicines for internal use.	Medicines for external use only.

Medicine for internal use is administered in several forms:

The patient swallows suck or chews the medicine. The medicine becomes effective after being indirectly distributed in our bloodstream by our digestive system:

The process starts in our mouth when we swallow the medicine

⬇

which proceeds down to our stomach. Part of it is absorbed in our blood.

⬇

The rest of it continues on to our small intestine. The vast majority is absorbed in our blood and is distributed throughout our body.

⬇

It heads for our large intestine, where a small part is absorbed in our blood.

⬇

It continues down and, in most cases, is eliminated from our body as feces.

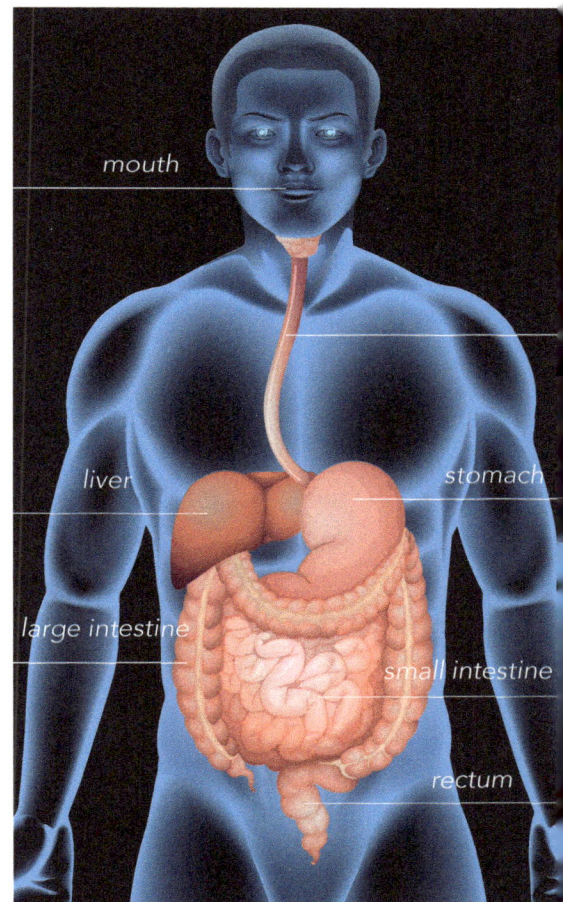

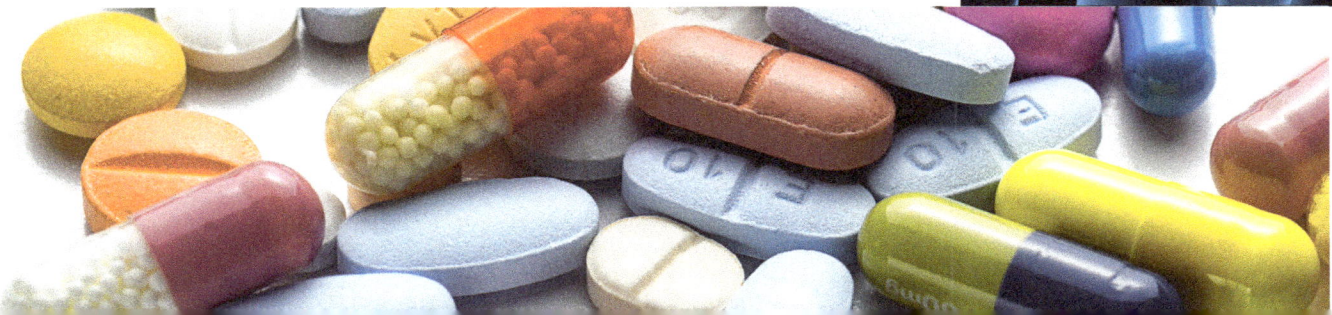

mouth

liver

stomach

large intestine

small intestine

rectum

Intramuscualr administration

- **The medicine is injected in solution form** into a muscle in our forearm or thigh, and does not involve the digestive system.

Intravenous administration

- **The medicine is introduced** into our body in solution form by infusion, through a needle stuck into a vein in our arm, and is distributed directly in our bloodstream.

- **The medicine is applied locally** to a specific organ, as in eyedrops and eardrops.

Medicines for external use only.

Various kinds of ointments and special solutions are applied externally on the affected part of the body.

This is important

Different medicines work in different areas of our body.

For a medicine to be effective, it must reach the area that it is intended to heal.

Certain medicines can have undesirable side effects. When this happens, not only do they not improve the patient's condition, but they also cause undesirable consequences.

To avoid side effects, it is important to read the patient information leaflet that comes with every medicine, and that describes such possible undesirable consequences.

Infusion

(A) Prescription medicines

What is a medical prescription?

A medical prescription is a notification in writing by a doctor, addressed to a pharmacist, to give the patient a specific medicine, and to attach to it the doctor's instructions.

The doctor's instructions indicate:

For whom the medicine is intended.	**The correct way to use it.**

Did you know?

A pharmacist is a person who is professionally trained to supply medicines and to guide the people receiving them on how to use them correctly. In professional language, the pharmacist's role is to dispense medicines.

Important!

You need a doctor's prescription in order to purchase most medicines.

Examples of dosage forms in which medicines are administered

Medicine can be administered in several different dosage forms:

1. As a pill, tablet, or granule:

The medicine is a small mass that looks like a tiny ball, tablet, or granule, and is given to the patient to swallow.

2. As a capsule:

a. The medicine, in liquid, granular, or powder dosage form, is inside a gelatin-coated capsule that dissolves in our stomach when we swallow it.

b. The patient swallows the capsule whole, and does not feel the unpleasant taste of the medicine.

3. As a suppository:

a. The medicine is in the dosage form of a tiny cylinder or cone, and melts after being inserted into our rectum. It gradually spreads over the lining of our lower rectum, where it is either absorbed into our bloodstream and scatters throughout out body, or acts directly on the area where it is inserted.

b. Suppositories are medical preparations that are used when it is difficult for the patient to receive the medicine through her mouth.

4. As a syrup:

a. Medicines that come in the dosage form of a syrup are sweet and thick.

b. Patients who find it difficult to swallow tablets receive the medicine in the dosage form of a syrup.

5. As an ointment:

a. A medicine that in the dosage form of an ointment is applied if you have a sore or a skin disease.

b. The ointment is spread over the affected area to prevent an infection from developing, or to heal one that has already developed.

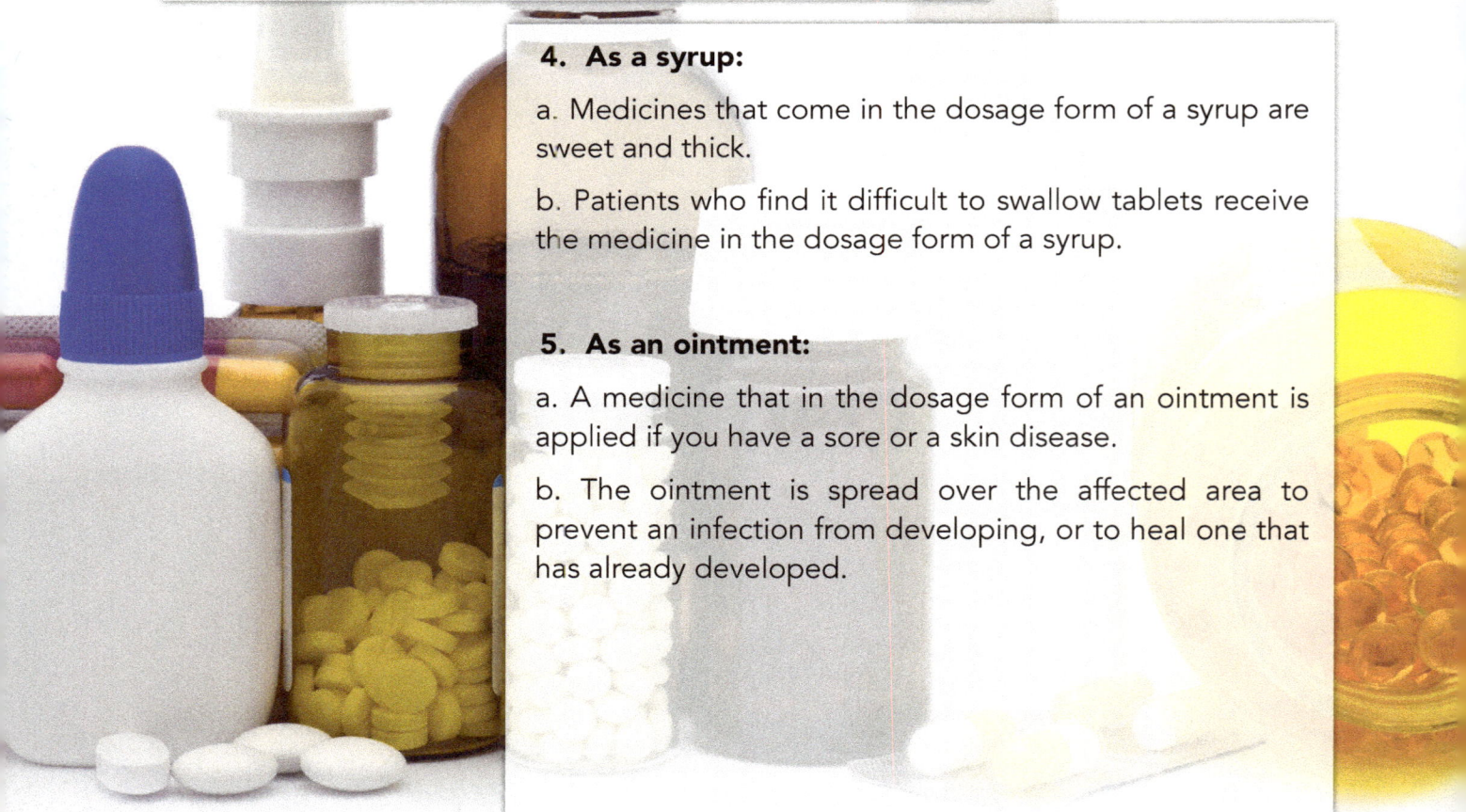

(B) Non-Prescription (Over-the-Counter) Medicines

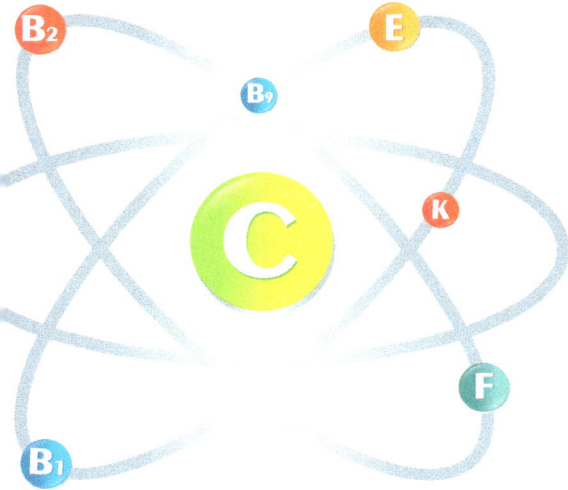

Two kinds of non-prescription medicines can be bought without having to see a doctor first:

- Medicines that are only allowed to be dispensed by a pharmacist at a pharmacy.

- Medicines that have been specifically licensed by countries' health ministries to be sold in stores that are not necessarily pharmacies. This authorization is relatively new in Israel and in the world.

Interesting!

Certain substances, called food supplements, can be purchased that are neither a food nor a medicine. Food supplements contain particular kinds of nutrients, such as carbohydrates, minerals and vitamins, whose active ingredient is essential for the body cells of specific population groups to function properly. These food supplements are intended as dietary supplements.

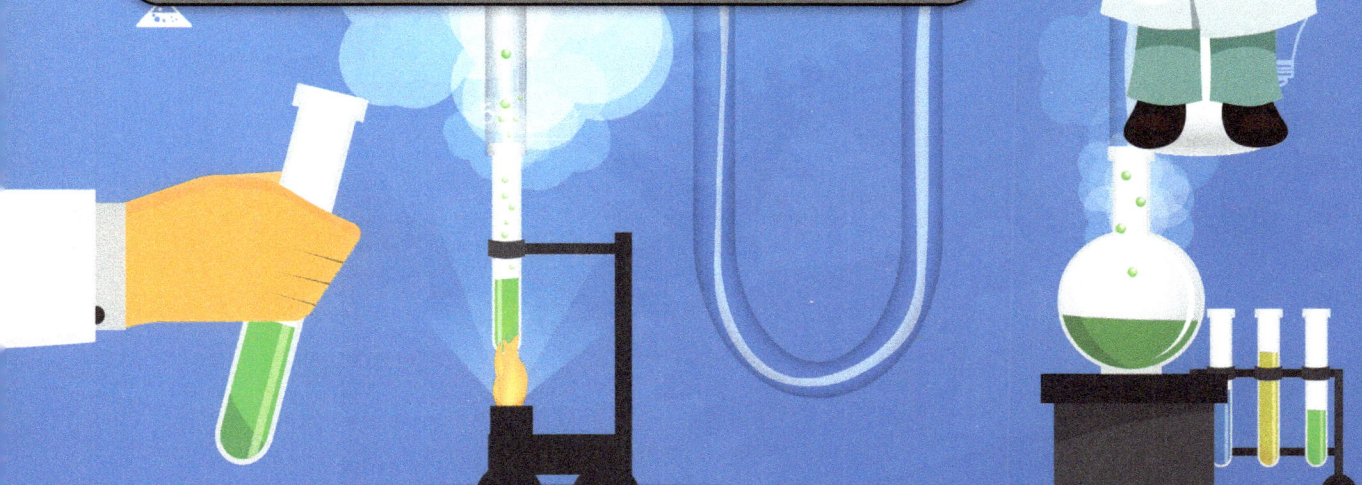

Two fun assignments!

Assignment A: Information and publicity

Choose several newspapers that cover a range of subject matters. You'll definitely find articles on medicines in each of the newspapers. Read them carefully.

Here is a question:

In which articles were you able to find information on the proper use of a specific medicine?

Sort the articles into two groups:

1. Articles intended to provide information on specific medicines.

2. Articles intended to encourage the consumption of medicine.

Summarize your conclusions.

Assignment B: Find the 10 medicines and dosage forms hidden in the word search:

Medical advice: Dr. Nadine Khatib, Clinical Pharmacist and Senior Officer, Tel-Aviv Sourasky Medical Center, Tel-Aviv.

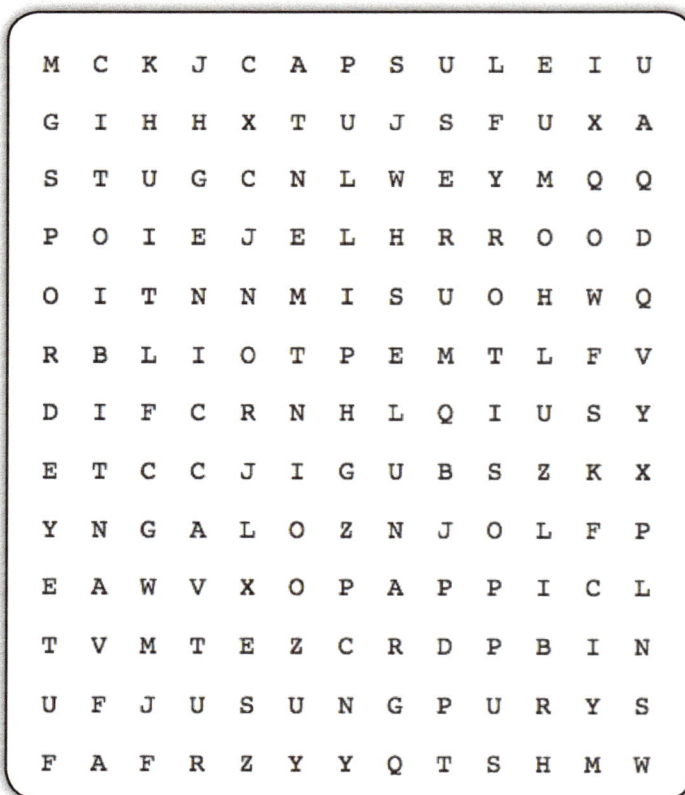

M	C	K	J	C	A	P	S	U	L	E	I	U
G	I	H	H	X	T	U	J	S	F	U	X	A
S	T	U	G	C	N	L	W	E	Y	M	Q	Q
P	O	I	E	J	E	L	H	R	R	O	O	D
O	I	T	N	N	M	I	S	U	O	H	W	Q
R	B	L	I	O	T	P	E	M	T	L	F	V
D	I	F	C	R	N	H	L	Q	I	U	S	Y
E	T	C	C	J	I	G	U	B	S	Z	K	X
Y	N	G	A	L	O	Z	N	J	O	L	F	P
E	A	W	V	X	O	P	A	P	P	I	C	L
T	V	M	T	E	Z	C	R	D	P	B	I	N
U	F	J	U	S	U	N	G	P	U	R	Y	S
F	A	F	R	Z	Y	Y	Q	T	S	H	M	W

Journey's End (For Now)

Dear Reader,

My desire was to present you with a little something from the world of medicine.

Now that you've come this far, I am sure that you are as impressed as I am by the wonders of this world, whose essence is the relationship between the organs of our body, and the identification and healing of illnesses.

I fervently hope that the knowledge you gleaned from this book will help you to look after your body, now and in the future. If it also imbues you with the desire to further deepen your knowledge of medicine, you have my wholehearted blessing!

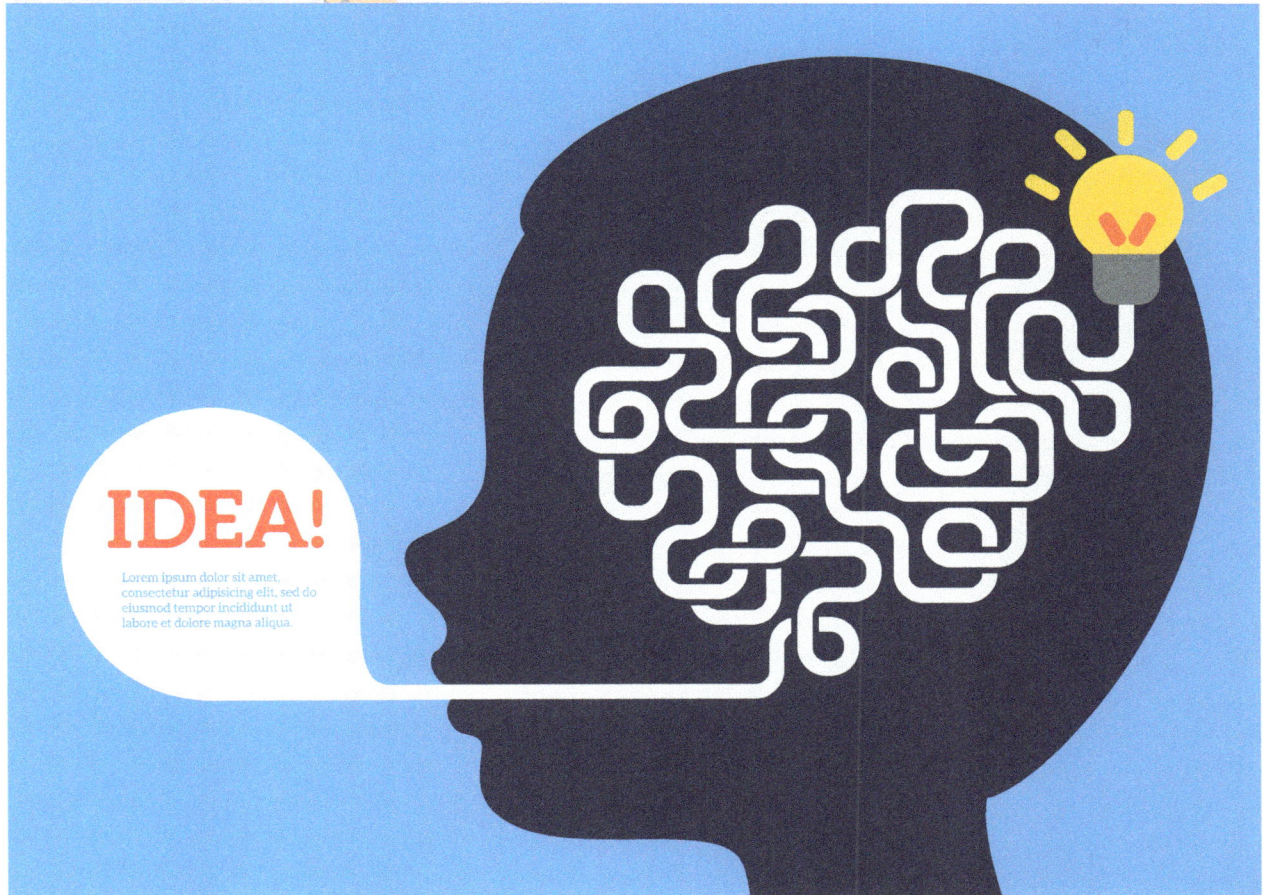

List of Professional Advisors

Chapter 1   **The Immune system**   **Dr. Yael Levi Vice** Director of Immunology and Allergy
Schneider Children's Medical Center of Israel

Chapter 2   **Pathogens - Germs**   **Prof. Itamar Shalit** Previous Director of Medicine
Pathogens - Viruses   Schneider Children's Medical Center of Israel

Chapter 3   **Fever**   **Prof. Yitzhak Versano** Previous Director of Internal
Medicine Schneider Children's Medical Center of Israel

Chapter 4   **The Stethoscope**   **Prof. Benjamin Volovitz** Specialist Paediatric Pulmonology
In the service of the   Schneider Children's Medical Center of Israel
pulmonary system
The Stethoscope   **Dr. Boaz Geva** Specialist, Internal Medicine and Cardiology
In the service of the heart

Chapter 5   **Heart Decoder - The heartbeat**   **Prof. Ovdi Dagan** Director of the Intensive Care Unit
Heart Decoder - Blood   Schneider Children's Medical Center of Israel
pressure gauge
Heart Decoder - Electrocardiography

Chapter 6 - 7   **Research the circulatory system**   **Prof. Yaakov Amir** Director of Internal Medicine Schneider
Syringe and injection   Children's Medical Center of Israel

Chapter 8   **Researching Ear and Pharynx**   **Prof. Yitzhak Versano** Previous Director of Internal
The Otoscope   Medicine Schneider Children's Medical Center of Israel
Researching Ear and Pharynx -
The Pharynx and the Tongue Depressor

Chapter 9   **At the imaging institute**   **Mr. David Tveta,** Director School of Radiographers,
Kaplan Med. Center, Rehovot

Chapter 10   **Medication**   **Dr. Nadine Khatib,** Clinical Pharmacist and Senior officer
Sourasky Med. Center, Tel-Aviv

Lightning Source UK Ltd.
Milton Keynes UK
UKHW052355061218
333592UK00006B/105/P

9 789657 589212